ETERNAL GAMBIT

KELLY ST. CLARE

Eternal Gambit
by Kelly St. Clare

Edited by Melissa Scott and Robin Schroffel
Cover illustration and design by Amalia Chitulescu Digital Art

ETERNAL GAMBIT

Exosia
Kentro
Maltu
Selkie's Cove
Pleo
Portum
Syraness
Febribus
Charybdis
Neos
Zol
Caspian Sea

Dynami Sea

Davy Jone's

Medusa's Lair

N

W

E

S

Exosian Realm

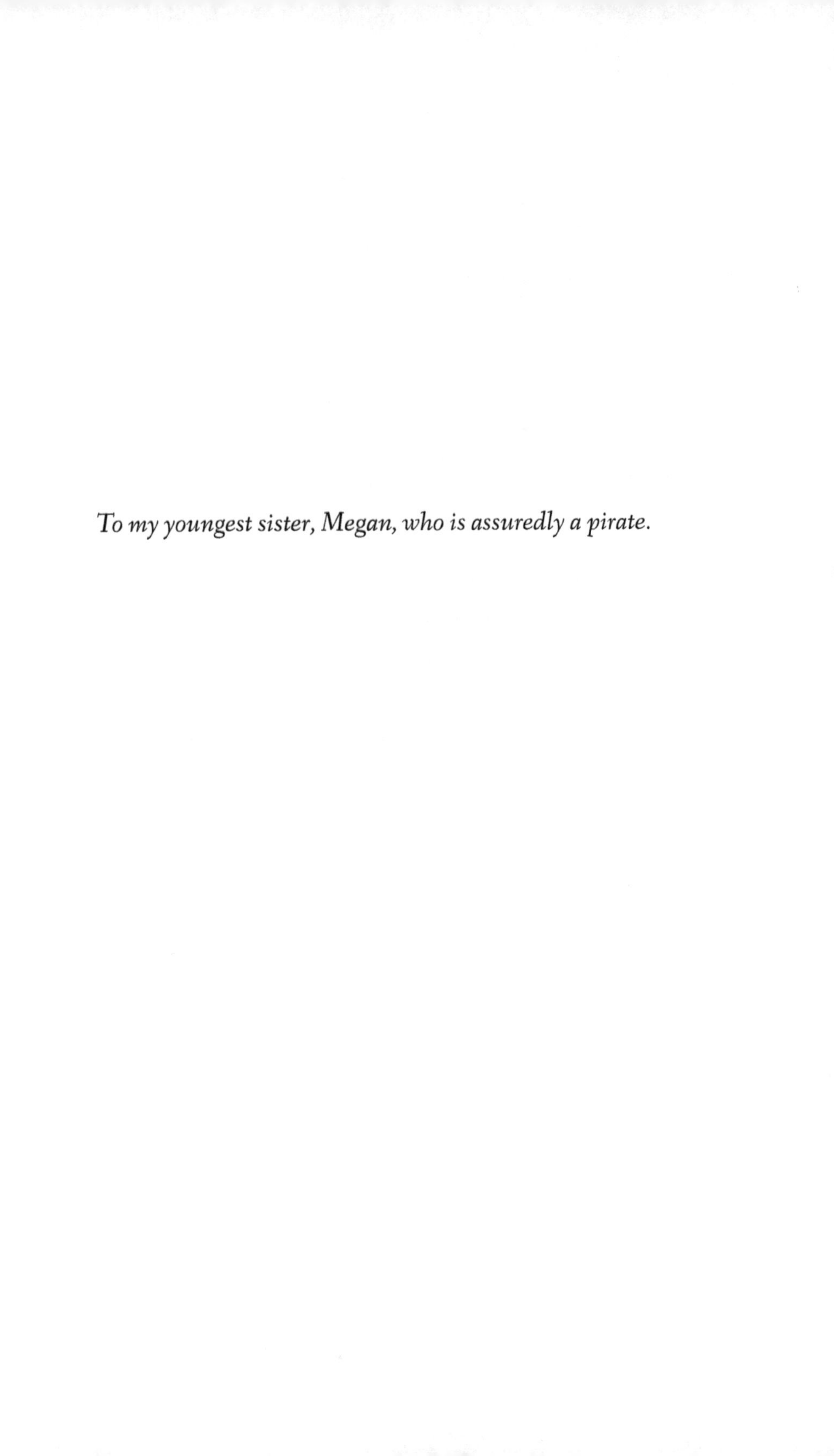

To my youngest sister, Megan, who is assuredly a pirate.

ONE

While saving the realm from the pillars of six, many hellish things had happened, but Ebba had never actually *gone* to hell.

She shuffled along, wedged in the middle of a single-file line of her crew. Her limbs felt heavy, as though sand filled them. Her eyes gritty, her breath labored as if an anchor crushed down on her chest. Her very thoughts waded through mud.

Leading the procession were three tainted pirates she'd never thought to see again—in fact, Ebba was certain she'd killed them on Exosia.

So far, hell lived up to its name.

Ebba placed her hands on the cliffs either side of the crevice they walked through. The black stone of the cliff walls possessed an angry red tinge and extended so high she couldn't see the sky . . . if there *was* a sky in this place. The strangled light in the crevice was just enough to make out her feet. Sand covered the uneven ground—the only remnant of the Dynami Sea on the other side of the rock wall they'd passed through. The rock wall they'd been unaware was the entrance to Davy Jones' Locker. Here, there was no wind, no sound of sea, and no smell of salt.

When she'd first passed through the rock wall, Ebba thought she was in another world. She didn't know exactly what hell was classified as. But she knew they definitely weren't in the Exosian realm any longer.

"Do you think they're ghosts?" Caspian whispered low in her ear.

She half-turned to look back at him as she walked. "Nay, not ghosts." Pockmark, Swindles, and Riot were as physically real as any of her crew.

But dead.

And in hell.

Unanswered questions whirled through her mind, but one thing she knew.

And Ebba wished she didn't.

An attempt to overthrow Pockmark and his two cronies had crossed her mind many times as she squeezed through the black-and-crimson stone crevice. In a passage so narrow, and with their enemies at the front, all the crew needed to do was simply turn around and run back to the entrance.

There were a couple of problems with that, though, the chief one being that not everyone could *get* out. Plank had tried and failed. If leaving Davy Jones' Locker had anything to do with whether or not a person was tainted, then only she, Caspian, and maybe Grubby had any chance of escaping. Leaving her fathers wasn't an option, and after what the love cylinder, *amare*, had shown her, not even one hour ago, leaving Jagger behind wasn't an option either.

So they followed the tainted trio.

"My grandfather be right excited to meet ye," Pockmark crowed from the front of the single-file line. His cold voice echoed back through the tight passage. Despite the steamy heat, a shiver worked its way up her spine—and it had nothing to do with the skimpy blue silk shift she had on.

None of her crew answered, and the three pirates sniggered at their silence.

They were about to come face-to-face with her fathers' biggest fear. A person who broke each of them in turn, haunting their minds in death for twenty years. None of her fathers had spoken since Pockmark had uttered the words: *Mutinous Cannon.* Not one peep. She could only imagine the thoughts running rampant through their skulls. The person they'd thought dead and gone was resurrected.

Or had ended up exactly where he belonged.

Her hands shook at the thought of seeing Cannon in the flesh, the last pirate to stand against King Forge Montcroix in the Battle for the Seas.

Her entire body shook.

With anger.

Ebba was going to tear the bastard's head off. She'd sat and listened to each of her fathers' stories in turn, barring Plank, and as she contemplated seeing the unscrupulous pirate who'd done such things to her parents, all she felt was all-consuming, churning anger. That rage might not have risen to the surface before. But now, with the person who'd nearly destroyed her fathers inside and out nearby. . . .

. . . Her anger had risen, all right.

"Ebba, are you okay?" Caspian whispered in her ear.

"Aye," she said. "Why?"

"You're breathing really hard."

She switched her focus to the rise and fall of her chest. Toothless sharks, she was.

"I'm workin' myself into a rage," she informed him.

"I see," he mused. "That rage won't get us in further trouble?"

Honestly, it might. Her temper only worked out around fifty percent of the time. "I won't be doin' anythin' to put yer lives in harm's way." Not intentionally.

She knew they had to be very, *very* careful.

The pirates leading them were tainted—exactly as they'd been in life.

Pockmark's eyes were yellowed and streaked with blood. Riot and Swindles' pupils were flooded black, their bodies emaciated. Their dark *Malice* uniforms hung loosely over their skeletal forms. Weeping wounds, like small popped boils, covered their faces and visible skin. And the presence of black eyes meant Riot and Swindles were contagious. Which was why Jagger, the immune, walked behind the tainted trio.

He was the only person in the realm who was resistant to magic and able to beat back the taint, given time.

"I know that," the prince said softly. "And I'm afraid we inadvertently did that with yours. Some rescue attempt that was."

Ebba snorted. That was putting it lightly. If the rescue had gone according to plan, they'd be away from the Satyr and still on their quest to collect the sixth and final part of the root. Except, she had a mounting feeling the last piece was in *here,* so maybe they would've always ended up right in Davy Jones'.

"Quiet," Swindles snapped from ahead, rounding to peer down their line.

Stubby, the first behind Jagger, said, "Keep yer wig on, matey."

The tainted pirate ripped one of the pistols from his sash and aimed just over Jagger's shoulder at her father's face. The hammer was drawn back with an awful, ringing *click.*

Ebba's heart stopped as her father held up both hands, taking a step back. A tiny, terrified sound escaped her lips, and Grubby turned back and squeezed her hand, giving her a toothy smile.

Swindles sneered. "Aye, that's right, old man. Ye step back, like a good wench."

Pockmark and Riot had halted, but now Pockmark strode forward and gripped Swindles' shoulder. "Enough. Mutinous be expectin' us. Mercy on anyone who keeps him waitin' overlong."

A dark wariness settled over Swindles' face an instant before he released the hammer and holstered his pistol back in his sash.

Ebba closed her eyes, chest loosening as the immediate danger to Stubby dissipated. Sink her, she *hated* when her loved ones were placed in danger.

Pockmark glared at them. "When ye come afore my grandfather, ye'll all kneel. If I see a speck o' a wrong thought on yer face, ye'll find a hole in yer chest in a scant second."

She wondered if he'd intended the words to sound ominous and threatening. To her, he sounded nervous about displeasing Cannon.

"I can't kneel," Peg-leg called from the back. "I'll never stand after. My body feels all heavy-like since I got here."

"I second that. If I go down, I shall require a hand up again," Barrels added from just in front of her.

Grubby said, "Don't ye worry, m'hearties. I can be kneelin' for all o' ye."

"Listen to that one, lads. He's still only got a skull half-filled o' rum," scoffed Riot.

Heat crept up Ebba's neck, but where once she'd tried to attack the *Malice* pirates for a similar insult, she was willing to let it slide right now to exact revenge at a later date. Plus, when the *purgium* had healed her father's head injury, Grubby turned out smarter than even Barrels . . . before sustaining a second head injury.

"Ye'll all kneel when I say," spat the *Malice* captain, whirling and pushing past Riot and Swindles.

"That ain't likely," Locks told Pockmark. "But how about ye keep orderin', and we'll keep pretendin' to obey?"

His remark might've lacked wisdom, but Ebba felt only glee as the color in Pockmark's face changed from a sweltering pink to a tight-lipped white. Her fathers planned to fight back. If not physically, then with sheer gall. She hadn't known what to expect. When the beast, Ladon, first brought up Mutinous Cannon all those months ago, her fathers nearly lost themselves. She knew that since then, they'd been plagued by the pasts they'd locked away in a box. To hear they weren't going to cower and lose themselves gave her hope that one day they'd be better. Even if the taint within them couldn't be cured without the *purgium*, and even if they couldn't bring themselves to touch *veritas* and lessen their taint, *even then*, they'd have their defiance to cling to.

"Brave words," Pockmark replied through gritted teeth. Unlike the other two, he had greater control of his anger, probably because he didn't appear as tainted. "Let's see how ye act when ye're afore him. He's been tellin' me tales of yer little crew. Of how path'tic ye were. How ye cried and screamed and begged like little girls."

In her life, she'd seen women giggle and fawn over a man to secretly save another's life. She'd seen Verity sending her fathers scrambling to do the dishes with a tiny narrowing of her eyes. She'd seen Caspian's youngest sister pinch one of Marigold's grandchildren so hard it drew blood. To her mind, if a girl was crying, begging, or screaming, the person causing it should watch their backs. Not for a day, but for the rest of their lives. Weak males insulted women to cover their fear. That was why brave men never did it.

"Ooh, Ebba, look. There's a sign up ahead," Barrels said.

She squinted past him and caught sight of the square wooden sign nailed into the stone up ahead. "So?"

"Go on, read it aloud?" he asked.

Ebba withheld her groan and then a grin at Caspian's muttered '*Are you serious?*'. Her father was a *tad* overzealous with her reading lessons and didn't pick the best times and places.

And he'd heard Caspian's comment.

"There is *always* time to read," Barrels said, sniffing. "Even when you are walking into hell." Judging by the snapping edge to his words, the criticism on reading upset him more than their current location.

As they drew alongside the sign, Ebba focused on the words, sounding them out quietly so the *Malice* pirates wouldn't hear and laugh at her efforts. "Dah-oo. Do. Nnn-oo-tt. Do not. Ee-nn-tt-err. Do not enter," she said, smiling brightly. That was pretty quick, too. "Oh, there be another one ahead." Ebba focused again. "Yah-oou. You. Wuh-ill. You will." She trailed off at the next word.

"Surely," Barrels supplied.

"Nay, it ain't," she countered. "Shore has an 'H' in it."

"Yes, my dear. Like a lot of other words, there are two ways of spelling the same sound, and they mean different things. You are sure something will happen. Or you are rowing into shore."

Her head would *shorely* explode all over the *sure* in a second. With a sigh, she glanced back at the sign. "You will surely duh-i-e. You will surely die!" She put both messages together. "Do not enter. You will surely die. . . ."

She trailed off.

Barrels cleared his throat. "Poor reading material."

Just a little.

The only material she really wanted to read was the scrapbook her fathers gifted her for her eighteenth birthday. They'd managed to save some of their belongings from *Felicity*. They'd secured everything in water-tight barrels and tied them to a rowboat that the kraken hopefully still towed around.

Ebba hoped everything was still with Matey. Though, being in hell made that issue seem quite small.

The crevice passage widened, and some of the darkness lifted—her bare feet were now visible, anyway.

They filed out to stand upon a platform that looked down over a cavern. Ebba gasped with the others. At first glance, Davy Jones' appeared to be on fire. But it was just the effect of the light tugging out the deep red embedded in the rock. The buried red in the black stone was akin to dark, molten flame crawling over the charred remains of wood.

The entire cavern was made of the stuff. The ceiling, walls, and floor were all formed of the black-and-crimson stone. There wasn't a sky in here.

"Best get used to this sight," Pockmark said with undisguised glee. "The Locker be yer new home."

The semi-circular platform they stood upon was large enough to fit four rowboats in pairs. Ebba inched up to the edge of the platform. A howl of wind blew down the passage they'd entered through. The pitch catapulted, soaring to a scream as it entered the cavern. The gust exited at a full-blown shriek that lifted the hairs on the back of her neck.

Ebba peered over the edge of the cliff face.

A purple stream split the cavern in two, running from north to south. The space on the east side of the water was much smaller than the west. She eyed the curling steam and bursting bubbles arising from the odd waterway. Crossing a boiling river of purple water wasn't high on her list of ways to survive this ordeal and escape Davy Jones' with her crew and the five parts of the root in their belts.

"There be a shipwreck down there," Plank said, pointing.

Ebba shifted her attention from the river to the larger western half of the cavern. Plank was right. In the far corner, wedged in the midst of towering boulders, were the remains of a ship.

Locks' voice was low. "Never be mindin' the ship. Look at the people sleepin' on the east side o' the cavern."

What? Her neck protested as she whipped around to look. Ebba sucked in a breath, hearing Jagger do the same from behind her.

There *were* people down there. Filthy people. They were sleeping . . . or dead. The griminess of their clothing and skin made them merge in with the churning red-and-black quality of the ground and surrounding cliffs.

Were these people the damned?

Wordlessly, Ebba turned to Jagger. He had the most experience with dark things.

. . . He was also integral to another issue that she considered just as problematic as being in hell.

What the *amare* had shown her on the rocky jetty they'd walked over from Satyr Island was no joke.

Ebba forced that aside, asking him, "What is this place?"

She knew the *name* of where they were, but what were the rules? What could this place do to her, to her fathers, to Jagger, and to Caspian? What could the damned do to them? How long could they stay here before *none* of them could leave?

Her breath came fast, and Jagger lowered his head to her.

"Aye, Viva," the flaxen-haired said. "This be a brand new barrel o' fish. Don't worry yer head. We'll be figurin' it out just like everythin' else."

Was that how he saw their lives over the last months? He thought they'd gotten through all that by *figuring it out*?

Despite herself, a part of her believed him. Or maybe in his confident tone. The other part that Calypso recently awakened was solely interested in Jagger's muscles. He was bare-chested—having gifted his tunic to her on Satyr Island. All of his breathtaking tribal tattoos were on display. They covered his chest from the outer tip of each collarbone, leaping whenever he moved.

Blow her down.

And he smelled like bloody sea salt and rope.

Ebba turned from him, wrapping her arms around her body.

Being in hell *really* wasn't her only problem.

TWO

On the left side of the semi-circle passage platform were steep steps. The steps were cut into the black cliff face and led to the bottom of the cavern. They didn't zig-zag to the ground in a switchback that would've made sense. Instead, the stairway had been carved in a straight line so sloped that Ebba knew she'd be nearly crawling if climbing up. The steps proved both slippery and treacherous, and Ebba didn't have time to dread what was coming as she clung to Peg-leg's belt for fear he'd slip and fall to his death.

They descended fifty feet, and the knots in her shoulders didn't ease until their group reached the bottom. The uneven floor of hell was made entirely of the black-and-crimson stone, as she'd glimpsed from above.

Pockmark led them over the rocky ground and parallel to the purple stream. To her right, on the other side of the stream were the grimy people she'd seen from the platform. The ground over there was mostly flat. But on this side of the water, to her left, were boulders of the unusual stone. The closest boulders only rose to her knees, but they became larger and larger toward the cliff-face borders of the cavern. From her vantage point on the passage platform, she knew the shipwreck was nestled in those boulders at the top-left corner.

The heavy sensation in her gut increased as Pockmark turned away from the purple water and led them between the boulders in that direction.

He was taking them to the ship. And Ebba could guess that Mutinous Cannon would be waiting for them. Her rage seemed to have left her hanging as the fear over what might happen to her fathers swelled into panic territory.

The stone underfoot had a distinct worn look that told her their current path through the boulders was the common route between the ship and the purple stream. And as she'd seen prior, the height of the black boulders grew progressively. Soon, they towered over her.

They continued winding down the path toward the top-left corner of hell. Ebba tilted her head back, peering up at the black stone ceiling and cliff faces as they drew nearer.

How had they landed themselves in this?

She shook her head, facing forward as the path opened into a larger space.

At the far end of the circular space, the mostly-intact stern end of a ship was wedged between numerous boulders. The mast had snapped off just above the lowest boom; the bilge door was still there, as were the bulwarks and wheel. The rest of the ship lay in pieces scattered around the edges of the flat area where they stood.

The boulders underfoot had been hacked and chipped away with brute force, by the uneven, sharp look of the ground.

But those small details were lost as pirates—*tainted* pirates—began to creep out of the bilge door of the shipwreck like cockroaches out of cracks in a wall. They climbed out through the gun ports dotting the hull and emerged from behind the ship. Her heart pounded as the black-eyed pirates shuffled forward, some of them stopping at the base of the splintered ship deck, and the rest of them pushing around behind her crew, blocking off the path they'd entered on.

Black eyes. All of the pirates were contagious.

Her fathers rearranged themselves around her. Ebba elbowed her way between Stubby and Plank. She wasn't having any of that shite.

The pirates erupted into hoots and jeers, and Ebba lifted her chin as she surveyed them. Gold fillings, yellowed teeth, and pirate garb blackened with filth. They waved rusted cutlasses in the air, hands resting on their pistols.

"Come on then, ye sorry excuse for misbegotten smallpox," she shouted back at them.

Barrels cleared his throat. "More of them than us, my dear. More of them than us."

Aye, Ebba just didn't want to look like she'd go down without a fight. Which one of them was Mutinous Cannon? Her rage was back again.

She was good for a few rounds.

"Caspian," Barrels said. "What does the *veritas* say? Is everything around us tainted?"

If so, they'd already have caught it. Which was bad, bad news.

Amongst other things, the *veritas* showed the truth in any present moment. Goodness and truth were shown as a shimmering white quality. Anything evil or false gained a shadow.

Caspian took hold of the sword's hilt above his belt, and they waited, ignoring the catcalls of the pirates. At least the scum hadn't advanced from the edges yet.

"Uh, not . . . great, I'm afraid," Caspian answered quietly.

Stubby sidled closer to him. "How 'not great' are ye talkin'? Have we already caught the taint? Out with it, lad."

"Everything barring the black-and-red stone is tainted. The ship, the pirates are absolutely crawling with shadows. The taint in Pockmark is confined within him, not escaping through his skin yet, but he's the only one."

Which they'd known because Pockmark's eyes weren't black.

"Stay back, ye blackened scum," Pockmark roared at the tainted pirates.

The tainted scuttled back like rats over rotting food. Every single one of them.

"Go get Captain Mutinous," he ordered Swindles.

She whispered to Locks over her shoulder. "Cannon ain't here yet, I take?"

"Nay, lass. He always did like to make an entrance."

"So what be the plan?" she hissed at her crewmates.

Locks' emerald eye blazed. "We be in Davy Jones' Locker, lass. There ain't such thing as a plan. But Mutinous never did anythin' for the sake of just doin' sumpin'. The Satyr gave us the parts for a reason, and I can be guessin' who the parts be for."

Ebba had put together as much. And if the taint was here, it meant Cannon wasn't really the one in charge. His actions would be governed by the pillars of six.

Stubby turned to them. "Ye heard Caspian. Nothin' but the stone be safe to touch. Most o' the cavern is made o' the stuff, but we need to stay away from the tainted pirates and everythin' else."

Fear stirred like nausea in her stomach. She didn't need to be told twice. She'd vowed to never be tainted again. Ebba knew what she was made of, and she wasn't sure if she could survive going through that twisted terror a second time.

Pockmark whistled, and the jeering pirates immediately skulked back to the shipwreck, disappearing in the same scuttling way they'd arrived that drew bile up through her gullet.

Once back inside the ship, some of the tainted crew peeked out of the gun ports at them.

"On yer knees, *Felicity*," Pockmark sneered, strutting before them.

"Are we still called *Felicity*, lads?" asked Peg-leg. "She did sink."

The question made her heart ache with the memory of watching her beloved ship disappear to never be seen again. She hadn't even had time to properly mourn the loss of their home. Her eyes slid to Plank of their own accord to check his reaction to Stubby's comment. He'd been acting strange, almost lifeless since *Felicity* sank. Sure enough, his lips were pressed firmly together, showing angry white.

"Yer ship be sunk?" Pockmark asked. He threw back his head and laughed. "Ye always were sorry excuses for pirates. Then again, yer ship was a sorry excuse for a ship, too."

Ebba jumped at an inhuman roar from Plank, who lunged for the *Malice* captain with both hands outstretched and a wild look in his rounded eyes.

That was it, then.

She and Stubby leaped for Riot, Barrels and Grubby not far behind. The others rushed to Plank's aid. But they couldn't touch the tainted pirates. Only Pockmark wasn't contagious.

"Ye measly coward," shouted Plank, chasing after the younger pirate. "Why are ye runnin' from me? Stand and fight."

Pockmark scrambled to stay out of his reach.

Crack.

A pistol fired.

She stilled alongside the others, whirling in a panic to see if any of her loved ones had been shot.

"My, my," a mild voice said. "What is all this, Pockmark?"

Heart thundering, mouth suddenly bone-dry, Ebba faced the base of the splintered shipwreck.

THREE

Mutinous Cannon wasn't what Ebba had expected. Though clearly a pirate from his garb, he had an air of distinction, further reinforced by his purple-and-gold doublet and black tricorn hat. Where Pockmark was the kind to choose the hat with the largest feather, this man seemed inclined to choose practicality. His boots were clean but well used; his dark gray hair was confined in a leather tie at the base of his neck, much like Barrels wore his. Rings adorned most of his fingers, but these were his only jewels aside from the gold hoop in his ear. He clasped his hands behind his back and drew his shoulders back to display his full, lean frame, about the same height as Plank.

All in all, if Ebba had met him in a tavern, she might not have thought anything amiss, barring one thing: his yellowed, bloodshot eyes made her insides feel like ice. They changed him from a normal pirate into someone she'd never turn her back on for fear of a dagger finding a home under her ribs. In his eyes, she saw the taint, she saw the pillars' control; she saw the end of her life and everything she cared about.

This was his domain, and she wasn't in charge here.

Pockmark was panting hard, sweat trickling down the sides of his face from the cloying heat. "They attacked. . . ." He trailed off as Cannon turned his head and rested his attention on his grandson.

"Another excuse, I see," Cannon said, tutting softly.

Pockmark's face fell, but he straightened his tunic and strode to Cannon's side. Ebba ran her eyes over the older captain, wondering how Pockmark appeared almost harmless when placed beside a pirate like Cannon. They'd really gotten themselves in shite this time.

Mutinous Cannon hadn't come alone.

Three black-eyed pirates stood either side of him on the deck. Ebba stole a peek at her fathers. Sink her, they weren't looking too flash. Caspian and Jagger seemed okay.

. . . In fact, Jagger appeared almost curious.

Typical. His survival compass needed calibrating.

Cannon gestured around the shipwreck clearing. "But are the pirates of *Felicity* not happy to see me?" He smiled for the first time, and Ebba's insides stirred in warning.

"I could be angry at ye, I s'pose," he said. His entire face warped into a snarl that was gone as quickly as it had appeared.

The warning in her gut intensified. Beneath Cannon's mild manners was a vicious, snake-like temper.

Cannon rearranged the simple ruffles of his clean tunic. *Clean.* Everyone else was filthy. "Ye did desert me right afore the battle that took my life. But," he added, "seein' as ye've brought me—"

"Sorry, matey," Ebba interrupted. "It be soundin' like ye have a whole lot to say. Who are ye exact-like?"

She listened to her fathers' muffled gasps, all except Plank who snorted loudly. A sound behind alerted her that one of the crew had shifted to stand at her back, but Ebba didn't shift her attention from Cannon.

Honestly, his reaction didn't give her as much satisfaction as she'd anticipated.

Cannon settled his full attention on her, and it felt like hot oil pouring over her head. She managed to keep her gaze levelled on him. Just.

The pirate stepped off the shipwreck and onto the black stone ground, approaching her. "Ebba-Viva Fairisles. Princess o' the Pleo tribe. Adopted daughter o' six o' my old crewmembers. Eighteen years old, quick to anger, slow to put things together, and adamant-like that she be a pirate." His eyes shifted to her chest and then over her hips to her bare legs. "I see ye dressed for the occasion—in a dress, as ye should be."

Did he mean to hurt her by listing her traits and heritage? She'd come to terms with that identity long ago. He'd clearly received his intel from Pockmark.

"Aye, I did at that." She smiled right back at the bastard, struggling not to fidget.

His gaze shifted behind her, and Ebba took a shaking breath.

"Jagger, I presume. Prior first mate to my . . . grandson." Cannon glanced at Pockmark. "And from what I can tell, far worthier o' the title 'captain' than he'll ever be."

Phew, harsh. Ebba almost felt sorry for Pockmark. Then she saw the hate-fueled look Pockmark directed at Jagger. That was Cannon's game, then? Just like he'd done with her fathers, he was manipulating his grandson, breaking him into a malleable mold for future orders.

Jagger didn't answer.

"Then we have the six o' my old crew who betrayed me," Cannon continued. "Here we are, mateys. Now, ye're all as old as me. There's one thing to be said about Davy Jones'," he said, gazing around at the sheer cliffs. "If ye get old and die, it's hard to be eternally imprisoned for yer misdeeds, ain't it?"

The pirate ambled down the line, stopping before the prince.

"And last, but not least, we have Caspian, *king* o' the Exosian realm. What an honor." Cannon bowed low. The black-eyed pirates behind him followed.

Horror trickled through Ebba. Davy Jones' was the worst possible place for the prince to be. Royals and pirates didn't mix. And Caspian was the son of the man who'd beaten Mutinous Cannon in the final Battle for the Seas. She stilled, not daring to look at her friend.

Instead, she scanned the filthy, rag-clad pirates before her. Pockmark was slightly cleaner than the others, but dirt covered the rest from head to toe. Their hair was limp and greasy. Their souls belonged to the pillars, so self-care was probably a barren concept to them.

"We have a gift for ye, my one-armed *liege*," Cannon said.

Swindles and Riot were carting a box down the deck. The box appeared to be made of the black-and-red stone too. They set the heavy box on the uneven ground at Cannon's feet.

She jolted as the captain kicked the box. The stone lid clattered on the ground, and the object within flew out to land with a ring as it bounced over the hacked, uneven ground.

A simple golden crown landed with a clatter, ten feet from Caspian.

Ebba gave up the battle and cast a look at the prince. He stared back at Cannon, expression smooth.

"Please, King Caspian, won't you put it on?" Cannon said, throwing a cruel grin over his shoulder.

The pirates behind him laughed, as did the tainted peering out of the gun ports. Ebba heard the sound echoing within the shipwreck as the message spread to the rest of them lurking in the hull.

Caspian took a step forward. "Certainly."

"Oh, but ye can't walk, King Caspian. Ye'll be needin' to crawl. Ye should be used to that with naught but one arm, methinks."

Caspian arched his brows. "It's actually surprisingly hard to crawl with one arm."

Ebba choked on a laugh.

"Let me make the choice easier for ye," Cannon snarled.

Faster than her eyes could track, the pirate had a pistol out and pointing at her head. Her fathers surged forward with a chorus of yells.

"Stop," Cannon ordered them. "Or I'll put a bullet through yer pretty daughter's skull."

Her fathers froze on the spot.

Ebba stared down the barrel of a black pistol, breaths shallow, no longer able to pretend she wasn't afraid.

"Crawl, great king." Cannon slid his yellowed gaze from her to Caspian. "Ye be a servant o' the people, after all."

Ebba closed her eyes. Why did this have to happen to her friend? After everything he'd been through, every time she thought Caspian might be getting back on his feet, something happened to crush his confidence.

She opened her eyes and found Cannon was smiling at her, his cold, bloodshot eyes filled with triumph.

His cocky smirk filled her with trembling rage.

"It be nothin' to crawl," she informed him. And promptly sank to her knees.

Silence filled the clearing in the boulders before the shipwreck. It filled the space up to the black stone ceiling and the surrounding cliff faces.

"My legs be right tired all o' a sudden," Stubby announced brightly, doing the same.

Locks lowered with a groan. "*Much* better."

"I thought we weren't kneelin' because we ate sand bags and were fat," Grubby said, sitting cross-legged on the ground. "Did we change our minds?"

Barrels and Plank sank to their knees without a word.

The crew looked at Peg-leg.

"Ye know the humid heat affects my joints," the cook complained.

"We're makin' a stand for Caspian, ye lazy bugger," Locks hissed, emerald eye flashing.

"I *am* standin' for him," Peg-leg argued, gesturing down his body. He gazed over them again and sighed. "Fine."

Ebba cast a look at Jagger.

"I ain't doin' that." The pirate shrugged.

That. Right there. That was why the *amare* had to be wrong. Sure, she was intensely attracted to Jagger, and she'd accepted that without issue, even feeling a jolt of excitement about it. But all-consuming *love*?

The *amare* was drunk.

"How quaint." Cannon watched them. Ebba remained silent, perceiving he was peeved to no end over their show of comradery.

Caspian swallowed hard when she glanced at him. *Thank you*, he mouthed. She nodded and didn't comment as he lowered to his knees and crawled to the crown, hopping slightly to replace the anchor of his missing arm. The prince picked up the crown and straightened to a kneel to place it on his head.

"Now, that wasn't so hard, was it, King Caspian?" Cannon said, replacing the pistol in his holster. "Really, the show from the rest o' yer crew wasn't needed. I think ye'll find we'll all get along fair well, especially if threatenin' Ebba-Viva here has such a reaction every time." His lips curled.

Shite.

Still kneeling, Ebba formed tight fists, feeling more hate than she'd ever felt in her life. She would kill this man. For everything he'd done. For what he was doing now.

"If ye don't harm a hair on her head, ye'll find us obligin'," Peg-leg told the captain. "The minute ye do, we'll all be takin' turns wringin' the life from ye."

Cannon crossed the uneven rock at a leisurely pace and stopped immediately before her father. It was the first time he'd put himself within five feet of her crew.

"Ye have my word," he purred.

A pirate truth if she'd ever heard one. It went both ways. If an opportunity arose to kill him, she'd take it.

The captain turned and strode to the shipwreck once more. He didn't stop but kept walking up the old deck. Only when he was halfway did he turn back. "Oh, and I'll be needin' those shiny-like magic parts from yer belts. All five. My masters will be *most* pleased to be reunited with them."

Ebba closed her eyes. She'd known it was coming, but her heart sank nevertheless at the confirmation the pillars were involved. The parts *were* for them. Her crew weren't just fighting Mutinous Cannon but a much greater foe.

As soon as Cannon disappeared from sight, Pockmark rounded on them, fury etching the lines of his face. "Ye heard him. All five o' the magic things. Pass them over. No funny bus'ness."

Ebba covered her mouth, gagging as one of the wounds on his face cracked open and pus dripped down his cheek.

She shared a long look with the others.

To her way of thinking, there wasn't any wriggle room. Right now. First, they had to figure out how to get the tainted members of their crew back through the entrance. Handing over the objects wasn't ideal after everything they'd been through to secure them, but she suspected the alternative was a bullet in her innards, which was less conducive to escaping.

"Nothin' for it." Jagger grunted.

Stubby hummed in agreement. "Nay. Not for now."

Jagger's hand went to the *amare* tucked in his belt. He was still bare-chested. She focused on one of his many intricate tattoos—a gleaming diamond in a wreath of flowers and feathers.

A wrinkle formed between her brows.

The lean muscle of his torso tapered into a V low on his hips. Funny . . . she'd never noticed that before. It probably wasn't important in her current situation, but it interested her . . . *greatly*.

Jagger glanced up. She didn't move her eyes, however. He'd caught her staring at his body a few times in the last week and hadn't seemed bothered. Plus, when it was just attraction she felt, Ebba felt excited and shy. Now that things between them had taken a more serious, *accidental* turn, she was pissed off.

She'd look her damn fill.

He glanced at the *amare* and then back at her, quirking a brow.

Sink her, but that reference to the latest part was enough to make her look away. Her gut churned in memory of the wonderous feeling that had overcome her mere hours before when Jagger touched the *amare* to her skin. As the bearer, he wouldn't have felt a thing. But prior to the incident, there *was* an occasion where she'd touched the tube to him.

What had he felt?

And would knowing the answer make her more or less angry?

Grubby tossed the *scio* to the ground.

With an apologetic look at Grubby, Plank did the same with the *dynami*.

Caspian frowned at the sword, and Ebba knew he would consider passing over *veritas* as a failure to his father's memory.

She'd better toss the healing tube over.

Brightening suddenly, Ebba extracted the *purgium* from her belt. Swindles' back was turned, and she threw the cylinder, whistling sharply.

The pirate whirled about and raised his hands to protect his face. Ebba grinned as he caught the *purgium*. He seemed confused at first, but then his face and body contorted. Black fissures joined the boils on his face and the pirate screamed.

Ebba stumbled back with her fathers for fear he'd explode. But then he just *stopped*.

His skin smoothed of any blemish. For a second, his black eyes cleared to a bloodshot yellow, and then a healthy white. Until his eyes turned glassy and staring. Until the life escaped his body and he sagged into a crumpled heap on the black-and-crimson stone, the *purgium* falling from his grasp.

Locks clapped her on the back. Honestly, she kind of felt bad about doing that, even though it was Swindles. Still, at least he was healed of the taint. Ebba would rather be healed and dead than living like him. Not that she'd done it for those reasons.

"Y-ye," Pockmark uttered, staring at Swindles. His breath came fast as he turned to fix yellowed eyes on her.

Ebba eyed the black encroaching on the edges of his gaze, quelling her uneasiness at his rabid intensity. "Just followin' orders."

He took a deep breath, and the black receded. "Pick the tube up and put it in the box."

"Well, why didn't ye say so?" she said reasonably. Crossing the space, she held down the back of her short blue shift and crouched to pick up the object. Picking her way over to the box that had held the crown, Ebba placed the *purgium* inside.

"Bring the box," Pockmark snapped at Riot.

Without hesitation, the pirate strode to pick up the lid and placed it securely on top. Riot and Swindles had been attached at the hip for as long as she could recall, but Riot didn't even glance at his dead friend.

"Ye can be sure I'll be alertin' my grandfather to what just happened," Pockmark said coolly.

Aye, and if he didn't, then one of the twenty or so tainted peering out of the gun ports would.

Ebba cocked a hip out, arms folded.

"The captain has arranged special quarters for ye," Pockmark then announced, smirking.

She didn't like the sound of that. Not one bit. If they were locked up, getting out of here just became even more impossible.

His leering smile displayed rotting teeth. "Won't ye follow me?"

FOUR

Pockmark led them away from the shipwreck and back down the worn path to the stream. Riot followed at the end of the procession, pistol out and trained on Peg-leg's back.

The heaviness she'd felt since entering Davy Jones' Locker had steadily dissipated during the walk. Most of the dryness had left her mouth. Her mind felt clearer, her limbs lighter.

That Ebba had already acclimatized to hell was faintly disturbing.

To her surprise, Pockmark veered off the path well before the water. They walked down a different path—one smaller and not as worn. Looking up, she tried to get her bearings, but the boulders here were still taller than her.

The shipwreck had been in the northwest corner of the cavern. Now they moved directly west.

They weaved between the towering boulders all the way to the base of the cliff face. The crimson twinkled deep within the rock, again giving her the sense that the entire cavern was aflame.

"Follow the steps up," Pockmark ordered. He rounded a jutting part of the cliff and jerked his head.

She trailed after him.

Similar to the passage platform, steps had been cut into the black stone. Ebba craned her head, following the stairway twenty feet up where the steps looked to stop. Well, at least her crew now knew the stone wasn't tainted.

"Ye're to stay up there unless sent for," Pockmark told them. "And don't bother tryin' to escape. The passage be guarded. Ye'll never make it back to the entrance."

Barrels cleared his throat. "Food and water?"

Pockmark snorted. "This ain't a saloon."

With that, he ambled to stand beside Riot, hand resting on his pistol.

Ebba sighed and faced the steps, standing back when Plank squeezed in front of her.

"Jagger," she whispered as he came up behind her. "Can ye mind Peg-leg on the way up?"

"Aye, but if he falls, I ain't goin' down with him."

Ebba scowled over her shoulder.

The *amare* was wrong. It *had* to be wrong.

Or was she so angry because deep down she knew the part was right? Whatever the answer, her current confusion had made her realize she knew little about the silver-eyed pirate. He was twenty, had spent two years on *Malice*. Being the immune gave him resistance to the taint and all types of magic. He wasn't infallible but could only be affected by magic with high and unrelenting exposure. Even then, he recovered in time. When he was young, Caspian's father killed his parents. And he was only alive because a servant had put him in a boat, which ultimately drifted onto the shores of Neos.

He had tattoos that her eyes found irresistible. And he was a prized sod. Though a predictable sod. Jagger would do whatever was necessary to save his tribe family.

"Ye may want to think twice on that, matey," she told him. "Peg-leg is integral-like to the quest. Might affect yer tribe if he dies."

Jagger's eyes gleamed. "A new approach?"

Aye. Ebba shrugged nonchalantly and settled her attention on the steps. There was nothing for it.

"Hold on. Hold on," Stubby called. Her father tugged off his tunic and tossed it to her. "Wrap that around yer waist, lass. We don't want any eyes where they shouldn't be." The last part was entirely aimed at Jagger.

Her cheeks heated, but she accepted the tunic and obeyed without comment. The idea of Jagger staring at her butt all the way up was grossly unsettling.

That done, Ebba began to climb.

Her view from the base of the cliff face proved correct. About twenty feet up, Ebba crawled onto a wide ledge. There was more than enough space on the ledge for each of them to caulk with ease, but the perch formed the welcome mat for a dark cave.

"Yikes," she whispered.

Ebba walked onto the ledge to stand beside Plank. Her father scanned the Locker, and she did the same, turning away from the cave.

Everything was visible from here.

At the southern end of the cavern were the passage platform and the steep steps where they entered. The entire length of the boiling purple stream was visible, as were the damned on the opposite side of the water.

The only thing she couldn't see was Cannon's shipwreck. Though this cave and the wreck were along the western wall of the cavern, the cliff curved slightly, blocking the tainted pirates from view.

A good vantage point, all in all. They'd be able to spot danger approaching.

Ebba left Plank as the others joined them at the top. She tossed Stubby his tunic back and then stepped just inside the cave.

She paused to give her eyes time to adjust to the dark, muttering, "They could've given us a torch."

But in short measure, Ebba was able to make out a few jutting boulders in front of her. Only the height of her knees. Edging into the dark with her hands extended, Ebba strode from the right cave wall to the left.

She called out, "It be the width of our sleeping quarters on. . . ." *Felicity.*

"Be careful, lass. Caves can drop off fierce-like," Stubby warned, his voice echoing.

She worked deeper into the cave, but Stubby's warning wasn't necessary. "It ain't really that deep," Ebba told them.

The inside of the cave was about the same size as the perch outside. They could caulk in here without issue too.

"There are some trunks here," Caspian called from the opposite wall.

Ebba edged over to him, hands still outstretched. "Really?"

"I think it's clothing. . . . Do you think it's safe to touch?"

Inside the cave, the temperature was a lot colder, and the temptation to shrug clothing on was strong. Ebba wrapped her arms around her body. "It ain't worth the risk, matey."

Her fathers entered the cave, stumbling around in the dark.

"Are you cold?" Caspian asked her.

She squinted through the dark, making out his outline before her. The thoughtful question upset the balance of too many surges of energy, fear, and panic from the last week. Ebba laughed, high-pitched. "Aye, Caspian. I be cold. I'm in naught but a tight pillow case."

His reply was low. "I noticed."

Her stomach twinged. Not in a good way; in a 'we need to have a serious talk' kind of way. Caspian carried a deep regard for her, and a while back, she'd promised to be open to the idea of returning that regard. Then she'd had a run-in with Calypso, which led her to discover she was fiercely attracted to Jagger and only felt friendship for the prince. And now, after touching the *amare*, things had become a lot more complicated.

Ebba was transported back to the flash of intense feeling when

Jagger touched the *amare* to her skin. How it had bolted through her with the force of a cannonball, pooling between her hips, flushing all thought from her skull. Sink her, she really needed to explain the situation to her friend, yet she barely understood what had happened herself.

The last thing Ebba wanted was to lose their friendship because she botched the conversation.

"Here, take my tunic," the prince said, reaching overhead to pull it off.

Her stomach twinged again. She rested a hand on his arm. "Nay, I'm right without it."

The prince stilled and lowered his arm. "You're sure?" Caspian leaned in, and her stomach twinged for the third time. "When I thought I'd lost you to the Capricorn. . . ." He sighed. "You have no idea how frantic I was. How frantic I *am* with you in this horrible place."

Ebba squeezed her eyes shut, guilt churning within her. Not because she couldn't return his feelings. She'd never promised to do such a thing. But she truly feared what would happen when she confessed the truth. For so long after losing his arm, experiencing the taint, and then losing his father and his kingdom, Caspian had been almost despondent. Drawn in on himself and just *less*. For her friend, Ebba would do mostly anything to prevent him returning to that state. That included picking the right time to tell him everything.

"Ye don't fight for me," she shot back, harsher than intended. "Ye fight because there be people who need ye—yer kingdom, yer sisters. That's who ye're fightin' for, matey." She straightened away from him. "And I be sure about the tunic. I'll survive."

The gold circlet on his head caught at what little light existed in the cave.

"Ye can take that off, ye know," she told him. "There ain't no one to see."

Caspian shifted in the darkness. "I could. I'd rather keep it on. I am a king, after all."

If his tone wasn't so forlorn, she would've been overjoyed to hear such words out of his mouth.

"Aye," she said fiercely. "Ye *are* king. And ye're the only person who decides how kingly ye feel." Curse Cannon for making him crawl.

He reached out and took her hand, squeezing it tight. "I'm just so glad you're safe."

This time her laugh was genuine. "Caspian, we be in Davy Jones' Locker. Safe has naught to do with it. Unless there be two meanings to that word as well."

Leaving him, she helped Barrels to sit on a low boulder.

Groaning, her eldest father sat down. He patted her hand. "Thank ye, my dear."

In short succession, all of her fathers found a pew, and for a full minute, no one said a word. Like her, were they absorbing the huge and dire change in their circumstances?

Ebba sat crossed-legged on a mostly flat slab of stone and tilted her head back, feeling her dreadlocks brush the bottom of her bare shoulder blades. What a week. From *Felicity* sinking to the Capricorn's attack. Then the Satyr and the *amare*.

Now, they were literally in hell.

That seemed like rock bottom. She was emotionally drained, physically exhausted, and wanted a hug from someone she could depend upon.

Ebba glanced to the wide ledge outside.

Jagger hadn't entered the cave but sat with his legs dangling over the edge of the perch. He didn't like dark places after his time on *Malice*. The cave must qualify in the same category as 'below deck.'

"So," Locks drew out.

Peg-leg sniffed. "So."

"Are ye all okay after seein' Cannon?" Ebba whispered.

The pregnant silence all but echoed in the dark.

Locks was first to answer. "Ye know, I did a whole heap o' pretendin' at that shipwreck. He affected me more after twenty years than I care to admit. But I was able to pretend, and that be a lot more than I was able to do in the past. Now the first meetin' be over, I'll be better more prepared-like for what's ahead. I ain't sayin' the sight o' him doesn't stir up awful feelin's, but I can handle it. If anythin', the feelin' o' the taint while aboard *Eternal* was worse. In my memories, the taint and Cannon were the same thing, but I be seein' now that the ugliness I felt all those years ago was just the taint. And Cannon was a bully addin' to that ugliness."

Ebba released a shaking breath. She'd been prepared to hear much worse. That they'd be propelled right back to the bad place she'd been trying to drag them from through sheer determination. But Locks' revelation was huge.

"That about sums it up," Barrels said.

The rest of her fathers added their agreement, and the knot in her gut loosened.

Ebba glanced toward the very back of the cave, waiting for Plank to add his 'aye.' When it didn't come, the knot in her gut turned to a churning anger. He was still isolating himself. It had to stop. *She'd* stop it. But Ebba was too exhausted to trust what she might say to him tonight. Or whatever time it was.

"The larger issue be that we're in a bucket o' fish guts," Stubby declared.

Grubby laughed.

Barrels spoke. "What's our plan?"

"We need to figure out how to get back through the entrance," Ebba stated. "In the meantime, we'll retrieve the parts o' the root. The jetty path back to Satyr Island only shows once a day when the tide changes, recall? So we'll have to time our escape."

Caspian answered, and she jumped, realizing he sat directly behind her. "There is also the issue of the Satyr if we make it across the jetty to their island."

She tapped her bottom lip. "Grubby could tow a few o' us. Except that depends on us gettin' the rest o' ye through the entrance anyway."

Stubby hummed. "Maybe Matey will be on the other side? Or Sally and the Daedalion."

"Can't depend on that, though, can we?" Peg-leg grunted.

No, they couldn't.

"We ain't dead," Locks said.

"Well done, matey," Stubby said sarcastically.

Locks cursed at him. "I mean, we *ain't dead.* If Mutinous only wanted the parts o' the root for the pillars, then he'd hardly be needin' us. So why are we still alive?"

That was a pretty good point.

Caspian blurted, "You believe Mutinous has kept us alive for some other purpose?"

"Aye," her fathers chorused.

Well, *most* of them. Again, she pushed down her frustration at Plank.

Ebba frowned. From her fathers' stories, she knew Cannon to be cunning and manipulative. Sink her, she'd glimpsed that herself with the shite he'd stirred between Jagger and Pockmark in the clearing before. And with the Caspian-and-crown nastiness.

"What can he be cookin'?" she mused aloud.

Why would he need them?

She, Caspian, and Jagger were the three watchers who could assemble the weapon to destroy the pillars. Basic pirate logic would conclude that killing the three of them would secure the pillars' power forever.

"Do the pillars need to use us for sumpin'?" she asked.

No one answered. Simply because none of them could possibly know.

"Anythin' to add, Plank?" Stubby called to the back of the cave.

"Nay," her father whispered after a beat.

She felt the tight irritation of her other fathers at his lack of interest in their plight. Seeing any of her crew sad and despondent didn't sit well with her. But the warning in her gut from Plank's behavior had reached a whole new level. It was like he'd checked out of living. And that wasn't allowed.

Ever.

"Okay, here's what I be thinkin'," Peg-leg said.

Locks shot back, "Shite, ye're thinkin'? Dangerous stuff that."

Ebba snorted with the others. How people got through tough spots without humor, she had no idea.

Peg-leg growled. "Are ye done?"

". . . Aye," Locks quipped.

"We be sittin' ducks until Cannon shows more o' his hand. All we know is that he's operatin' on the pillars' orders. And we know what *they* want—the root o' magic. Mutinous has a plan to get the parts to them, and all we need to do is sit back, keep quiet, and figure out how he's goin' about that."

Which was sound logic.

. . . But Ebba highly doubted their escape would be so easy.

And she could say with near certainty that their escape would take more than sitting back and watching.

FIVE

Howling screams woke her.

Ebba jerked upright, clutching at her face until remembering she was in a cave in hell. And then she continued clutching her face because that was what her nightmare had been about.

But it wasn't her fathers screaming. The sound came from outside the cave. The wind.

She held her breath and listened for a few stuttering heartbeats, but her fathers and Caspian hadn't stirred from slumber.

Ebba blinked sleepily and hugged her knees to her chest. How much time had passed? Even on the uneven rock of her cave bed, she'd been dead to the world as soon as her eyes shut. But she was absolutely freezing in this silk shift. Perhaps that was what gave her nightmares.

She had to move.

Urging her cold limbs to obey, Ebba managed an awkward crouch and picked her way to the wide ledge outside so she could pace and get the grog in her veins moving. She could do with some grog, too. That and food. If Cannon didn't plan on feeding them, their 'wait and see' escape plan wouldn't be worth too much.

Glancing up, she halted at the sight of Jagger still perched in the same spot, his legs dangling over the ledge.

Her heart squeezed at the sight of him, and she had a near-overwhelming urge to seek comfort in his arms.

As much as the revelation shocked her, Ebba couldn't ignore what the *amare* had shown her. When the tube was touched to a person's skin, their true feelings were confirmed. That meant that the *amare* hadn't just shown her a love that could be. It meant that Ebba loved him already. The tube had shown her the exact depth of that feeling, too. Without him, her life would be less. *With* him by her side, she would be the best possible version of herself. They would fit as though designed for each other, neither of them as strong or as full without the other.

And that pissed her off because that was too good to be true. Her fathers had hammered a few tips into her. One was that she should always start sixty percent up when selling something. The more pertinent advice was that if a thing sounded too good to be true, it was.

The *amare* had gone on a massive bender, like Sally, and was broken.

. . . Surely.

What Ebba *did* trust was the attraction she felt for Jagger—a burning lust, just as she had encountered with Calypso—but without any of the fear. The challenge and promise in Jagger's eyes enticed her in a way nothing else ever had. *That* was something she wanted to explore. But knowing what she did about loving him took all the exploration out of it.

She already knew how the quest ended.

Was that what made her most angry? That she hadn't been allowed to fall in love at her own pace? And if that was what angered her, was that really Jagger's fault?

The *amare*'s revelation had felt so very real. Ebba had never experienced something so . . . breathtaking . . . so certain.

And yet it just couldn't be true.

"Are ye goin' to sit by me then? Or just breathe all hard-like?" Jagger's voice washed over her like the first fresh whiff of the salt air.

Ebba's entire body tightened in response.

Her voice was husky from disuse. "I'll just be pacin' a bit. I'm cold."

The bare-chested pirate twisted to look at her, tracing up her bare legs to her face. "I gave ye my tunic, where did it go?"

"Took it off when I was savin' Barrels and Peg-leg outside the Locker."

He quirked a brow at her, silver eyes dancing. "Well, I be warm enough for the both o' us if ye'd care to join."

She glared at him, wanting to take the offer but held back by the *amare* weirdness. "Thanks," she replied. "I'll pace."

Their cave ledge was about ten strides from end to end. Ebba reached the southern end and spun, returning to the northern end of the ledge where the steps were situated. She passed by Jagger again.

Peeking at him, she stumbled.

He'd turned his back to her. Now closer, she saw that not one inch of the skin on his back was unmarred by abuse. Where his skin was usually a pale gold to match his straggly hair, the ropey scars on his back, from shoulder to hip, were faint white, thick, and raised. *Licks* had been his pirate name on *Malice*. Jagger told her months ago that he'd survived one hundred and fifty lashes. For the first time, Ebba saw the proof of what he'd suffered at Pockmark's hands. She'd seen the front of Jagger's chest plenty, but he'd always been so very careful not to display his back. To her, at least. He either walked where she couldn't see the wounds or covered his back with a tunic or feathered cloak.

Her breath took a while to come steady.

Ebba collected herself and swallowed before walking toward the pirate. She sat on the black-and-crimson stone next to him, shivering.

"How much time has passed?" she asked him.

"I be thinkin' it's the next day," he answered, stiffening. "Hard to tell without the sky, but it went dim for a bit. The wind howled through the entrance passage just afore, and then the cavern lightened a mite. I'm guessin' it never gets truly dark, though damned if I know where the light comes from."

Jagger leaned back, and Ebba scooted closer to him, feeling the warmth emanating off his powerful frame. He really was warm. She inched closer. "How can ye stand to be near Pockmark when he did that to yer back?"

Jagger didn't shift his gaze from the passage platform at the south of the cavern. "Because he a'cidentally made me stronger by doin' it."

Hugging herself, Ebba turned to look at him.

He mirrored the movement. "It was during the first few months on the ship when I was too obvious-like with my quest to save my tribe. The lashes on my back were a lesson I took serious. And I've never made the same mistake. Pockmark taught me the cons'quence o' not usin' my head. I can be handlin' the scars because I know Pockmark understands what he did. He might not've for a long time, maybe not until he landed up in this place. But now he knows I'm stronger than him. And that be enough for me."

And Jagger was just offering all that up because. . .? Ebba was confused.

Normally, their conversations centered around one of them shouting about being king or queen of the crow's nest. So why *was* he casually spilling his guts on a silver platter? Ebba thought back to the moment she'd passed him the *amare* on the rowboat. He'd had a strong reaction, but never told anyone what he felt. At least, he'd never said anything to her. Had that strong reaction triggered his change of heart?

Had Jagger felt what she'd felt?

Not knowing was agony.

She shuffled closer so they were thigh-to-thigh. Galloping seahorses, he was like a hot drink. Sighing, Ebba leaned into his body. "Cannon pitted Pockmark against ye back at the shipwreck yest'rday, ye know."

"Aye. I ain't sure what his angle be. If he be tryin' to wear Pockmark down or if he's ensurin' it be harder for me to make a move."

"Last night, the crew decided to watch and wait," Ebba told him.

"I heard well enough. And I wasn't agreein' to anythin'."

She lowered her voice. "Truth be told, I ain't sure waitin' will work. I don't see what we can do otherwise just yet, but I don't feel we be havin' the luxury o' sittin' back on this one."

Jagger cast her an amused look. "Goin' against yer fathers, Viva? I didn't think ye had the guts."

"I ain't goin' against them," she retorted. "Whatever move I do or don't make, it won't be against them. They'll know o' it. Considerin' what we've been through with ye, I'd be hopin' ye'd lend the same courtesy to them."

"Aye, I can be alertin' ye to anythin' when I do it." He searched her face and then lifted an arm, watching her as he wrapped it around her shoulders.

She was in Jagger's arms. And her stupid heart was on the fritz.

The action didn't distract her from the fact Jagger had just told a pirate truth. "Nay," she said after a scant second to adjust to their new position. "That ain't good enough. Ye need to discuss the matter with us ahead o' time. With the entire crew."

Jagger scowled. "Who put ye in charge?"

Ebba sniffed. "Don't get snooty because ye're used to workin' alone. Yer actions affect all o' us; it's the least ye can do. We won't be ruinin' it."

"Not even Grubby?" he said, sliding a look at her.

She choked on a laugh. "Aye, well, it's usually a roll o' the die with Grubs. Sometimes when he blurts out sumpin', things work out, though."

"Just like ye." Jagger grinned and looked out over Davy Jones' again. She wrapped her arms around his torso and felt him peer down at her.

"This is purely survival," she told him.

He snorted. "Sure it is, Viva. And walkin' into hell be a trip to the beach."

She decided to take the high seas and ignore the pirate.

They fell into silence, and Ebba's body defrosted.

"I can't believe we be in the Locker," she said, scanning the fiery cavern below.

"It ain't so bad, really, is it?" Jagger replied. "There be all the tainted pirates. We'll need to be avoidin' them. But with the stone as a safe point, it be better than some places I've ventured."

And by that, Ebba could glean he meant *Malice*. "Jagger, there be sumpin' wrong with ye if ye be thinkin' this place is okay."

The man beside her stilled.

She could take a hint. Despite his candidness, Jagger wouldn't be spilling his guts about everything. And it occurred to Ebba that the pirate might really believe what he'd said. Maybe the Locker seemed like a haven compared to two years on *Malice*. Then again, he'd spent time on *Felicity* and with his tribe on Neos, so he knew there was better. He remembered how all that felt, didn't he?

"Ye know ye deserve better than this, aye?" she asked him.

"Do I?" he said. "I be tainted. My tribe might be dead and gone. I haven't even avenged my parents."

She wasn't going there with the last part because avenging his parents meant killing Caspian. "Ye did everythin' ye could for yer tribe. Ye killed *Ladon* for them. They can't be askin' more o' ye than that. At some point, people have to help themselves. Why do ye take such a burden on yer shoulders?"

"Because only I could save them, and only I could kill them," he said after a beat. "If I didn't mind my actions, they would die. That was how Pockmark kept me docile."

She untangled herself and scanned his high-boned features and silver eyes, which had darkened to pistol metal.

"I hated the burden of bein' respons'ble for my family's lives," he said softly.

Jagger watched her as he spoke the words, and though he hadn't asked a question, Ebba got the sense her answer mattered to him very much.

She pursed her lips. "I can understand that. It be natural for a person to begrudge the chains on their freedom. And the chains ye wore for two years were heavy ones. It don't mean that ye don't care for yer family."

Jagger closed his eyes at her reply. A small smile curved his full lips. Just for an instant before he smoothed his features, masking his emotions again.

Her gut was flipping like a bloody dolphin on brandy. She had to say something about the *amare*. It was killing her. In the past, there were times she'd been certain she loathed Jagger with the force of a thousand currents. But there were things about him, unexplored depths—like his unfaltering loyalty to his tribe—that had always made him somewhat of an enigma to her. That depth had scared her for a long time. It was only when *veritas* confirmed she could trust Jagger that she'd opened herself emotionally to the pirate.

If a man like him ever loved her, his love would be infinite.

Ebba sucked in a breath that made her gut explode with nerves . . . and something other than anger.

"So," she said, easing into the subject, "what did ye feel when I touched ye with the *amare* that time? Anythin'?"

He grinned again.

Jagger peered down at her lips. "Why do ye ask, Viva?"

His deep silken voice made her entire body coil. She shifted her gaze away from his. "Just passin' time."

Ebba peeked back up through her lashes.

"Mmm," he said, scanning her face again. "I be an immune, as ye know. I have to be holdin' the tubes for some time for them to work on me."

Drat, she'd blasted forgotten about that. Ebba gripped the ledge with both hands, huffing. Then she recalled his face when she touched him with the *amare*. "That's bullshite. Ye felt sumpin'. I know it."

"Ye seem put out, Viva. What was it that ye felt with it?" Jagger said, his voice low.

She turned back to him and inhaled sharply as their mouths nearly met. Sea salt and rope assailed her. His silver eyes were all she could see. The world around them disappeared. Longing swept through her with the cloying heat of a thousand hells.

"Viva?"

"Viva. What?" Ebba said thickly. She winced. "I mean, nothin'. That I hate ye, that is."

She shrugged off his arm and shuffled away to put distance between them.

"Which is it then?" Jagger rumbled, his eyes liquid pewter. "Because I can't do much about nothin', but I can work with hate."

What did that mean?

She searched the angled planes of his face as he closed the gap. Only the width of a few fingers separated them.

Agony. Fire.

Ebba licked her lips as his gaze dropped to them again.

She said hoarsely, "What does this mean?"

Jagger pushed closer until a mere whisper separated their lips. Ebba's breathers stopped working altogether. Who needed to breathe when they could feel this? Her body tightened again. She'd never experienced such delicious, heart-pounding anticipation.

Ebba's eyes were wide on his.

She knew what happened next. But knowing and doing seemed as different as flying and swimming. With one, they could pretend the *amare* meant nothing. With the other, it felt like they'd have to accept everything the tube had to say.

Jagger whispered, his gaze touching the deepest parts of her. "Hate it is."

SIX

Jagger stood, striding into the cave without a backward glance.

Ebba sat staring at the space where he'd sat. They'd been about to kiss. She was sure of it. One second before, that was where they were going. The next, not.

She gaped at the empty air before shutting her gob. Scrambling to collect herself, she cast her gaze out over the fiery cavern.

Why hadn't he kissed her?

And what did he mean, 'Hate it is'? Did Jagger mean that he was going to work with it? And what did *that* mean?

Ebba groaned and put her face in her hands. She'd just sat there like a codfish. She might die of the shame. Was he having a good laugh now?

The *amare* must have given Jagger a completely different feeling. Or maybe he really hadn't felt anything because of his resistance to magic. Where did that leave her? Did that mean he *didn't* feel anything for her?

She wanted this thing figured out. It was like a speck in her head she couldn't get rid of, a scratch she couldn't itch.

That was the problem. Jagger was a disease. That was probably how she should think of him. Then there'd be no repeats of the almost-kiss and cryptic comments. *And*, she recalled with a second groan, kissing Jagger would have hurt Caspian. Ebba had told herself things with Jagger wouldn't go further until she spoke to the prince and cleared up the situation between them.

Her cheeks heated. As soon as Jagger had gotten into her personal space, she'd forgotten all about her friend. How was that possible? She had to do better next time.

No. There wouldn't *be* a next time.

"Ebba?" Caspian asked.

She jolted.

Shite.

"Ahoy," she greeted him, not looking back. Had he seen anything? He'd slept right by the entrance of the cave.

"Aren't you freezing?"

Not anymore. "Aye, I awoke freezin' my rear off."

". . . You should have woken me. I'd have given you my tunic like I offered," he said, sitting beside her on the opposite side from where Jagger had sat only moments ago.

"Ebba?" Stubby called.

That was her cue! Like the coward she was, Ebba leaped to her feet and rushed inside the cave.

"Aye?" she answered her father. "Do ye need sumpin'? What do ye need? I'll get it for ye."

"Uh . . . nay, lass, just wonderin' where ye were. Ye didn't need to . . . sprint in here."

"Oh."

"Are ye feelin' okay-like?" he pressed her.

For a coward, yes. She felt pretty bad for not saying something more to Caspian just now. That had been the perfect time to tell him all. But the guilt over delaying their talk warred with protectiveness over the prince's state of mind. And she'd been all flustered from the encounter with Jagger.

"Aye, fine," she told her father.

Ebba sank onto a stone near the entrance, staring out at her friend who remained where she'd left him, peering down at the cavern below.

Alone.

She didn't want him to be alone.

Caspian sprang to his feet. He jogged to the cave.

"Food and water," he called in.

"Speak sense, or shut yer gob," Locks snapped from where he still attempted to sleep.

Jagger melded out of the shadows. "Where is it?"

"Three pirates are carrying it through the boulders toward us," Caspian replied.

Her stomach grumbled, and Ebba scowled. "Well, if the tainted be touchin' the stuff, we can't eat it."

The prince left the cave, Jagger one step behind. Despite her words, Ebba hurried after them, Stubby and Barrels hot on their heels.

Once out on the ledge, Jagger leaned against the cliff wall so his back was turned away from the crew.

The action made her realize just how purposefully he'd always positioned himself to keep his back out of sight, especially during the last two days. His scars were faint, but visible within five or six feet. Clearly, something about the scars still shamed him if he felt he had to hide them.

He scowled at her staring, and she scowled right back before joining the others to peer down to the base of their cliff perch.

Three pirates were weaving toward their cave. Ebba squinted at the blond head of the one on the left. That looked an awful lot like...
.

"Swindles." She gasped. But she'd killed him yesterday with the *purgium*—how was he back?

"I did wonder how that would go," Barrels said, tying back his salt-and-pepper hair.

She turned to stare at him with the others.

Her eldest father shrugged. "How do you die if you're already dead?"

"So what? Ye think he just . . . got up after a while?" Jagger asked, joining them at the edge, rotating slightly so his back wasn't visible to the crew.

"Not sure," Barrels replied. "Swindles didn't get up immediately, so I'm inclined to believe a certain amount of time passes before they regenerate. Or get up, as you say."

"Great," Stubby said. "So we can't be killin' the sods in here. Good to know, I s'pose."

Ebba had felt slightly bad for killing Swindles, but she felt cheated that her efforts to dent Cannon's numbers had backfired. If the occupants of Davy Jones' couldn't be harmed, that was mighty bad news for her crew.

"Oi, two o' ye come down. Only two!" came a shout from below. Riot, by the sound of the slight whining tone.

"I'm goin'," Ebba declared, already halfway to the stairs.

She had to see how dead Swindles was.

Ignoring the calls behind her, she started down the black stone steps. When out of sight from above, Ebba paused. Stubby descended behind her in short measure, throwing a glare her way.

"What's wrong?" Ebba asked, eyes wide.

Stubby flicked her cheek, and she sniggered, turning to continue picking her way to the bottom.

At the base, she swept her gaze over the three pirates.

Pockmark was absent today. Riot, Swindles, and an unknown pirate who looked more dead than alive stood behind a two-foot-by-two-foot case made of the black-and-crimson stone.

Ignoring the case, she surveyed Swindles. Yesterday, when he'd healed and died, his skin had cleared of the weeping blemishes caused by the taint. Today, all of the pus-filled wounds were back. Like nothing had ever changed. He didn't move with difficulty after what had sounded like an excruciating ordeal with the *purgium*. His eyes were still black. Nothing had altered.

As Barrels had theorized, Swindles appeared to have regenerated.

"Surprised to see me?" Swindles sneered at her.

He didn't seem happy about being killed. "Dying hurt then?" she asked. "Good."

His face contorted into a snarling fury, and Stubby shifted forward to stand beside her, but the tainted pirate didn't move off the spot.

"Food and water," Riot said, kicking the stone case.

Stubby spoke. "And how do we know it be safe to eat?"

The pirate's lips curled. "Cannon thought ye may be havin' hes'-tations. He said to tell ye that the Capricorn were droppin' off the food into the stone case just this mornin'. It be safe to eat. He was also sayin' that if ye chose not to eat, that be yer choice. Whether ye be dyin' or no is o' no cons'quence to him."

That Cannon was feeding them seemed to contradict the last part. But . . . she glanced at her father. The black stone couldn't be infected with the taint. They'd seen that with *veritas*. Back on Satyr Island, she'd glimpsed small amounts of taint within the Capricorn, but their eyes hadn't been black. They weren't contagious, so eating food they'd touched was safe.

She nodded at her father, and he pressed his lips together before doing the same.

Stubby faced the tainted pirates. "Anythin' else then?"

"Aye," Swindles said, smirking. "Cannon be desirous o' seein' the wench. Said she'd be better put to use servin' him lunch."

Ebba would serve him a bullet in his innards if she got the chance. Even if he'd regenerate. Before she had time to form an answer, her father was charging the three pirates.

"Ye ain't flamin' well takin' her, ye cowardly sods," Stubby roared at them.

The three pirates threw themselves out of her father's way, rolling away and dodging to put the boulders at their backs.

Ebba ran forward and gripped Stubby's wrist. "M'hearty," she said in a hushed voice. "Come back with me now."

Stubby glanced over his shoulder. She held his gaze, drawing him back.

"Ye know what Cannon said," she said in a low voice, stealing a look to make sure the three pirates were still stuck to the boulders. "He'll try to control ye all through me. This is naught but a game."

"But what if he hurts ye, lass? I won't let him harm ye." Stubby closed his eyes, dragging in a breath.

Cannon had killed Stubby's father. By separating her from the others, Cannon was digging at old wounds as well as making fresh ones.

"We be needin' more inform'tion. I'm goin' to get it," she told him firmly, quelling her nerves at the thought. "And if I get hurt, that be on my noggin', not yers."

Stubby blinked at her, and Ebba shifted on the spot, tensing as the other pirates neared again.

"When did ye get so old?" her father whispered.

Ebba snorted. "Hard to know, ain't it?" Crawling through the kraken's six mouths had aged her ten years at least. Not to mention the Capricorn's attack, which probably added fifteen. She was probably as old as some of her fathers by now. Surprising that she still found any enjoyment in life, really.

"Aye, ye can tell Mutinous that I'd be right chuffed to serve him lunch," she called to Riot, Swindles, and the pirate who hadn't spoken.

The three pirates stood warily, tensed like they expected Stubby to leap at them again. Why were they so skittish? They couldn't bloody die.

"Someone'll be here to collect ye when the wind next howls," Riot said.

Ebba frowned. "How can ye know when the wind'll do that?" Was that how they told time in here?

Swindles jerked his head to the others. The pirates left without answering her question. As they reached the path, Riot turned. "I'd be rationin' that food-like. I doubt Cannon'll be givin' ye any more."

Their laughter echoed around the sheer cliff faces back to her and Stubby long after they'd disappeared back through the boulders, out of sight.

Stubby approached the black stone case. She did the same and peered down. Inside were three full waterskins, dried seaweed, and raw fish.

They both sighed.

"Ah well," Ebba said, wrinkling her nose. "Could be worse."

"Could be cooked by a sulky Peg-leg," Stubby agreed with a hasty look up to the cave.

She reached for the handle.

"Hold on, lass." Stubby removed his sash, already devoid of weapons. He wrapped the material around her hand. "Just in case they got taint on it."

Once done, he rounded the other side and gripped the second handle with his bare hand.

She threw him a dark look. "Double standard, matey."

He shrugged. "Aye, but we already be tainted."

"And ye could've pulled yer tunic sleeve down, regardless-like," she shot back.

Stubby arched a brow at her and let go, tugging down his sleeve to cover his hand before gripping the case once more.

They heaved the case off the ground together.

"Heavier than it looks," Ebba puffed, already thinking of the stairs.

Stubby grunted.

Ebba took the harder position, opting to go first and walk backward. "And just so ye know," she said, slowing as Stubby navigated the first of the steep steps, "I don't like that ye think just because ye're tainted that it don't matter what be happenin' to ye. It makes me right angry."

"Does it?" he panted.

"Aye, it does," she snapped. "Ye should want to help yerself."

Stubby fell quiet as they struggled up the black stairway.

"Ye know," Stubby said between puffs, "we are tryin', lass. It might not be as quick-like as ye want, but we are. Peg-leg and Locks've touched *veritas*. And afore we were caught, the rest o' us were goin' to have a go. What ye said in the rowboat after *Felicity* sank. Ye were right. We've been scared o' the truth for far too long. And I don't know how much we can be fixed. But startin' with the truth seems a right good idea. After that, mayhaps we'll think o' sumpin' else to help us even more."

Ebba's arms burned, but the tightness in her chest wasn't just from the strain of carrying the heavy case.

"That means a lot to hear ye say such things." More than a lot. That her fathers had talked with each other about touching *veritas* made her feel almost joyful. The decision not to ignore the truth anymore seemed like huge progress.

"We know ye worry over such things," he puffed. "Ye always were a worry-wart when it came to us."

"That be Grubby's fault. And it'll never change," she replied, reaching the top and stepping back onto the platform so her father could join her.

Stubby smiled at her, sweat dripping down the side of his face. He peered past her shoulder and spat, "Fat lot o' help ye all were gettin' this back up. Should've left yer portion down there. Or mayhaps this'll be all for me and Ebba. Ruddy sea cows."

Ebba set her end of the case down with a groan of relief, moving back as Locks and Grubby took over, taking the black stone box farther onto the ledge.

"Fresh water, seaweed, and fish," Barrels said, sounding about as excited over that prospect as she and Stubby had been.

"Raw fish?" Caspian repeated, face falling.

Jagger selected a fish, bending it in half to split the skin and expose the flesh beneath. "Ye ain't never had raw fish, Exosian? Too fancy for it, I s'pose."

Caspian threw him a withering look and grabbed a fish as well, repeating Jagger's action. He stared down at the pink flesh, and Ebba could definitely detect a green tinge to his gills.

Striding forward, she reached for a waterskin and uncorked it, taking several gulps before shaking it in Plank's face. He blinked and took it after a few seconds, taking one sip before passing it on to Grubby. Anger simmered within her, and she took a few dried pieces of the seaweed, handing two to Plank.

"Eat," she said forcefully.

He lifted his gaze to hers, his eyes searching her face. Movements slow, Plank brought the seaweed to his mouth and took a bite. He'd never been like this in her life. A daydreamer, yes, but barely functioning, no. If he didn't snap out of it soon, she'd explode. She opened her mouth—

"What did the tainted pirates say?" Jagger asked.

Ebba stilled, closing her gob.

"Would ye like to tell them, Ebba-Viva?" Stubby asked her, an evil glint in his eye.

Narrowing her eyes at him, she cleared her throat. "Well, they said a few things. And I be fair interested in a couple o' things they *didn't* say."

Barrels fixed her with a flat look. "We want the full version, my dear, not the pirate version."

The pirate version used to be enough.

"I was gettin' to it," she said, rolling her eyes. "Well, first off, Swindles be lookin' like he was never healed. I think ye were right about him, Barrels."

"I wonder how long it takes for them to regenerate," Barrels mused. "That we can't kill them isn't ideal. But if we seize the right window to strike against Mutinous, then it might aid our escape."

"Aye." Peg-leg hummed. "Though I ain't even sure how they be tellin' time here."

"They mentioned sumpin' about collectin' Ebba when the wind next howled," Stubby said.

The ledge quietened.

Locks faced Stubby. "What be this about collectin' Ebba?"

"When the wind howls," she answered quickly. "Which seems odd-like to me, don't ye think? It must happen each day at the same time. Or a few times a day. . . ." She trailed off, seeing the rest of her crew weren't taking the bait.

"What are they collectin' ye for?" Jagger demanded, dropping the remains of his raw fish back into the stone case.

She took another bite of the seaweed and chewed in silence.

They all waited, though Jagger appeared the closest to exploding, Peg-leg right behind him. Or maybe Jagger would explode and trigger explosions in all the others, like dominoes.

She swallowed.

Sink her, they knew enough about her stalling tactics. "Don't overreact-like, but Cannon wants me to serve him lunch. In-and-out job. I'm goin' to get intel." Ebba aimed the last bit at Jagger with a pointed gaze that didn't appear to have any effect on his simmering rage.

Crossing to her side, Caspian took her hand and turned to the others. "She can't go alone."

"*She*," Ebba cut in with an irritated glare at her friend, "is."

Caspian dropped her hand, bewilderment crossing his face. "I'm sorry, I didn't mean to cut you out of the conversation."

Ebba's temper wasn't only due to him speaking about her rather than to her. Her angst over their relationship was rearing its head. She squeezed his shoulder. "I know. But it be my choice. We need to know more. And I'm thinkin' that ye know the benefit o' pretendin' to be a servant," she said.

He chuckled. "Touché. Though I don't believe Mutinous will let down his guard, knowing who you actually are. I just don't want you to be hurt."

"It's a good idea," Jagger announced.

Locks took a swig from a waterskin. "Nay, lad. Makin' ye walk the plank would've been a good idea. But not this. I don't like it. I say we put it to crew vote."

They'd vote against her.

"Nay," she said, heat creeping into her cheeks. "I've already made my mind up. I'm goin'."

"Ye can't just change the votin' system to suit ye," Locks countered.

"Not every choice needs to be a crew decision," she shot back. "I can be makin' up my own mind."

Stubby whistled, and Locks and she each took a step back.

"She's grown, lads," Stubby said to the others. "Look at her. It's just like Barrels' book said. She's assertin' herself."

"Chapter Twenty-Three: The Crow Leaves the Nest," Barrels said. "I'd hoped to never see it."

Caspian's lips trembled. "Is this from your *How to Raise a Child at Sea* book?"

Her fathers nodded gravely, and Ebba closed her eyes briefly, realizing they were having a weepy co-parenting moment.

Peg-leg sniffed and half-turned from the group, wiping at his face.

Stubby cast her a look. "But I'd like to ask everyone to vote on the issue anyhow. Raise yer hand if ye say aye to Ebba goin'."

Jagger raised his hand. Barrels sighed and did the same. Stubby added his, then Grubby and Plank. Ebba stared at them, stunned at their vote. She'd expected a blanket nay from the lot of them.

Stubby punched Locks' leg, and he grumbled, waving a hand overhead before dropping it. They turned to Peg-leg, who fluttered a hand behind him.

"I ain't ready for her to leave the nest," he choked.

"I'll be back in a couple o' hours," she said, exasperated. Though an ember of warmth had flickered to life within her at their show of support.

Ebba had grown up on a ship as the only child. After the Maltu brothel abandonment incident, her fathers had always included her in the voting of major decisions. From that point on, she'd been added to the captain-of-the-month roster too. Since her stint on *Malice*, they'd actively asked for her opinion. But for them to trust that she was capable of protecting herself through a run-in with *Mutinous Cannon*, even if they hated her decision, was more than she'd anticipated. Even if they didn't trust in her capability, they respected that it was her move to make.

Ebba blinked several times to dislodge the burning in her eyes. Then she peered at Caspian. "No hand to raise?" she asked.

He frowned at his hand. "No," he said. "I know you wish me to say yes. But I care about you too much to agree to that. I'm sorry, but I also won't change my mind just because it might upset you."

His reply soothed and annoyed her all at the same time. And, now she thought of it, why wasn't Jagger saying no? Out of anyone here, Ebba might have been most gratified if he'd voiced some discontent over her sacrificing herself. He'd barely waited a second to throw his hand in the air.

The wind tore through the entrance crevice, screaming high as it entered the cavern.

Ebba whirled toward the sound, gazing over the hundred-foot gap between them and the passage platform. Her insides clenched as she shifted to look directly down. A pirate was making his way through the boulders again to their cave.

She swallowed, already thinking of marching to the shipwreck to meet Cannon and his tainted crew by herself.

"That be my cue," she said lightly.

And strode to the steps once more.

SEVEN

As soon as Ebba stepped into the shipwreck clearing, the illusion of safety that had built in her mind was shattered. In the cave, her crew was separate, and ignoring that they were in hell was easier. That safety peeled away as Pockmark marched her to the base of the splintered deck.

Ebba fixed her attention on not tripping over the hacked-away remains of the boulders as she picked her way toward the shipwreck.

"Stop there," Pockmark barked.

No worries on that count. Ebba didn't need encouragement to stay off the tainted ship. Especially—she glanced at the dark brown skin of her toes—as she wasn't wearing shoes. Pockmark hadn't uttered any insults on the walk over, which had surprised her. Nothing but orders had crossed his lips. In that respect, he'd greatly changed from the pirate she'd first encountered on Maltu. For Pockmark, the days of selfish indulgence and meaningless cruelty seemed at an end. Ebba suspected that was due more to Cannon's tight control than to any change of heart.

Ebba wasn't sure how far it was wise to push Pockmark. She *did* know that pushing him was a fair chunk safer than pushing Cannon.

"Did granddaddy tell ye to mind yer beh'vior then?" she asked him. "Do ye do everythin' he says now?"

Pockmark stiffened and turned to face her.

Ebba sniffed dismissively. "I recall that feathered hat ye used to wear. That's gone, too, I s'pose? Granddaddy told ye to take it off?"

"Keep talkin' and see what happens," he spat, rounding on her.

She planned to. Ebba had no doubt she was faster than Pockmark. "Cannon seems mighty disappointed in ye," she continued. "Can't say I'm blamin' him. Ye always were a stupid bugger."

The pirate clenched his fists, and Ebba held back a gag as the skin between his knuckles cracked and oozed yellow pus.

"Ye're one to talk o' stupid," Pockmark said. "Ye ain't got more than two coins rattlin' in yer skull."

"Aye," she said, lifting a shoulder. "But I can rub my two coins together. Ye can only do it if Cannon says ye've been a right good lad. He probably only lets ye use yer noggin' when the wind whistles through the passage. How many times is that? Twice a day?"

Black flooded Pockmark's eyes, and Ebba tensed her legs, ready to spring out of the way. Pockmark took one step in her direction.

"*Mercer*, collect yerself."

Ebba shivered at the stone-cold voice and tilted her head to see Mutinous Cannon standing near the bottom of the shipwreck. How long had he been there?

Pockmark breathed hard, his eyes fixed on Ebba.

"Ye heard him, Pockmark," she whispered with a smile. "Be a good lad and heel."

With a roar, the pirate lunged at her, both hands outstretched.

Ebba leaped to the left, one eye on Pockmark, the other on the sharp rocks underfoot. His clawed fingers swiped at the air where her head had been a scant second prior. As she spun out of his reach again, he paused to draw his cutlass.

Ebba searched the ground for a weapon. A chipped bit of stone the size of her fist lay to her left. Crouching, she swooped down to pick it up.

"Enough." The sharp word shot through her ears like an arrow.

She didn't remove her eyes from Pockmark, who still breathed like a rabid dog, his rusted cutlass half-unsheathed.

Cannon ambled over to them at a leisurely pace, not paying Ebba any mind. His eyes were fixed on Pockmark, and his long, weathered fingers rested lightly on the butt of his pistol.

"Ye know the order o' our masters," he said to Pockmark. "Ye know what they command."

Ebba hung on his every word.

Pockmark's black eyes shifted to Cannon, who leaned in close to his grandson. She stepped closer on light feet to listen.

"You are not to touch her," Cannon whispered low.

Pockmark looked past his grandfather at her, and Ebba smirked at him. There was a roar as the pirate lost control again, and then the sharp retort of a fired pistol.

Ebba leaped away from the pair, heart catapulting into her throat. Eyes wide, she watched as Pockmark thudded to the ground, a gaping hole in his stomach.

"Waste o' a good bullet," Cannon said with a weary sigh. He holstered his weapon and turned to her.

"Ebba-Viva Fairisles," he said, regarding her with displeasure. "Did ye not see fit to dress in the clothes I provided?"

He meant the garments in the cave? "How can I be knowin' if they're tainted or not?"

Cannon gave a mocking bow. "Why, my word, of course. Is that not enough?"

"Nay," she answered. He'd just shot his grandson. Even if Pockmark regenerated, it didn't make the act any more palatable.

He straightened, the cold attempt at a smile fading from his lips. "I see. And yet ye walk on sharp stones that might cut yer feet. Don't ye know the surest way to succumb to the taint be for it to infect a wound?"

Ebba did know, but why was he telling her that?

"Ye want me to wear shoes?" she asked, confusion filling her.

This was some twisted version of the numerous times her fathers had said the same thing.

"I would think ye'd be eager to remain away from the taint. Pockmark told me o' yer time on *Malice.* And yet ye also were able to leave Davy Jones', which shows ye ain't tainted any longer. Ye touched the *purgium,* I take?"

Uh-uh, that's not what we're here for, Ebba thought. She was drawing information from *him.* "Mayhaps I just be immune to it."

"No, Ebba-Viva, there is only one immune, and that honor falls to Jagger and Jagger alone." His eyes gleamed as he spoke, and uneasiness skittered down her spine. So Cannon knew about the pillars, the parts, *and* the three watchers.

She may never know, but she needed to figure out how many times the wind came through the passage each day. If her crew knew that, then tracking when the path to the Satyr's island was exposed would be easier.

"It must get rep'titive in here," Ebba said, noticing Cannon watched her.

He stared, head tilted as though searching for a crack he could drive a wedge into. It interested her to suppose the captain thought she had more than one crack. Maybe she had a while back, but her fathers were the only vulnerability that would make her do anything. And surely Cannon had discovered that already.

"It does," he answered with an indulgent smile, like he'd granted her a boon. "I'm a pirate. I ain't meant to be in a place such as this. I'm meant to sail the seas, free."

The answer struck her with force, if only because he mirrored her exact desire, yet they were two completely different people. "Maybe if ye'd sailed the seas a different way, ye wouldn't be in here."

His smile widened, and he clasped his hands behind his back, crossing closer to her. Ebba held her breath, but the pirate stopped three feet away, bloodshot eyes glinting. She'd seen that look in Ladon's eyes when he'd intended to devour her soul and those of some of her fathers and Jagger. She'd seen the same look in Pockmark's eyes. She'd felt that undiluted evil exuding from the six shadows who'd manifested on *Malice.* And she felt it now as Mutinous Cannon stared down at her. Ebba couldn't look anywhere else or appear weak. Yet to not look elsewhere and show she was aware of how glancing away would look seemed equally weak. Alone, without her crew at her back, without the *dynami* in her belt, or one of her magical friends in the wings ready to rush to her aid, Ebba felt an awareness of her slight frame creep upon her.

Cannon didn't say a word. He just stared.

"Is this the part when we don't speak then?" Ebba asked, tilting her chin.

"And the six o' *them* made a strong woman like ye," Cannon said, snorting. "Blow me down, who would've thought they had the guts."

Heat flooded her cheeks, and Ebba bit back her angry retort. Cannon quirked a brow, his finger lifting to her cheeks. He hovered his hands over her skin, and her heart pounded. His eyes were yellow, so he wasn't contagious, but Ebba would rather not run the risk.

"Rage," Cannon said. "A woman of passion. Rage, I understand. Rage is my constant companion in closed walls."

What was he on about? Why was he talking in cryptic nonsense? Or did he know that doing so would unsettle her more than if he held her at gunpoint?

"Because ye're tainted," she forced out.

Cannon made no answer. Facing away from the ship, toward the stream path, he said, "Come."

"No lunch?" she asked, walking after him.

"Not today," he said. "Yer attire ain't ap'ropriate."

Pirates weren't usually one for manners. What was his obsession with the clothing and shoes? And more importantly, he'd told Pockmark the pillars didn't want him to touch Ebba. Was that specific to Pockmark? Or did that apply to all of the tainted pirates? And in regard to her fathers, Caspian, and Jagger too?

Ebba strode after the captain down the worn stream path, breathing a sigh of relief when he didn't branch off toward the cave. Any situation involving Mutinous and her fathers was bound to work out badly. Where was he taking her?

Images of him pushing her into the boiling water reared up in her mind. But, Ebba thought as she straightened, Cannon hadn't touched her once.

That struck her as strange, now that she thought about it. At their first meeting, he'd lingered at the base of the shipwreck for the most part. And Pockmark had shouted at the other pirates to stay back. Her crew was then led to a cave of the black-and-red stone with clothing stored in large stone cases, a smaller version of the one their food came in.

Her crew had been so worried about catching the taint from the occupants of Davy Jones' they hadn't paused to consider that Cannon was doing everything possible to ensure they didn't catch it too. And if she was right, why did the infamous captain want or need them free of the taint?

A blur of flaxen gold between the towering boulders caught her eye, and Ebba peered into their midst. Silver eyes stared back at her, and she gasped.

"Did ye cut yerself then?" Cannon whirled, and Ebba wrenched to face forward.

"N-nay," she answered, clearing her throat.

A fury burned like midnight fire in his gaze. At her answer, the fire slowly died away. The captain continued down the worn path, and Ebba released a breath, stealing another glimpse at Jagger in the shadows of the boulders.

What was he blasted well doing? Had he followed her the whole time?

What are ye doin'? she mouthed at him.

He darted to the next boulder parallel to the path and merely grinned at her. She was going to kill him.

Ignoring Jagger lest she give him away, Ebba forced her attention to the path. Between the tapering boulders ahead, she glimpsed the purple stream. Wisps of steam from the boiling water rose in languid swirls. The boulders steadily shrunk in size; they were only to her hip now and becoming sparser. Just off the path, Jagger crouched behind a boulder that hardly covered him and gave her a curt nod. He couldn't go any farther. Despite being unaware of his presence until a few minutes ago, Ebba dreaded continuing without him.

Her sense of foreboding heightened as she strode after Cannon.

The boulders continued to shrink until they were only to her knee.

Cannon stopped beside the boiling purple stream, and she halted beside him, out of reach. Ebba glanced across the water and took an involuntary step back at the masses of faces staring at her.

Just like when she'd first peered down at the western half of the cavern from the passage platform high above, the damned on the other side of the stream blended in with the fiery stone.

Ebba covered her nose at the smell of waste and body odor piercing the steam to reach her eight feet away. The murky grime coated their skin and the creases on their faces. Dirt and slime blanketed their clothes, edging under their nails and between their teeth. If Ebba had to guess, she'd say they'd kept the exact form they'd died in. Some were old and frail, others strong and tall, and the face of more than one child caught her gaze. Their eyes were tired, dull, and downtrodden where the eyes of the tainted were black.

How did they get over there? Ebba glanced left and right and couldn't see any way across. Sheer cliffs lined their flatter and smaller half of the cavern. Only the passage platform interrupted the uniformity at the southern end. Maybe the damned had to climb down the cliff to get there?

Regardless, at least the inaccessibility and the boiling stream had saved the damned from the taint.

Pity rose within her at the sight of them, the emotion surprising her with the force and speed of its punch. The tainted pirates had been people once, but the damned here *were* people. They were cognizant of what happened. A young boy across the water reached for her, sobbing, tears trekking down both cheeks.

Yet to be here, they must have done terrible things. Or, were they just judged to be more bad than good by the thunderbird who sorted light and dark souls in the Oblivion? According to the entrance of Davy Jones', her fathers belonged here, yet Ebba knew they didn't. Her fathers were on the light gray side of good, not the dark gray.

How many of these people could be good if given a chance? Or if sorted by someone other than the thunderbird, who seemed to have a one-size-fits-all approach to sorting souls? He'd been ready to chuck Jagger in this place for killing a bird. Staring at such pitiful humans, Ebba's heart squeezed, wondering if they truly deserved eternal suffering for the choices they'd made.

"Pitiful, aren't they?"

His words echoed her thoughts, but the context couldn't be more opposite. Cannon sounded almost gleeful about their sad, depressive state. Ebba didn't answer. She didn't trust her voice not to shake.

"When we arrive here, we turn up at the entrance, the rock wall you walked through. We stumble through the crevice passage into this cavern. Let's just say, anyone who ain't a pirate is encouraged to climb down to the other side."

Ebba shook her head. "Yer point?"

"The point bein' that there ain't no pirates over there. Everyone there be a murderer, a thief, and all o' them have a black heart. They scream and groan, but they turn on each other in the blink o' an eye. Every day. And they hate pirates. If a pirate were to venture in there. . . ."

"Ye're goin' to put me over there?" she asked, a dull ringing in her ears.

Cannon glanced at her and smirked. "Nay, it ain't ye who deserted me afore the final battle." His face changed, and Ebba's chest seized at his flash of white-lipped fury.

"It ain't ye that mutinied and trapped me here for two decades." The pirate cut off, spinning from her to look toward the entrance.

He whirled back and stepped closer than he'd yet dared.

Would he touch her? Or would he refrain? That would be a sure way to know if her working theory was right or wrong.

Cannon bent his head down to her, and Ebba set her jaw, refusing to budge.

"Most people fear their loved ones dyin', but not ye," he said, scanning her face.

Ebba frowned. That wasn't true. If they died, if they were taken from her, Ebba would cease to exist.

"Ye fear yer fathers not *livin'*," Cannon said. "That be what ye fear. So listen wisely, Ebba-Viva Fairisles, because ye've likely heard I ain't one to give out warnings. Ye harm one o' my pirates again, think to venture a comment that ye feel makes ye strong, or see fit enter my company again without wearin' the clothes I've seen fit to grant ye, then I'm sure ye can guess where yer fathers will end up. And I can tell ye sure-like, none o' ye be dead. Yet. But if the vagabonds across the water kill yer fathers, they will be. And ye can guess where they'll stay for all time."

Ebba fisted her shaking hands, dropping her gaze. Eternal desolation. That's what Cannon intended for her fathers. Whether it would be because she stepped out of line or whether he intended to take his revenge regardless was unclear.

As for the rest, she could abide not killing any of the tainted pirates. Hardly a point if they just came back. She could even still her tongue if push came to shove. Though it wouldn't stop her taking jabs at Cannon's underlings when he wasn't around.

But the clothes.

"I don't trust why ye want me to wear the clothes so bad-like," she said, meeting his yellowed gaze again. "And I don't trust that they ain't tainted."

"Then ye've decided," Cannon said, straightening.

"Nay," Ebba blurted, an idea coming to her. "There be a way to prove ye're tellin' the truth."

The pirate had turned from her and craned to look up at the passage platform again. How many times each day did he look toward the entrance? He'd admitted hell was repetitious. He'd spat the word '*trapped*' just before. Cannon had confessed he wasn't meant to be in here and that pirates were meant to sail the seas, free.

She'd barely had time to think on the matter when a trail of pirates appeared high up on the passage platform. Swindles and Riot were there, and Ebba squinted as Riot held a hand in the air, fingers spread wide.

Two.

What did that mean?

Cannon merely nodded and pivoted back to her.

Two, what?

"I'm listenin'," he told her.

Huh? Oh. "The sword. *Veritas.* With it, we can see what the taint be infectin'."

How much Cannon knew about each item was anyone's guess. And Ebba didn't want to give him more knowledge than she had to. But a stint with the sword to peer through Davy Jones' in more depth than the quick glimpse Caspian had stolen yesterday might help them uncover more answers.

"We'd know if the clothin' were all right, and I'd have no problem wearin' them," she added. *Or the shoes.*

Cannon crossed his arms, the lines of his weathered face deep and shadowed as he loomed over her. "And why should I do this for ye when I can just throw yer fathers over the stream with the damned?"

Ebba shrugged. "Ye don't have to, I s'pose. But there may be sumpin' I can help ye with. Ye've been out o' the realm for a long time. Things have changed."

The pirate's eyes glittered. "Ye offer me useless inform'tion in exchange for an object o' immense power? The pillars see through my eyes. Through all of the tainted eyes. I get ample information of the outside realm from the tainted beings who arrive here."

Right.

"It'd be no skin off yer back to let us have it." She redirected the conversation. "Lend it to us for an evenin' to check the clothes, cave, and food over, and that'll be enough for us."

"One minute," he countered.

Ebba shook her head. "That be unreasonable, and ye know it. One hour, and we'll be hard pushed to get everythin' seen to in that time."

A scream rent the air, and she clutched her chest, spinning toward the water, fearful of being ambushed. What awaited was worse.

One of the damned had jumped into the boiling water. The man's scream was a sobbing wail of agony, spanning the huge distance to the ceiling, spreading out to fill the fiery cavern, overwhelming her every sense.

The skin was melted from his body, and all she could do was stare in horror at the man as his eyes rolled back in his head and he slumped back into the water, disappearing from view.

She dropped to her knees, eyes riveted to the spot where he'd disappeared. Bile surged up her throat. She gagged, clutching her stomach and her mouth in a bid to keep the burning liquid within.

Too late, Ebba regained control of her eyes and squeezed them shut. The image of his shrieking face and melting body were seared on the backs of her eyelids.

"He jumped in there to die knowin' he'll be back in half a day when the wind howls," Cannon said, crouching beside her. "Such is his torment that he was willin' to be boiled alive for the reprieve from this place. He's not the only one. If ye listen closely, ye'll hear the same screams over and over. How many times do ye think yer fathers will jump in there to escape the emptiness?" he asked.

She couldn't open her eyes. Right now, Ebba couldn't look at

Cannon in the way she wanted or needed to. She didn't feel capable of resistance. She felt . . . weak.

The volume of his voice lessened as he stood again. "I agree to yer terms, Ebba-Viva Fairisles. One hour with the *veritas*. Soon. Look at all ye need because ye won't be seein' the sword again after." He paused. "I trust ye can be findin' yer own way back?"

EIGHT

"I saw," was all Jagger said as Ebba tripped along the worn boulder path.

She stepped off the walkway into the shadows where he stood, sighing to see a familiar face. Or his face in particular.

Ebba swallowed thickly. "It was. . . ."

"Aye, Viva. I know."

He opened his arms, and she fell into them, hugging him as she rested her cheek against his hard chest. One of his hands splayed between her shoulder blades, the other coming to stroke over her dreadlocks and beads.

His hands bunched in her hair after. "Tell me."

"Oh, just a threat. He'll chuck my fathers in there if I kill another pirate or mouth off. And I need to wear the clothes he put in the cave. We all do."

She felt Jagger tense.

His voice was tight. "Why?"

"Cannon seemed awful bothered by me not wearin' shoes. Said if I cut my foot, I could be infected with taint. I'm thinkin' he needs us untainted for some reason."

Jagger was quiet as they stood embracing in the shadows of the boulder. Had they ever hugged before the last couple of days? Ebba couldn't recall being aware if they had. Not like this. She could feel the rise and fall of his chest and hear his heart.

Ebba was glad to hear evidence he had one. In the past, she'd wondered. He was warm; the heat of his body reached through her shift to seep into her skin.

She was only wearing a thin shift.

Ebba let her arms drop and stepped back. Jagger searched her face as she did so.

"Ye said ye'd share any thoughts goin' through yer sly head," she told him.

His lips twitched. "Those weren't my words, nay. I said I'd tell ye o' plans that might be affectin' the rest o' yer crew."

Her hands went to her hips, and she pinned him with her gaze.

"That be a mighty fine look on ye, Viva," he said with a grin. "Have I told ye I like it when ye're mad? Makes those green eyes o' yers as bright as new ferns."

Jagger said things like that sometimes. More and more in the last few weeks.

"Why do ye say that stuff to me?" she whispered, hands twisting in the sides of her shift.

Jagger took a step closer and bent his lips to her ear. "Because not only do I like it when ye're mad, I like it when yer lips form that surprised little 'o.'"

"Nay," she blurted, turning to him in shock.

He looked ready to burst out laughing. "Aye, Viva."

"But why do ye *like* those things?" she pressed, tilting her head back. She searched his handsome face, tracing his high-boned cheeks.

Jagger's breath hitched.

He wanted her. She wanted him. They both knew it.

Her lips neared his.

Jagger leaped back like he'd dipped a toe in the boiling purple stream. Ebba jolted, her heart leaping in her chest. She'd been about to lay one on him! What was he doing running away?

He couldn't say her eyes were like plants one second and then freak out when push came to shove.

Was he messing with her? Because she hadn't read that wrong.

"Ye're actin' strange, Jagger," she snarled at him.

Ebba set off down the path toward the cave.

Her mind was in a twisted mess from all the things she'd just seen, let alone Jagger's games. Ebba didn't even *know* what she'd found out with Cannon. But she'd be able to mull that over with the others' help.

Jagger grabbed her hand. "Wait."

She peered back and waited, brows raised. "What? We've got problems to be sortin', and if ye're bein' yer usual secr'tive self, then I won't be wastin' time mullin' them over with *ye*."

He took a deep breath and exhaled heavily. "Aye, then. Let's get back. I was only hearin' bits and pieces o' the talk by the ship. After that, I was too far to hear."

He really wasn't going to tell her why he'd freaked out back there?

Ebba veered off the main path and onto the cave path. She weaved between the boulders at a fast clip. "Why were ye followin' me anyhow? He said for *me* to come. Who knows what he might've done to ye if he'd spotted ye."

"Ye think I'm stupid enough to get caught?" Jagger countered.

No. Just stupid in general.

"—And I came because I wasn't about to let ye walk into that alone."

. . . "Stop sayin' things like that if ye don't mean them," she hissed as they reached the bottom of the cave steps.

"But I do mean them."

She whirled and stared at him. "Then why didn't ye. . . ? Nay, I don't want to know. There be too much in my head tonight without ye playin' tricks."

"I'm not playin' tricks," Jagger said after a beat.

Aye, he was. Or had some plot of his own.

"Whatever," she muttered. Her cheeks heated, and she faced the steep stone steps again.

. . . Suddenly, her silk shift seemed very short.

Ebba pivoted back. "Ye need to go up first."

Jagger leaned against the cliff, lips curving. "Why would that be?"

She stared at him, scowling at his widening grin. The hot, joyful feeling surged through her afresh, except this time, it wasn't bile, and Ebba was inclined to think it'd be preferential if it was.

She squinted over his shoulder and blanched. "Pockmark!"

Jagger whirled, and she did the same, sprinting up the steps while his back was turned. She heard his shout of laughter when he found her gone and kept up the scrambling pace all the way to the top, knowing if he caught up, he'd see the very sight she'd been intending to hide from him.

Breathers bursting, she reached the ledge and tugged down her shift. How was it possible she was nearly laughing after what she'd just seen? The thought sobered her. As did the sight of her fathers and Caspian sprawled out over the wide ledge, looking at her like she was half a skull short of rum.

Clutching her side, Ebba took gulps of air and waved at them, laughing a little.

Jagger appeared behind her in the same condition.

She didn't dare look at him.

"Got heaps to tell ye," Ebba said, putting distance between her and the flaxen-haired pirate. She avoided Caspian's gaze and picked a spot to sit between Plank and Stubby.

No one spoke.

Odd.

Was it just her imagination, or did the ledge feel awkward? Why was it awkward? Ebba wanted to glance at Jagger to see if it *was* just her. Except she suspected the awkwardness would increase if she did that. They'd just run up the stairs. They hadn't spoken loudly at the bottom, so it couldn't be their conversation that had inspired the uncomfortable tension.

Ebba shook her head.

"Viva and I be thinkin' that Cannon doesn't want us to be tainted. Either all o' us or just Viva. We ain't sure yet."

We? Viva and I? Was he doing that on purpose?

She refused to look at him. "Aye, Pockmark went for me, and Cannon said, 'They told us not to touch her' or sumpin' close, and then he shot Mercer."

"I told ye it was a gunshot," Peg-leg threw at Stubby. "'*It's just falling rock.*' We should've gone to check."

Stubby ignored the cook, looking at her. "That does seem odd-like."

"And he be right intense about me wearin' the clothing in the cases here," she added. "I made a deal with him over it. We get the sword for an hour tonight so we can see what's tainted." She left out the 'if I don't, he'll chuck you on the other side' part.

Her fathers were still tense, but some of the silent heaviness dissipated.

Barrels shifted. "What else, my dear?"

Ebba thought. "When someone here be killed, they reappear in twelve hours. Mutinous said half a day. I wanted to figure out if the timin' o' the wind was the same each day, but didn't think it wise to push too hard."

"But knowing even that is very useful," Barrels said.

Ebba nodded. "While we were by the stream, a group o' pirates arrived back from the entrance."

Locks said gruffly, "Aye, we saw them from here." He glared at Jagger.

Ebba blinked at her father. Why was he glaring at Jagger? She scanned the others, saying, "When the tainted pirates returned, Riot held up two fingers, and Cannon dipped his head."

Jagger shot her a surprised look. “I didn’t see that. What do ye think it meant?”

“I have no idea,” she said truthfully. “A signal. Or a count? I’m only guessin’.”

“They’d returned from the entrance to Davy Jones’,” the flaxen-haired pirate mused. “What’s the link between them goin’ there and the number two?”

“No notion,” she replied, shrugging.

He frowned. “Me neither. But it seems important-like.”

Stubby took her hand and squeezed it. “Ye did great, lass. We have sumpin’ to go on.”

She hadn’t put that together alone, but her fathers didn’t seem eager to acknowledge Jagger, and Ebba had a sinking feeling why. It might also account for the fact that Caspian hadn’t uttered a single word.

“Now the question be: Why doesn’t Mutinous want us tainted?” Peg-leg said.

Good to know she wasn’t the only one stumped by that.

“It don’t make sense,” Locks said. “The pillars become more powerful the more people they taint. So why keep us safe from it?”

Ebba glanced at Barrels, who shrugged and said, “I’m afraid I can’t make hide nor hair of it.”

“Mayhaps the sword’ll tell us more.” Jagger rounded the circle of her sprawled fathers as he spoke.

Ebba finally deigned to look at him.

Something was amusing him. Greatly.

Jagger caught her eye and jerked his head in the direction of the stream.

Her sinking feeling grew as she peered over the ledge. At the boulders below. She’d already guessed at the source of the awkwardness.

She’d forgotten about her crew’s vantage point from up here. The stream was visible. They would have seen her fall to her knees. They might've heard the man scream, too. She was certain they would've seen him die. But that wasn't what bothered her.

Ebba traced the boulder path with her eyes. Though she couldn't pinpoint the exact spot where she and Jagger had embraced in the shadows, it didn't matter because the entire first section of the route, with the smaller boulders, was an open book from here.

Shite, shite, shite!

Dread settled heavy in her heart. She'd just screwed up big-time. Big, big-time.

"Excuse me."

Ebba winced at Caspian's voice. Her fathers' conversations cut off, and she turned back toward her crew.

Caspian's hard amber eyes were set on her, and Ebba had only a single beat to realize that what was coming didn't bode well before he asked, "Could I have a moment alone with Ebba, please?"

Her eyes went to Grubby.

He smiled at her and Caspian. "Sure," he said. "That be fine with me."

Dammit.

She bit back her groan, shifting to look at each of her fathers in turn. The sods weren't meeting her eyes, and their message was received loud and clear. She was on her own. Only Jagger seemed inclined to stay. He watched her, apparently content to ignore the royal only feet from him.

It was only that the pirate *was* willing to stay that made Ebba understand he couldn't. If Caspian had seen them hugging earlier, no matter what hadn't happened, she owed her friend an explanation. It was past time to set the matter straight between them. She'd already screwed up.

"Are ye okay, Viva?" Jagger asked.

Fury churned within her, all of it aimed inward. "Aye," she replied. *No.*

"What do you think I'd do to her?" Caspian said irritably. "I'd never harm her."

Jagger's jaw was clenched tight as he replied, "There be di'ferent types o' harm, as ye well know."

With another concerned look her way, Jagger stalked into the cave. A faux privacy. If her fathers and Jagger wanted, they'd be able to hear every word.

Ebba stood and squared her shoulders toward Caspian—the friend that only a couple of weeks ago, she was open to seeing as something else entirely. Calypso had changed that. He'd opened her eyes to Jagger. Even before she'd touched the *amare*, Ebba had resigned herself to tell Caspian the situation had changed. But to tell him she didn't feel anything for him was one thing. To tell him she felt attracted to another was something else. And to tell Caspian that she felt the deepest of love for Jagger seemed plain cruel.

"We saw you and Jagger," he said, drawing closer.

He gestured to the edge, and she took the hint, sitting down and waiting for him to sit beside her before replying, "Aye, I gathered."

"And?"

What did he want? An apology? Ebba felt like she owed him one and also didn't. "We hugged."

"Yes, it appeared like quite the hug from here. Not to mention the kiss."

"Nay," she said. "There wasn't a kiss." But there nearly was. And it wasn't her that stopped it. She lowered her voice, too aware of Jagger close by. "But it could have happened."

Caspian sucked in a ragged breath. "How long has this been going on?"

A lump rose up in her throat. "I can assure ye it took me just as much by surprise."

"I doubt that."

She'd give him a run for his money. Mentioning Calypso and her deep attraction didn't feel right somehow. Although mentioning the *amare* seemed cruel, not mentioning it felt dishonest as well.

Ebba whispered, "Ye remember on the way here, Jagger was

holdin' the *amare*? Well, the tube touched me while he was touchin' it, and . . . I felt sumpin' . . . for him."

Caspian stilled. "What kind of something?"

Ebba's insides clenched just at the memory of it. *Love.* "Hard to say. I ain't rightly sure. Just that I ain't exper'enced the like o' it afore. But it was strong." Ebba clutched her cheeks and stared at him, wondering if this was making matters better or worse.

Caspian swallowed hard, his Adam's apple bobbing up and down. She watched as he blinked furiously and cleared his throat.

The minutes passed unchecked until he said hoarsely, "You're in love with him."

Ebba closed her eyes against the pain in his voice. A pirate truth balanced on the tip of her tongue. She could scoff at his claim of love and downplay what she'd felt, but Ebba bit back the lie. Her friend deserved more than that. He'd been with her right from the start in Governor Da Ville's mansion.

"All I know is that I do feel a deeper regard for him. And that it is likely real."

Caspian scowled, and Ebba's breath seized in her throat at the dark look. Her heart sank as she came to understand just how fierce the prince's regard for her was. In his expression, Ebba could see that if she handled this wrong, he could very well come to hate her. She was too selfish to let that happen.

He watched her. "But . . . you can't know what powers the *amare* has. We haven't fully explored it. And you know Jagger. He plays games. He can't be trusted."

The words held a speck of truth, and doubt churned within her. She'd wondered herself if the *amare* was glitching somehow. Was he right? Had she misinterpreted everything? Yet a simmering anger sparked within her at the prince's accusations too. Ebba exhaled steadily to release her irritation. "Ye know that Jagger be used to workin' on his own to protect his tribe. Surely ye can understand why he's secr'tive. At least in part." Caspian might not know about the scars on the pirate's back, but he did know the rest.

"And now you're defending him. You must be in love with him," he said bitterly.

Heat crept up her neck. Caspian was lashing out. The prince was usually the voice of reason, and if he couldn't be that right now, Ebba would have to put on her big pirate slops.

Rising, she said, "I'll be leavin' ye to mull that over, methinks. Mayhaps ye're right about the *amare.* I ain't sure if what I'm feelin' be the truth. But if that's what regard is s'posed to feel like, Caspian, then I be sorry to say it ain't what I feel for ye. And Jagger has nothin' to do with that. I regret that there couldn't' be more between us, I do, but that seems like the way it is."

He didn't utter a word.

Ebba shoved away the urge to hug Caspian and tell him she'd try again. With a heavy heart, she said, "I hope we can still be friends."

"I don't know if that's possible," he muttered, only his shadowed profile in view. "At least not for a while."

A lump rose up her throat. "Fair enough," she whispered hoarsely.

That was it then.

Ebba turned and froze when Caspian caught her hand.

"Ebba," he said, voice low and urgent. "Just, don't rush into anything. As you say, you haven't touched the *amare* before. You don't know if it works. Just, please don't pursue this thing with Jagger until you're sure. I don't want him to take advantage of you."

The *amare* had inspired motherly love in the Jendu. It had inspired friendly love in Barrels for Locks and sisterly love in Caspian with regards to the princesses. With all of them, it drew out their true feelings, so why would the tube mess up when it came to Ebba?

"I'll have my wits about me," she replied, freeing her hand.

His eyes flickered to her face and then away as he dropped his arm. "Ebba, I'm feeling rather sorry for myself at the minute, so I'll ask you this only once, and I want you to be completely honest with me."

Her heart hammered faster. Soon it would beat right out of her chest, she was sure. "Aye?"

Caspian murmured something so softly she missed it.

"Huh?" Ebba pressed.

The prince closed his eyes. "Is it because I only have one arm to hold you with? One arm to protect and love you with? Is it because I'll always be a fumbling fool?"

Horror struck her dumb. The silence extended long enough that Caspian had opened his eyes and turned to her.

"Nay," she said on an exhale, stepping toward him—uncertain whether she should make contact. "Nay. A thousand times nay. Please, never think that. Ye know that ain't how I see ye. I never have and never will."

He shrugged his shoulder. "And yet that is exactly what a person would be pressured to reply."

"Or is it what ye want them to say because ye think it yerself?" Ebba said fiercely, a jolt of triumph striking her as he started.

She continued, her cheeks burning with temper now. "By yer logic, I'd think less o' Peg-leg for only havin' one leg. Or less o' Locks for only havin' one eye. Or Grubby for havin' half a mind. Is that what ye're sayin?"

Caspian held her gaze. He was angry; she could see it. His soft amber eyes now held the same serrated edge as Ebba had associated with his father, King Montcroix. Would she be the person to unleash that in the kindest, most empathetic person she'd ever known? Would he let things come to that?

"No," he said finally, turning away again. "I don't."

"Then why do ye think I would think less o' ye for the trials ye've been through? If anythin', I think more o' ye for them. I look at ye and see someone who understands hardship. And someone who has found the strength to go on. That makes ye a rarity."

His words were dark. "And all of that I would erase if only you would love me in return. Yet how could I ask you to love me when I do not even love myself? A son who dreams of more and a prince without an arm to protect his people. An exiled king, forced to wear a crown and crawl." He reached up and made to drag the golden circlet from his head.

Ebba stayed her friend's hand. "Nay, don't take the crown off. The joke be on Cannon and his cronies, recall? The only way that circlet be comin' off yer head is if Cannon orders ye to crawl to his feet and remove it. And ye'll do it if he asked because ye know a crown don't make a king as surely as two arms aren't makin' a man. And if sumpin' like a little crown can be undoin' ye, mayhaps some practice at lovin' yerself wouldn't go astray."

The sounds of Caspian's choked breath undid the last of her restraint, and Ebba squeezed her eyes shut as a few hot tears spilled over her cheeks.

Removing her fingers from the circlet, she stood back and watched Caspian's shaking shoulders before turning for the cave with dragging steps.

She'd made a right mess of everything.

NINE

Eyes blurring, Ebba edged into the cave, hands outstretched in the darkness. The black was a welcome relief to hide her distress after the conversation with Caspian.

A calloused hand reached out and gripped her elbow, steadying her a few feet into the cave.

She glanced up into silver eyes.

"Are ye all right?" Jagger asked quietly.

Ebba sniffed. "Aye."

Pulling her elbow free, she continued into the cave, dashing away her tears as she did so.

"So we get *veritas* for an hour, lass?"

She tilted her head to the sound of Locks' voice, her chest relaxing. They weren't going to have a chat with her about Caspian. Good. Ebba wasn't sure she could do that.

"Aye," she said, clearing her throat. "He just said soon, so I ain't sure when we'll have it. We get an hour to look at everythin' we want. No more. I was thinkin' the sword might give us some clue about what's happenin'."

Peg-leg sighed heavily from the opposite side. "It's a good plan. I can't be makin' head nor tail o' his game. May as well try the sword."

"And you said that Cannon mentioned the people here regenerate in twelve hours if killed?" Barrels asked.

There was movement behind her. "If I were him, I'd lie about that," Jagger said.

How close was he? Awareness filled her at his warm proximity. Ebba tensed and bent down, locating a rock to perch on to get away from Jagger's intensity.

Jagger continued. "I'd tell ye more time than was true, in case ye tried to use the knowledge against me."

"A lovely insight into your mind," Barrels replied drily. "But in this case, I must say I agree. Was there anything else, my dear?"

Ebba wouldn't share the part about Cannon chucking them over to the other side. "He went on for a bit about not likin' ye. He said ye'd trapped him here for two decades."

"Trapped him here? Nay, we didn't. King Forge was the one to kill him," Stubby mused from the very back of the cave. "But that makes it seem like he means to get out. . . ."

"Aye, he was talkin' about bein' a pirate meant to sail the seas," Ebba repeated as more of the conversation came back to her. "And he kept lookin' up to the passage, but now I'm wonderin' if he was just waitin' for those pirates to return from the entrance."

"And why they were there be a mystery," Stubby said.

"I can't blame them for wantin' to get out," Grubby said. "It ain't that nice in here. No place to swim."

Ebba smiled. They were quite literally in hell, and Grubby was only irked about the lack of a swimming pool. "I love ye, Grubs."

"I love ye, too, Ebba. . . . Was it ye that said that?"

Stubby snorted. "Her voice be a smidge higher than the rest o' us, matey."

"Nay, sometimes Peg-leg sounds like that, too," Grubby countered. "And Locks when he's talkin' to Verity."

Ebba laughed with the others but checked the sound, realizing Caspian was still outside and wouldn't know what to make of it.

"Plank," Stubby said. "What do ye think o' everythin'?"

Suddenly, she didn't need to check her laughter. It was just gone. Everyone listened for his reply.

"I be thinkin' the same as the rest o' ye," he rasped.

Peg-leg's reply was sarcastic. "Oh good, matey. Good. A solid ad'ition to the talk at hand."

"What would ye like me to say?" Plank snapped.

"Seven heads are better than one," Locks replied. "Jagger's, too, I s'pose."

Really? Because his tone implied that Jagger's head could be rolling and it wouldn't matter. Ebba winced. They'd definitely seen as much as Caspian, and she knew better than to believe they'd let things lie. Perhaps she should warn Jagger.

Plank shuffled, and she stared at the back of the cave, willing herself the ability to see in the dark.

"I don't know what to make o' anythin'," Plank eventually said.

Ebba couldn't take it anymore. "Just this sit'ation or more?" she demanded.

"Ebba. . . ," Barrels warned.

"More, little nymph. Defin'tely more." Plank stood and shuffled in the dark, drawing closer. When he made to pass her by, Ebba gripped his hand, stopping him. "I love ye, Plank."

"I love ye, too, little nymph. Never doubt it."

His words had the opposite effect. "But I do. Why are ye so sad after *Felicity*?"

One of her fathers sucked in a breath.

Plank tried to tug free, but Ebba held tight, digging her black nails into his skin. "Tell me. I don't understand why ye're bein' like this, bein' so withdrawn and broodin'. Please tell me why."

His hand relaxed in her grip.

Ebba swallowed as Plank knelt before the rock she perched upon, bringing his face closer until she could see the gleam of his hazel eyes and the shadowed planes of his face.

"Ye want to know?" he asked her, breath ragged.

"Plank, ye be keepin' yer head now," Peg-leg said. "It ain't Ebba who was doin' the deed all those years ago, so don't take out yer anger on her."

Ebba stared into her father's eyes. "This be about your wife. Cannon killed her."

Ladon had said as much when they met him on Neos Mountain. That Plank had been married was complete news to her at the time. That he'd carried so much heartache in silence her entire life had caused her to doubt if she even knew him. With Plank, there was something special. They'd always been the sole occupants of the ship who'd entertained the thought of magic. And they'd shared a love of clothing and trinkets. At least, Ebba thought the interest was shared. He was a dreamer, intelligent and discerning.

She relied on all of her fathers in different ways and liked to think that they relied on her, too. They all depended on each other. Without one part, the pyramid would crumble, and that was what she felt now. That the pyramid was crumbling without Plank—like a ship without a rudder. Ebba had no idea how to reach her father, yet she had to reach him and bring him back. To do that, she had to understand.

"Tell me," she told him, not releasing his hand.

She winced at his brash tone when he did. "I had a wife once. A beautiful, kind, wise woman who agreed to be mine."

Plank pulled his hand free but didn't stand. "I took her for granted, drawn by dreams and riches to the sea. Cannon threatened her life to keep me on the ship, to do his biddin'. At least at first. Ye likely know that afore long, I needed less and less encourag'ment to stay. But unlike yer fathers, barrin' Locks perhaps, I always remembered my wife. The feel o' her, the smell o' her hair, the sound o' her laughter. Even tainted, she was with me. And where was I?" he said harshly.

"Ye were savin' her life by stayin' put," Ebba said. "Just like Jagger did to save his tribe."

Plank continued. "And then we took ye from Pleo. I was the first to fall in love with ye, little nymph. Only because I could already remember what it felt like to love another with yer heart and soul. We ran with ye, the plan bein' to get ye to safety afore I went to collect my wife, if she hadn't moved on with another."

Ebba knew she'd died, and her gut warned that she didn't want to hear the rest.

"Dead," he said flatly. "I'll spare ye the details, but murder wasn't the only wrong done that night." Plank stood abruptly.

Ebba gathered her courage to continue. "And ye've carried the guilt o' that with ye all these years."

"Guilt," he said as though tasting the word. "Guilt, aye. Regret, aye. But that be nothin' on what I recall, little nymph."

Ebba knew nothing good would come of asking, but she did. "What can ye recall?"

"The feel o' her. The sm—" He broke off. "The smell o' her hair." In the dark, she watched her father clutching his chest, the area over his heart. "The sound o' her—"

"The sound o' her laughter?" she finished for him in a whisper.

Plank didn't respond. Still clutching his chest, he staggered out of the cave onto the ledge.

She waited until he sat down outside before curling her hands into tight fists that longed to hurt, to beat, to sink into flesh. "I'm goin' to kill Mutinous Cannon."

There was a *tap, tap, tap* as Peg-leg made his way to her. He gripped her shoulder. "Ye'll need to get in line, I'm afraid."

True. Whatever anger she might feel, the wrongs had been dealt to her fathers. They were the ones who had to bear the suffering over decades. The justice was theirs first. If they ever got the chance.

"Will he be okay?" she asked in a small voice.

Locks answered, "Truthfully, lass, we've only seen him this bad once—when we first found her . . . remains."

"But he got better in the end," she said, straightening on the stone. "He can do it. How did ye manage it when I was young?"

"Ye needed us then," Stubby said.

Ebba crossed her arms, very close to tears again. "I need ye all now."

Barrels broke the silence. "We negotiated a deal of sorts with him."

"What was the deal?" Jagger said, making her jump.

She glanced at the pirate but could only make out his outline in the dim light. He'd heard everything, but it didn't occur to her to be ashamed. He'd seen her in worse states by now.

"Well," Barrels said mildly, "we extracted a promise from him. As long as the ship was sea-worthy, he would sail her. If we were attacked and the ship sank, then likely as not we'd all be killed anyway. And if not, the ship was fresh enough to last several decades, during which time he'd be accustomed to life without his wife."

But the ship did sink, and they'd survived. And two decades after the death of Plank's wife, he hadn't grown accustomed to life without her. Ebba was willing to bet he'd merely spent her lifetime daydreaming of his deceased wife.

"What was her name?" she whispered.

Though none of them could ever be sure how much Grubby took in and what he missed, he replied straightaway. "Her name was Felicity."

Felicity like their ship? With six fathers, she'd always thought of the ship as her mother. Her mouth dried. If Plank had still had his wife, Ebba would have known what having a mother was like. That was why he'd agreed to the deal? Her fathers named their ship after the real Felicity.

They'd manipulated his guilt to make him form an agreement and stay with the living.

None of her crew spoke, and as the quiet weighed down heavier with each breath, Plank's weary voice trailed in from outside the cave.

It was the ballad he always hummed while daydreaming, the melancholy melody without words. Except this time, there were words.

Plank sang:

From the sandy shores she sang unto me,
youthful as fall,
as lovely as spring.
She sang as I sailed off for ambition and gold,
"I will wait.
Just return to me."

Each year that passed on the harsh sea
her face grew lovelier,
her smile a plunderer's dream.
She sang each time I sailed away,
"I will wait.
Just return to me."

Hints of gray streaked her hair; faint lines graced her face.
Such a lovely sight
I could never replace.
She sang unto me, voice as soft as a breeze,
"I will wait.
Just return to me."

One woeful eve, I did return,
ambition long cold, soul twisted and raw.
The sandy shore lay empty;
No loveliness brightened its shore.
No beauty sang,
No beauty waited.
To no one,
to none

would I ever return.

I stumbled to where she lay on our bed;
A bed more hers than ours.
She'd been taken.
Killed.
While waiting for me.
My love had died alone.

Her smile was not immortal.
Too late, I saw.
And now I would remain behind
To sail these long, lonely days alone.
Me, who only paused to think on life
When love and light were gone.

Faded years drag on
And my heart remains on that sandy shore.
I sing to my love for evermore
Of how I wish I'd never left her.
Of how I wish I'd never denied fate.
Of how I wish
I'd simply returned
as she bade.

Whenever her tears had started, they were unabated by now, one tear flowing effortlessly after the next. Ebba let them fall.

A hand reached for her in the dark, and she knew it was his.

"We'll negotiate another deal," Jagger said for her ears alone.

Whether by a fresh deal or by another, Plank would come back to the crew. He'd done it once; he'd do it again.

And whatever else *veritas* might help them find, Ebba knew the sword might provide Plank with all the truth he needed.

TEN

"They're bringin' more food," Locks said, alerting everyone.

Ebba stirred at his voice, feeling as though someone had rubbed grit and salt into her eyes. That she'd fallen asleep at all was surprising, but the granted sleep had been plagued with dreams of murder, darkness, and screams.

Ebba winced at the stiff feeling in her lower back and legs and opened her eyelids a slit.

Jagger stared back at her.

Her eyelids flew open, her heart thundering beneath her ribs.

Peg-leg called to Locks, "So it's to be a daily thing? Feedin' us."

"Ye creepy bugger," Ebba croaked at Jagger, who lay on his side, one arm crooked under his head as a pillow. The rest of his tall frame was crammed between several boulders. She was petite enough to squeeze into mostly any nook, but Jagger must have just spent a night in hell.

She snorted. They *were* in hell.

"Why are ye sleepin' here?" she asked him, lingering sleepiness making her brave.

His voice was hoarse. "Why not?" A slight smile tugged at the corner of his mouth. Aside from that, he appeared drawn and . . . concerned. His eyes didn't seem inclined to fully open either, and the usual tension was missing from his frame, as though half of his skull still contemplated giving in to sleep.

The sight tugged at a floating sensation in the vicinity of her belly. Freshly swabbed ship decks, he looked really, really good right now. Mussed-up and adorable. Ebba could maybe resist silver-eyed Jagger, but not vulnerable Jagger. And really, she didn't want to resist either.

She smiled at him, and the curve of his lips widened.

The world faded. All noise muting but for the sound of her and Jagger's breathing. The weird focus was happening—the one where the rest of the realm disappeared and only the two of them were here. *The Jagger tunnel.*

Everyone else . . . *poof* . . . gone.

Boots appeared between them, bursting the intense bubble encompassing them. Rolling back slightly, Ebba glared after Stubby.

More boots replaced his—Grubby's this time. Then Barrels' buckled landlubber shoes replaced his.

Peg-leg tapped his way through, whacking Jagger in the shoulder with his peg.

The pirate across from her battled a grin.

"Wondered when they'd start up," he whispered to her, winking.

Blood filled her cheeks at her fathers' behavior. She was yet to fully grasp what was happening with Jagger and the *amare* and whatever. That was enough without the overprotective father routine.

Ebba tensed at more footsteps. They belonged to Plank, who cast a look at her.

"I'm sorry for last night, little nymph," he said, reaching down to brush the back of his hand against her cheek. "I'm sorry I gave ye nightmares with my song."

Sink her, she must've made a racket. Ebba bit back on a groan. She'd die of mortification. Right here. That sounded good.

"For ye, I'll try," Plank said to her.

Her eyes flew to his. "Ye will?"

'Try' was such an abstract word for what she wanted from her father. Part of her wanted to push him for details. What was he trying for? What would he do to *try*? Was it happiness? Was it dealing with his past like the rest of her fathers? What would it take, and what could she do to help?

"Aye," he said with a slight frown. "Ye have my word on that."

She didn't want a promise he'd try. She wanted a promise he'd succeed. Because a pirate didn't make a promise he couldn't keep.

Ebba squeezed his hand. "That makes my heart right glad. Thank ye."

He granted her the ghost of a smile and peered down at Jagger. "Thank ye."

Plank walked around her and Jagger instead of between them.

"What's he thankin' ye for?" she asked, eyes narrowed.

Jagger searched her face. "Yer nightmares stopped when I lied down next to ye."

Well, that explained why her fathers hadn't thrown him off the cliff.

Ebba dropped her gaze. "Oh."

". . . So what are ye goin' to do about Plank?" he asked, shifting onto his back.

The slightly larger space between them made it easier to breathe. He'd really slept all crunched up like that for her?

Warmth spread through her chest, and she tucked away a small smile.

"I'm goin' to make him touch the sword when Cannon passes it over," she confessed.

He watched her, eyes shifting as he seemed to mull that tidbit over. "Worth a shot, methinks."

"Ebba . . . Jagger, show a leg. There be sumpin' to see out here," Locks called.

Sure, and she had two heads. He just didn't want her in here with Jagger.

Convincing her body to move, Ebba crouched and then stood with a small moan, her hands going to her lower back. The cave floor was no good for her. Her fathers had to be smarting pretty badly.

Jagger, of course, got up without a peep. If the cave affected him, he didn't show it.

"Hold on," she said, turning mid-step. "Ye slept in the cave."

He shrugged.

No way was he getting away so easy. "But ye never sleep inside because. . . ." *Yer time on Malice haunts ye.*

"Between ye, Caspian, and Plank, there wasn't much sleep to be had. But yer nightmares were worst o' all," Jagger said, stepping closer to her. "I just thought to wake ye, but when I touched ye, ye stopped whimperin'."

"I don't whimper." Ebba tipped her head back to look at him. Her face was on fire, and she sincerely hoped the cave was masking that because her skin felt hotter than the boiling stream outside.

"Sure ye don't," he continued, closing the distance entirely. "When ye stopped whimperin', I lay down beside ye, which—I can tell ye—a pirate o' my size ain't s'posed to do."

She intended to grin, but with him so close, it came out as a shy smile.

"And somewhere along the line, I guess I fell asleep myself."

His brows were slightly raised as though Jagger himself couldn't believe what he was saying.

"And how did ye sleep?" she asked curiously, glad her voice wasn't betraying her. One part of her body was obeying at least.

Jagger bent his head, his eyes going to her lips. "Surpr'singly fair-like," he whispered.

Fierce heat swept through her. A heat she'd denied for too long. In the darkness of the cave, pretending only the two of them existed was easy. The Jagger tunnel zipped into place, and the world faded away.

She was sick of burying her feelings. This felt right. She wanted it, and there was no way he didn't. Jagger never pretended. In his honesty, she could trust; in his capability, his loyalty, and his intelligence. She'd been blind, and now her eyes were open.

Ebba-Viva Fairisles was going to grab the fish by the gills.

Lifting her arms, breath held, she intertwined her hands behind his neck, resting her black-nailed thumbs against the base of his skull. She raised on tiptoes. Jagger's eyes widened as she neared him.

"What?" She froze in the awkward pre-kiss position. There was no way she'd read his desire wrong.

Jagger wanted her.

. . . Didn't he?

"Ebba-Viva! Get out here," Stubby bellowed.

She jerked violently. The Jagger tunnel crumbled, and the world around them was reinstated.

What in Davy Jones' was Jagger about? He'd pushed his body against hers and talked all lovey-like about caves and nightmares and such. *Why wouldn't he kiss her?* That was three times by her count. And at this point, Ebba was definitely counting.

Flaming non-kisser.

She wouldn't do that again—the wrapping-her-hands-around-his-neck thing. Three times was enough rejection. If he wanted to kiss her, actually kiss her, he could bloody well go the full distance.

She glared at Jagger and spun on her heel, storming out of the cave.

"It be her choice," Plank was hissing as she neared where they sat on the ledge.

Stubby was pacing. "Nay, not in a cave with a pirate, it ain't her choice."

Jagger sniggered behind her.

What was it? Embarrass Ebba Day? And besides that, there was another person who might be affected by the conversation.

A quick scan told her Caspian was otherwise occupied, though the tips of his ears were pink. Bugger it.

He, Barrels, and Peg-leg were bent over a black case identical to the one holding food from yesterday.

Turns out there was genuinely something to see.

"I just ain't ready," Stubby said to Locks, who patted him on the back.

Locks replied, "Aye, matey, but don't ye be worryin'; it's just beginnin', and there be six o' us."

That was quite enough.

"I'm here," Ebba announced, striding out of the shadows and away from the still-sniggering Jagger. Distance between them was the best idea. Then maybe he could figure out whether he wanted to kiss her or not.

And now that she'd made an utter mess of things with Caspian, the only path left was to not shove the possible love situation down his throat. Win-win.

Ebba crouched between Barrels and Peg-leg. "What've ye got there?"

Barrels held a long and narrow piece of pale seaweed. Ebba had never seen the like of it before. On the pale seaweed were a series of ink blotches, dots and lines.

"We found this beneath the waterskins," Barrels said.

Looked dodgy to her. "I wouldn't eat it."

"No, my dear. It's the ink Caspian and I found more interesting."

And there it was; he'd said Caspian, and now she had to look at the prince. Peeking up, she stole a look at her hopefully-still-friend. Did they all look like seagull shite today? It was evident Caspian hadn't slept a wink. He glanced up. Denying her initial urge to quickly look away, Ebba smiled instead.

Caspian's gaze fell back to the pale seaweed.

Great. Frowning, she looked down too.

"Do you remember Matey saying that his grandfather kept records of magical history?" the prince asked.

So he'd talk to her, but not look at her? That didn't make too much sense. "Aye."

Much of what their kraken friend had said carried so little

substance that Ebba recalled everything that did. "He said they wrote with their ink. Ye think Matey wrote this?"

"Exactly," Barrels said.

The others gathered around the black case.

"The problem bein' that we don't read krakalacken," Peg-leg said.

Ebba took another look at the pale seaweed. The top half was a jumble that held no meaning to her. The bottom. . . .

Pointing to a straight line, she asked, "Do ye think that could be the rocky path?"

The response was dubious, even if not vocal.

"If I cross my eyes?" Grubby said.

Ebba traced her fingers over the many curly 'W's' either side of the straight line. "Matey knows we don't speak krakalacken. What if this ain't a note but a map? If that be the case, these be waves either side o' the path to Satyr Island. Mayhaps the note be about escapin' there. Matey could be outside the Locker, waitin' to help us get away."

"There be a lot o' maybes in that," Jagger said.

She wasn't talking to the non-kisser.

Barrels held the seaweed to his face, squinting before dropping it back into the case.

Ebba raised her head. "Can we send sumpin' back to him, do ye think?"

"With what?" Peg-leg asked.

Jagger pointed at Barrels' cravat. "That'd do. Write on it, roll it up, and stuff it in a waterskin. But," he added, "that be a risk. The Capricorn work for the Satyr. If the Satyr get hold o' the message or the tainted pirates, then—"

"We'll be right back where we started." Caspian interrupted him with more force than Ebba thought necessary.

Honestly, the hardest part of that plan wouldn't be delivering the cravat to the Capricorn; it would be prying the cravat off Barrels' body.

Plank stared at the note. "Ye don't think that the *scio* could help us? It helps us understand people talkin' di'ferent tongues. Why not the written type too?"

Stubby scratched his stubble. "Aye, I be seein' the logic o' that. But we ain't got the *scio,* do we?"

"We didn't have the *veritas* either, but Ebba talked Cannon into lendin' us that," Peg-leg shot back.

Ebba wasn't too optimistic that she could figure out a reason to get the *scio* on loan from Cannon. She'd rather not see the captain again unless it was to shove the *purgium* somewhere the sun didn't shine.

"So what's the decision then?" Jagger asked.

Caspian answered with a look around the circle. "I'm for risking a note back. A picture, more like. Even if Matey doesn't understand the note, he'll know that we've sent it. If getting out of here takes a while, we don't want him to move on. We should send notes every couple of days. And in the meantime, look out for a way to grab the *scio.*"

That sounded fine to her.

"All those in favor?" Peg-leg said.

Ebba raised her hand and called 'aye' with everyone else.

"Okay, well, I'll be in the cave," Barrels announced, standing.

Locks snorted.

Stubby blocked her father's path to the cave. "Yer cravat, matey. We'll be needin' it afore ye go."

Ebba wouldn't put it past him to hide it somewhere.

With a heartfelt sigh, Barrels tugged free his stained cravat. "It's all I have," he said sadly.

Stubby patted his shoulder.

"Look smart. We got company," Locks blurted.

"Hide the note," Peg-leg hissed at Caspian, who grabbed the seaweed and ran into the cave.

Ebba stood and walked to the edge, peering down.

Pockmark and his cronies had returned. And in their hands. . . .

"*Veritas,*" Jagger said.

At last. Ebba wanted to be in clothes again. Or just different clothes. She was bored of the royal-blue shift. And bored of covering her butt and breasts with every bend and jump. How females did it, she didn't know. Must get lessons.

"Oi," Pockmark howled. "Come and get it. Ye have one hour and not a second more."

Ebba was halfway to the stairs. Again. "I'll get it."

Locks bellowed, "Ebba-Viva, come back here."

She grinned as she ran. They never learned.

"She's *your* daughter," Barrels sniped at someone. Probably Stubby—he was the conniving father.

But this time her tail caught up a smidgen quicker. *Jagger*. Ebba ignored him and jogged down the remaining steps.

"Hey Pockmark," she greeted cheerfully. "Ye're lookin' pretty good considerin' yer grandfather killed ye."

His face contorted.

"The sword?" Jagger said, ambling to her side and cutting her a look that said something along the lines of 'shut yer gob.'

Pockmark jerked his head at Riot, who carried the sword in thick black material. The pirate tossed the sword down, material and all.

"Careful," Pockmark hissed, shoving the smaller pirate.

Riot shoved him back, eyes flooding black.

With a sigh, Pockmark drew out his gun and shot the pirate in the chest. "Berserk again," he muttered.

Then, to Swindles, he said, "Grab him."

"Nay, he's heavy," Swindles complained.

"We can't leave him here," Pockmark whirled to snarl. "Get him. Or join him." He glanced at Jagger and Ebba. "Yer hour be runnin' out."

True enough. Before she could swoop down, Jagger did the honor, grabbing the gleaming hilt of *veritas* and kicking the black material back to the pirates.

She resisted the impulse to roll her eyes at him. She hadn't been about to touch the tainted material.

Pockmark's bloodshot eyes fixed on Jagger, and his jaw ticked as the moment extended.

"Something to say, Mercer?" Jagger asked.

It was her turn to give him the 'shut yer gob' look.

"My grandfather would like a meetin' with ye and the mighty King Caspian," Pockmark eventually ground out. "Ye'll be comin' out with the sword. He said not to make the same mistake as *her*."

Her had a name, but she was much more distracted by the fact Jagger and Caspian would be going before Cannon.

"What for?" Jagger asked.

A cruel smile touched Pockmark's lips. "I be guessin' ye'll find out. I'll be there too."

"It's a date." Jagger smirked at him. "Come on, Viva."

Glancing at Riot's dead body once more, Ebba turned, glad to walk before Jagger this time because out of him and the pirates below, she'd much rather show her butt to the person she knew. Even if he was a non-kisser.

They hurried up the steps, and Ebba paused to catch her breath at the top.

"That was just as I imagined," Jagger whispered behind her.

He was talking. About her butt.

Ebba straightened. "Nay, ye don't get to talk that way when ye're actin' hot and cold, Jagger." If he decided to just run hot, she was open for business, as her friends in the Maltu brothel liked to put it. And Ebba wouldn't even charge Jagger anything to kiss her.

Really, it was a great deal for him.

"We got the sword," she announced, striding to her fathers. A glance back told her Jagger's eyes had followed her. There wasn't any cold in his gaze.

"All right," Peg-leg said, tapping over to snatch the sword from the younger pirate. "What now?"

"We need to look at the clothes," Ebba said. "And whatever else is in the cave. And then I was thinkin' everyone who hasn't already touched the sword should do so."

That was Stubby, Plank, Grubby, and Barrels.

Stubby had already expressed an interest in touching *veritas*. Grubby and Barrels shook their heads.

"Do we need to be votin'?" she asked, crossing to the food case. There was one fish left. Picking it up, she bent it in half and took a bite of the exposed flesh. *Steak, steak, steak.* Ebba swallowed, grimacing at the cold saltiness before taking a second bite.

"You didn't want a vote when it came to your choice. The word 'hypocritical' comes to mind," Barrels shot at her.

Ebba shrugged, swallowing the second bite. "There ain't no hippos about it. Ye all need to touch it. If only because ye might not get another chance." And then Plank would have to follow suit.

She took another bite, pausing to dig a scale out of her teeth.

Caspian cleared his throat. "I'd also like to touch the sword again. And we should take a chance to look around Davy Jones' while we're at it. Don't forget our original intention in negotiating for the sword."

The last comment felt aimed at her, but she didn't respond, chewing demurely on the fish carcass.

"I'll go first," Stubby said gruffly. "Pass it here."

Peg-leg sniffed, gripping the sword tight. "I see none o' ye have changed yer minds about my fish stew."

"How could we when we haven't eaten it since ye asked the sword last time?" Locks said.

The cook seemed to miss the heavy sarcasm and brightened considerably.

Ebba scolded them. "There be more important things to look at than whether people like yer stew."

"True enough," Peg-leg said. He held out the sword to Stubby.

"Hold on," Stubby said, jerking his hand away. "All o' ye get in the cave. I don't want ye to see."

She wasn't the only one to snort.

"Sod off," Locks scoffed. "I'm watchin'."

"Aye," Ebba echoed.

Stubby's face darkened. He ripped the sword from Peg-leg's

hand. They all watched as Stubby's gaze turned inward and his gray-blue eyes began to flicker side to side. He flinched, the blood draining from his face.

Locks hummed. "Did I do that? It almost be creepier than when he ate the mountain apple."

Minutes passed by, and Stubby flinched again, crying out twice before he stilled, and a brilliant smile crossed his face.

Her father blinked several times, glistening eyes focusing on the crew and the here-and-now again. "Okay, that weren't no swim in a lagoon, but not as bad as I thought it'd be."

"So. . . ," Peg-leg said, eyeing Stubby pointedly.

"I ain't tellin'," her father replied, wiping at his eyes. "Not my fault ye both blurted yer personal bus'ness, is it?"

They all waited.

"Sink me," Stubby said, bursting to his feet. "Ye're like flamin' piranhas."

"Good ship name," Locks said, brows raising.

Ebba hummed. "Aye, I wouldn't mind that one."

They turned back to Stubby.

"My father's murder wasn't my fault," he said. "Trippin' over my foot into the water didn't drown him. He was dead from Cannon's bullet afore he hit the water. I couldn't have saved his life."

The *veritas* confirmed truths a person already knew by showing them snippets of the past or future. It could confirm the truth of a present moment by showing goodness and truth as a glowing white and lies and evil as shadows. The sword could also show the truth of any moment a person had experienced *and* force truth from someone when the blade was rested on their skin.

"Did ye see that moment then?" she asked her father.

"Aye." Stubby shuddered. "But it was di'ferent, seein' it with these old eyes. More straightforward, I guess. It doesn't stop me missin' my father or from hopin' to honor his memory, but the sword did show me that what happened wasn't my fault and couldn't be changed."

Ebba walked to him and kissed his forehead. "I be right glad o' that."

She took the sword from him and looked at the closest of her fathers. Locks and Barrels stood beside each other, and she halted, staring intently at their chests. Each of her fathers had a cloud of darkness deep within their chest—the taint. Well, the taint inside Locks and Peg-leg was much smaller than the darkness within the others because they'd touched *veritas* a couple of weeks before.

Now, the others had to follow suit. She thrust the sword out at Barrels.

"Oh, I suppose I must, then," he said, curling his long, weathered fingers around the hilt.

He screamed, dropping the sword.

"Blimey, what is it?" Locks demanded, reaching for her other father.

"I look like a savage," Barrels said faintly. "An absolute ruffian."

Peg-leg muttered to himself before saying, "Ye're holdin' a sword o' truth and that's what ye decide to ask?"

"I was just thinking of it at the time," Barrels snapped. Bending down, he picked up the sword again, closing his eyes.

When he opened them again, a small frown wrinkled the area between his brows.

"And?" she asked him.

"I hardly know what to think, my dear," he said, pulling his collar out. "I am not a pirate, even after all these years."

They could have told him that. Her father much preferred numbers and books over treasures and a merry jaunt up the rigging. Ebba had an inkling there was more than that, but she didn't voice the observation as the others dissolved into loud hoots.

Ebba took the sword from him and stared intently at his chest. The taint contained there was less. The wispy black cloud within had shrunk by half. She was sure of it.

Hope exploded inside her at the sight. Truth *was* helping them heal. That was probably why Jagger had clung so strongly to the sword after leaving *Malice*. They'd been told that only the *purgium* could heal a person of the taint. Maybe the *purgium* was the only tube that could get *rid* of the taint, but clearly the healing cylinder wasn't the only part that could help.

"The taint in ye be less," she told Barrels. "Touching *veritas* helped ye."

He touched his chest. "Are you certain? I admit that I'm overjoyed to know I've stuck to my Exosian roots over the years."

He would be. She bit back her smile.

"Aye, I looked at ye afore and after," she said. "Ye're nearly the same as Locks now."

Barrels' hands dropped. "Locks is less tainted than me?"

"Only a mite."

"Because he loves Verity," Caspian blurted.

She glanced back and met his gaze. They quickly found other places to look.

"Aye," Ebba said, coughing slightly. "That's what I was wonderin' too. If love be makin' a di'ference too."

Locks interjected. "Ye know, I do feel lighter for lovin' Verity. The gold o' her hair—"

"We'll keep that in mind." Stubby cut him off. "Grubs, ye're next,"

Ebba walked to Grubby but wrenched to a halt, staring at his chest. "There ain't no cloud in ye." She ran the rest of the way to her part-selkie father, grinning. "Grubs, ye ain't tainted!"

"What? Let me see?" Stubby demanded. He grabbed the sword from Ebba and stared at Peg-leg and then Grubby. "Huh, the *purguim* did heal more than yer head, Grubs."

"My head?" Grubby answered.

"The kraken beat ye up, recall?" Plank reminded him gently.

Grubby's eyes rounded, his head drooping. "The mast hit me over the head. And I wasn't leavin' the grain bin open to deserve it either."

Was he referring to the first time he hurt his head? Because the kraken had caused the second injury.

"Aye," Stubby gripped his arm. "We know, matey. It weren't fair o' Cannon to harm ye."

Knowing Cannon, it wasn't. But the truth was, the *purgium* had healed Grubby's head recently, and none of them had liked the arrogant, selkie version of their crewmate.

Grubby reached out and took the sword.

He threw his head back and laughed, handing the blade to Ebba.

"Knew it," he said. Reaching for a bit of seaweed, he rolled it up.

Stubby cast a bewildered look at her. "What do ye know, matey?" he asked.

"That I be smarter than all o' ye," Grubby answered. Laughing again, he tucked the rolled seaweed behind his ear.

Well, they'd known that already. Kind of.

Glancing around the ledge, *veritas* in hand once more, Ebba was glad to confirm there was no hint of the taint in the black stone around the cave or on the ledge.

"We should hurry," Jagger said. "This be takin' too long."

Morbid curiosity struck her.

Dammit. Ebba couldn't *not* look.

What she actually wanted to do was rest the blade on Jagger's skin and ask why he wouldn't kiss her. But her fathers were here, so. . . .

Holding the blade, she stared at the pirate's chest.

Jagger's body glowed radiant white. Not a speck of shadow lingered within him—though that might not mean he was taint-free. His resistance to magic could be at play against the sword's power.

Her skull shot back to the moment she'd touched the *amare*. Her chest exploded with a trembling and overwhelming joy—like a thousand butterflies had been released within her. Pure joy made her lips tremble with the urge to laugh for no other reason than she just felt complete happiness.

She *had* to get to the bottom of this Jagger thing. Ebba focused her thoughts. Did she love Jagger?

A memory swept through her, warming her from the inside out. She closed her eyes, and in her mind watched as she sat in the hold of *Felicity*, stringing her beads back into her dreadlocks.

She'd loved him then.

Ebba focused again. Were they meant to be with one another?

Surety swept through her again, and she was catapulted back into the thunderbird's storm. Eyes already closed, she gasped, the past version of herself swinging in thin air over the Dynami Sea, Jagger's grip on her the only thing saving her from death.

Ebba squeezed her eyes tighter. Was Jagger the love of her life?

This time, the warmth erupted into an inferno as Ebba's mind was hustled back to *Malice*. Jagger was helping her to escape the tainted ship. She yanked him out of the gun port after her, sending both of them plummeting to the ocean below.

Swimming through the heady feeling, Ebba returned to awareness. The sword had confirmed truths she already knew deep down since the *amare*. Truths she'd been confused over and perhaps in a smidgen of denial about. It didn't feel right that a magical tube could tell her who she could feel for. And yet, looking back, her feelings for Jagger had steadily built for so long. She trusted him, respected him, and looked up to him.

When Ebba looked at Jagger, all she saw was him.

She loved Jagger with every fiber of her being.

ELEVEN

Ebba screamed her frustration and threw the sword away, watching it clatter and roll to a stop on the fiery stone just before falling off the cave ledge.

Locks reached her first and clutched her shoulders. "What is it, lass? What did ye see?"

She stared at the sword.

"Talk to us," Barrels urged her.

Lifting her eyes, she became aware that all six of her fathers surrounded her on the ledge in varying states of alarm. Jagger and Caspian hung back, but Plank alone appeared unworried.

"N-nothin'," she managed to say. The *amare* wasn't broken. Everything she felt was real.

"That wasn't nothin'," Peg-leg said with a snarl. "That was like ye'd been stabbed with a thousand knives."

He'd react like that, too, if he loved someone who wouldn't kiss him.

"Aye, I just found out that. . . ." She trailed off.

Between two of her fathers, she saw Plank's lips quirk. Ebba glared at him. He knew. Or suspected. She'd held the sword, looked at Jagger, and screamed for all of Davy Jones' to hear. Ebba was surprised the others hadn't put two and two together.

Perhaps suspicious was a better way to describe their obtuseness. A look at Barrels showed he was pale. A look at Stubby showed her he was scowling over his shoulder at Jagger. Right, it was a pretending thing. That worked both ways. There was no way she was confessing the truth to them. If she loved Jagger, she probably didn't want to see her fathers kill him with their bare hands. Unless the pirate didn't return her regard.

Ebba hooked the hand guard of the sword with her foot, kicking the sword across the perch in Plank's direction. "Go on then. Yer turn."

He shook his head, leaning back against a cliff face. "That ain't a good idea, little nymph."

That was enough to turn her other fathers on him.

"We've all touched it," Peg-leg said, crossing his arms.

"Aye, well, I just wanted to see ye do it," Plank answered with a gleaming smile.

The smile gave her pause. He hadn't smiled yesterday. Perhaps rushing him wasn't a good idea. Perhaps he should only touch *veritas* when he was ready. Their entire crew had pretended for a long time, and Ebba was once as afraid of the truth as they were. Her fear and the discomfort truth brought lessened each day, but she understood it wasn't a natural thing for any pirate. Would foisting the sword on Plank make him more afraid of seeking truth in the future? Or would he cope with whatever he saw?

"Touch the damn thing, ye spineless pufferfish," Stubby said, sitting down on the perch edge to dangle his legs over. "Ebba be right—we may not see the blade thing again."

She licked her lips. "Mayhaps he shouldn't if he ain't ready."

"I don't think time has anythin' to do with my truth," Plank said, his smile fading. "It won't alter or fade or darken."

"Okay, but we can only have one Locks in the crew," Barrels said, rubbing his temples.

Locks jaw dropped. "What does that mean?"

"It means your shanties about Verity are terrible. Once I considered jumping in the sea and swimming to shore to be away from them."

Uh-oh. The conversation was heading south.

Ducking down, Ebba reached for the hilt of *veritas* but paused, fingertips hovering over the hilt as her fathers squabbled overhead.

Plank left the cliff face and crouched beside her. Noise unfaltering above them, he reached out to cup her face. "Ye ought never be afraid o' love, little nymph. Esp'cially not a love that can span life and death and everythin' between."

Ebba sucked in a sharp breath. "Ye think I love him that much?" She hadn't asked the sword that question.

"I've had a true love. I'd never fail to recognize that emotion in my daughter. That's why I'll never come between ye."

. . . Unlike her other fathers.

He thought she and Jagger were. . . . "*True* love?"

"What? Ye believe in magic, but not that two souls can be designed for one another? What about the Daedalion lovers who jumped off the cliffs together?"

Aye, but they were magical creatures, and she'd never thought the same concept of soul mates or true undying love could apply to mortals. Or pirates.

Plank took the sword from her, and Ebba crouched, torn between curling into a ball on the ground and joining the world again.

She chose the ball.

Hands reached down and wrenched her back up on her feet. Ebba glared at Peg-leg.

"What'd ye do that for?" she demanded. "I was goin' to mope."

But he wasn't looking at her. None of them were. Not Caspian and not Jagger. Everyone looked at a swaying Plank.

He clutched the sword in two hands, head tilted upward toward the cavern ceiling and a smile on his face. A stark contrast to the grimace of immense pain squeezing the corners of his eyes, which were pouring with tears. It was though his joy was contained in molten coals that he could not touch without burning his flesh yet touched all the same.

The sight of his anguish was terrible.

In two strides across the black stone, Ebba was at his side, ripping *veritas* from her father's grip.

As she did, he lowered his head.

The smile was gone.

And Ebba knew, with trembling certainty, that she'd made a grave mistake.

"Plank?" she whispered.

He turned his face from her, extending his hand back. "Not now, little nymph."

Ebba hovered, sword in both hands as he'd just done, looking at the taint within her father. Horror rooted her to the spot. His chest was flooded with taint. Had he been that bad before? She hadn't gotten a chance to check him before he took the sword.

Gentle fingers pried the *veritas* from her grip.

"I'll check the inside for taint," Jagger said, his silver eyes dark as he searched her face.

Ebba barely registered him ducking into the cave. She watched as Plank staggered to the cave steps and sank down onto them, head in his hands.

Locks wrapped an arm around her shoulders. "Leave Plank be for now. He'll be right after a spell, ye'll see."

That sounded like a story parents told their children. But Ebba turned away, if only to hide from the growing knowledge that one of her fathers really wasn't okay. And that she, again, had no idea how to help.

"Grubby can get out of hell," Barrels said suddenly. "He could get out with Ebba and Caspian. And maybe Jagger if he's taint-free. They are the three needed to assemble the weapon. If we get them out with the parts, they can continue on with the quest."

Continue on without her fathers? Ebba wasn't listening to this.

She stormed into the cave after Jagger and stalled just inside in the shadows.

"Any good?" she called within.

"Aye," Jagger's low voice echoed back from the left. "All looks fine. There be a couple o' dresses in here. The rest be normal pirate garb."

Ebba could take one guess at what Cannon deemed appropriate for her. "How many sets o' slops are there?"

"Not many."

So it was a dress for her. She much preferred dresses of her own design, but gone were the days when she'd light fires to avoid being shoved into the things.

Ebba missed her slops. And her jerkin. She even missed boots. Which reminded her about Cannon's weirdness over her wearing shoes. "Shoes?"

"Aye, there be some child boots that should fit ye."

She listened to the smile in his voice. Ebba wasn't taking that bait, and she wasn't in the mood for Jagger's distraction techniques. His boots scuffed on the uneven ground as he worked his way back to her.

They really needed a bloody lantern in here.

"Here," he said, holding *veritas* out to her. "Take this and send Caspian in."

Caspian. That didn't bode well. "Why?" She drew out.

Jagger's teeth flashed in the dark. "Don't worry, Viva. I won't strangle him. We need to change for our meetin' with Cannon."

Her gut flipped. She'd forgotten about that.

"Unless ye'd rather stay and tell me what the *veritas* forced ye to admit to yerself afore?" he asked, raising his brows.

For once, *she* wasn't the one pretending. Ebba snatched *veritas* and stormed back out onto the ledge to join her fathers. It was a storming kind of day.

"I asked the sword, too, Viva," he called after her.

She stopped short. What? He did? Why wasn't he acting strangely then? And if he wasn't in shock, *why hadn't he kissed her*?

"Uh," Caspian said.

Ebba jolted and realized she was face-to-face with the prince in the shadowed entrance of the cave.

She shoved down the urge to march back to Jagger and kick him in the ankle bone.

"Ye need to go change for the meetin' with Cannon," she said to the prince.

This time, he looked at her. "What meeting?"

She rubbed her forehead. "Sorry, I forgot to say. When Pockmark comes back for *veritas*, he'll be takin' ye and Jagger with him to meet with Cannon."

Caspian stood, brows drawing together. "You didn't think to mention this until now?" He didn't wait for her second apology. "What else was said?"

She thought back. "That ye should dress ac'ordingly and that Pockmark will be there."

He nodded curtly and sidestepped her, entering the cave.

Locks whistled low. "Phew, he's right pissed at ye."

Ebba circled the wrist that held the sword. It was far too long for her and scraped along the stone. She wanted her cutlass again.

"Tell me about it," she mumbled, glancing to where Plank still sat, rocking.

"Don't worry, I find most people can get over love pretty well," Locks continued.

She wasn't taking advice from him on the subject of love. He'd had more girlfriends than she could count in her lifetime, and all because he was running from Verity because she'd hurt his feelings by calling him out on his promiscuous ways. And Barrels was right: his love shanties were shite.

Tuning him and her other fathers out, Ebba reached desperately for the meager wisp of privacy at the opposite end of the ledge to Plank. She sat heavily. Her mind was in turmoil, and her crew was wise enough to take the hint she didn't want company. Too much was happening that she didn't understand. It was all connected; she felt it as an almost tangible sensation in her chest. Plank's sadness, their reason for being here—for being on this unwanted quest, the reason she loved Jagger and not Caspian, the reason Caspian lost his arm. All of it had to *mean* something. For so many weeks, *months*, she hadn't let the lack of answers get to her. But now, the feeling of limbo had exploded into overwhelming territory. She needed to understand why such bad things were happening.

And yet that seemed impossible. To understand terrible acts, she'd have to understand the people who committed them. There was no rhyme to evil's reason.

Sniffing hard, Ebba scanned Davy Jones', sword in hand. She looked at the boiling purple stream, shivering in memory of the all-too-recent horrors there. The water wasn't tainted. She peered across the stream to the damned, who'd tugged so strongly on her heart. The people there weren't covered in shadows, unlike the tainted pirates. In fact, many of them glowed to varying degrees.

She continued scanning the damned on the far side of the cavern, from the passage platform all the way to the opposite, northern cliff face.

Ebba squinted.

Then blinked.

Whoa, one of the damned over there was glowing! Not just a subtle shine, either; radiance burst from the person in waves. Now that her eyes had found the brilliant light, she couldn't see anything else. The damned stood out like a beacon.

Ebba stared down at the sword in her hands. She was seeing truth or goodness. Across the stream. What did that mean?

Lifting her chin, Ebba stared again, watching as the light moved around, always staying toward the northern end of the cavern.

Who was it?

Movement directly below her snapped her attention back from across the stream.

Pockmark and Swindles weaved their way through the boulders toward the base of her crew's perch, but as concerned as Ebba was about Caspian and Jagger meeting with Cannon, she now had something of her own to do.

A glowing light in the middle of hell? That sounded fair-strange to her. More than that, the sword had shown it to her. That *had* to mean something.

And she was going to find out what.

TWELVE

Ebba rated the outfit a five out of ten. Not the worst she'd ever worn. And certainly not the best. The best being her slops.

The corset docked the most points. It sucked her waist in to a tiny V, which Ebba didn't mind. But it made her chest look about four times the size, which wasn't appreciated. Whether the V-waist or the new chest size was to blame for her trouble breathing, she wasn't sure. Beneath the black corset was a ruffled crimson skirt that gathered high on one side, exposing Ebba's thigh. Exposed thigh was better than exposed butt.

Under the black corset was a white linen shirt that would be perfect except the neckline was too wide for the garment to perch on her shoulders. Instead, both sleeves hung partway down her arm, drawing more attention to the boosted swell of her chest.

The boots had earned the outfit a few points, being that they were somewhat like her old boots except black and without the folded tops.

"I look like one o' Sherry's girls," she announced, swishing side to side.

Barrels had already been subjected to lacing the back of the corset and audibly shuddered.

Grinning, Ebba left her fathers to fumble around in the dark and change. Holding her ruffled skirt aloft as she neared the ledge, she glanced left to where Jagger and Caspian had disappeared far too long ago. What was Cannon doing to them? Driving the wedge between the pair further in? Or was he humiliating Caspian and playing Pockmark against Jagger? Probably all three.

She was uneasy that Cannon had met the pair by the tainted ship instead of leading them to the stream as he'd done with her. But that *did* leave the stream open for business.

"Ebba-Viva," Stubby said behind her.

She straightened at his tone. She hadn't done anything wrong. Yet. Turning, Ebba stopped short at the sight of her six fathers in a row outside the cave.

". . . Aye?" she asked.

"Can ye sit for a talk with us?" Stubby gestured at a rock on the wide ledge.

"Prob'bly not, matey. I can't do much o' anythin' in this corset."

Peg-leg shoved Locks forward, who scowled back over his shoulder.

"What be the matter?" Damn. She should have scooted down to the stream to find the source of the glowing light when she had the chance.

Plank walked to a stone and propped his foot up on it, eyebrows raised at the others. She watched him carefully for any sign of the anguish he'd displayed yesterday. But her father had either sorted through his strife or tucked his pain away so that none showed.

Her crew edged forward, not all of them electing to sit. But in time they lost the 'battlefront' appearance.

Ebba waited, resting her hands on the flare of her skirt just below her corset.

"There comes a time," Locks began, "when one person begins to look at another person as more than a friend."

Shite, she knew what this was about. Ebba eyed the ledge, wondering if she should take the risk and jump.

"And when that time comes, his or her parents should sit down with their child and explain the workings o' how one person loves another and the probable outcomes o' sexual intercourse."

She stared at Locks in mute horror.

Grubby frowned. "Ye said we wouldn't be readin' her the book."

Peg-leg hushed him with a fluttering hand.

This was about Jagger. She'd known it wasn't over. Sod it! They'd seen him hug her. They thought, like Caspian, that he'd kissed her. But luckily, there was one sure way to stop this conversation: by giving her fathers an easy way out.

"I ain't sure what ye think ye saw with me and Jagger," she said. "But Cannon showed me sumpin' ter'ible at the stream. Afterward, I was upset, and Jagger hugged me a little while. That was it. Nothin' to be worryin' over. I'm a pirate, recall?"

Stubby blew out a breath and strode for the cave. Plank yanked him back.

"Since we dropped you at the brothel, you've always been rather vocal about your identity, my dear," Barrels said. "And of late, to our disma— Well, you've been equally as vocal about being a tribe pirate female. So forgive us," he said, shooting Stubby a glance, "if we don't quite believe yer claims about Jagger."

"So now ye're all about the truth?" she shot back.

"*D'fensiveness be normal. Don't be put off,*" Locks whisper-screamed at Barrels.

Barrels stuttered. "Uh, yes. You convinced us of that. We thought we were protecting you, but we weren't. We're determined to no longer take the easy path. Especially when it comes to you."

He might not be a pirate, but he could certainly tell a pirate truth. He'd built himself an exit clause already.

They hadn't taken the bait. That left one route: Getting this over with as soon as possible.

"Allright then," she said. "None o' ye want to be here. I surely don't want to be. Say yer piece, and let's get it over with."

At a few looks from the others, Peg-leg hastened to say, "Good, right. Well. First off, we wanted to show ye the dif'erence between mere lust and love."

Ebba waved an arm. "The dif'erence between Locks' girlfriends and Verity."

"A-ah." Peg-leg blinked and looked at the others. "Aye, that's likely right. But sometimes when ye feel it, ye believe them to be the same."

She'd felt infatuation and then love. One after the other . . . a week apart.

Ebba told them, "I'm knowin' the difference. One feels empty, the other one whole."

Her fathers stared at her.

"That be . . . about right," Locks said, frowning.

Stubby was next up. "When ye think ye love someone, the best thing to do is to move slowly until ye know if it *be* love . . . on both sides o' the bulwark."

When Plank groaned, Ebba was inclined to echo the pained sound.

"Aye, I hear ye," she managed. This was about Jagger. They were trying to convince her against him.

"And," Stubby continued, "sometimes, ye need to learn to love what's good for ye rather than someone who might sail ye into a storm. It be the dif'erence between a good, kind lad and a shady, bad one with dubious morals. And ye know," he said, voice high-pitched, "not all the good ones be pirates. Sometimes they be landlubbers. Sometimes royal-lubbers."

This was beyond painful. Her fathers didn't know what she knew since touching the *amare* and *veritas*, but even then, falling in love with the wrong person or being misled by infatuation for a few months or years was her choice.

However, since Ebba planned to always have her fathers in her life, their opinion did matter. Most of the time, when they weren't forcing her to talk about drinking tea, Ebba respected their opinions.

"I know ye don't like Jagger," Ebba said, her face grim. "And I know ye like Caspian a fair sight more."

"He'd make a good captain," Locks interjected.

Ebba glanced at him, and he fell quiet. "Ye worry for me. For my happiness. For my feelings. Just as I do for all o' ye. But do ye think ye've raised a pirate who'd be taken in? And if I was taken in, do ye think I'm the sort to keep quiet about it and let it happen?"

Now they weren't looking at her. Except Plank, who was just amused and staring up at the surrounding cliff faces.

"Nay, lass. Don't take this to mean we don't have faith in yer strength. Ye know we think yer right fierce," Peg-leg said.

"I am," she said. "All o' ye made me that way."

"We be puttin' our nose in overmuch, I take?" Locks asked.

Ebba nodded. "Aye, ye are. Though it comes from a good place." Should she tell them about the *amare* and what she'd seen, doubted, and then been shown again by *veritas*? She peered from the sweat on Stubby's forehead to Peg-leg's nervous twitch.

Could they handle it today?

She thought of the way Jagger always pulled away. What if she told her fathers only to be rejected by Jagger?

No, she wouldn't tell them just yet. For now, it was between her, Jagger, Caspian, and Plank. Darn it, too many people already knew. Ebba opened her mouth then hesitated again. How should she tell her parents that she was accidentally in love? Or had been in love for some time and was forced to acknowledge it early?

Grubby stood and, in the absence of his usual cap, twisted the bottom hem of his roughly tucked tunic. "When ye have sex, there be certain herbs which will stave off pregnancy. Ye're much too young for children though we'd like a lot o' grandbabies one of these days. And also, there be diseases that Jagger might be havin'. That Caspian prob'bly don't."

Unfortunately for her, the yells of her other fathers came too late for a single word that spilled from Grubby's mouth to be lost.

She couldn't breathe. And it wasn't the corset.

Her jaw dropped. "Ye gave him all the hardest stuff to say!"

"Nay," Stubby attempted.

Ebba ticked off her fingers. "Pregnancy. Grandbabies. Diseases. Sex. Ye flamin' cowards."

"I don't mind, Ebba," Grubby said nervously. "Can I still see yer babies?"

"Of course ye can," she started saying. "Wait! I ain't bloody havin' babies." Then paused, thinking of cute mini-Jaggers with silver eyes. "Nay," she said, clutching her skull. "Nay, nay, nay. I've had enough o' this talk."

She turned away from her fathers, forcing away their bumbling apologies.

Their apologies faded to silence, and soon, arms wrapped around her.

Plank rested his head atop hers. "They be back in the cave now, little nymph. . . . I told them that was a ter'ible idea."

Ebba wasn't able to see the humor in it just yet. "They don't like Jagger overmuch."

"Nay, it ain't about that."

She rested back against her father, craving the contact more because of what happened with him yesterday than anything else. "What is it then?"

"It's about bein' replaced. With Caspian, it wouldn't feel like bein' replaced because he's no pirate. With Jagger, it does. Because we see how ye are with him. Even before ye touched the *amare*."

"Ye did?"

Plank nodded. "I saw it on Pleo. When he was holdin' that pistol to himself, wonderin' if he should shoot. Ye called a few words to him, and with just that sound, he decided to fight. I saw it again when he collected yer beads and gifted them back. I saw it when he risked his life to save ye durin' the thunderbird's storm.

And when he barely spoke a word when the Capricorn took ye hostage. That lad loves ye with all his soul. To me, it always seemed like he was waitin' for ye to realize the same. When Caspian showed an int'rest in ye, Jagger decided waitin' weren't good enough."

"I didn't notice any o' that," she admitted with a snort. "Ye really think so?"

"When we sat paralyzed in Medusa's lair, the others knew. Ye heard him, little nymph. I'd wager he was more embarrassed by that than he let on. Then aboard *Malice*, only the thought o' ye could reach Jagger's soul. He only kept going because he recalled yer joy. The need to preserve ye and to keep ye whole drove him to resist the darkness. I've lost count o' the times he's been there for ye, provin' himself. He reminds me greatly o' myself with. . . . Well, o' a younger version o' myself."

Hearing all of this baffled her. Because she remembered all of that. But at the time, she'd always thought the pirate was doing those things to mess with her. Was her father right? Had Jagger loved her all this time?

"Jagger be a better man than me, though," Plank said, kissing the top of her head.

Ebba turned and kissed his cheek. "Nay, father. Just immune."

"And in these times, who could be a better choice for our daughter?"

Ebba did her best to conceal her shy smile but lost. Bloody thing.

Plank searched her face for a beat and then kissed her forehead once more. "Would ye like a moment more out here? I'll tell the others they've upset ye big-time."

Ebba grinned, sweeping back a dread that whipped about as the howling wind came through the passage. "Aye, I'll stay out here. But Plank? Are ye okay after touchin' *veritas*?"

He paused and peered back at her. "I know what I have to do."

He did? She beamed at him. "I'm glad for ye."

Dipping his head, Plank strode for the cave.

"Plank?" she called again. When he turned, she said, "Thank ye. It means a lot that ye like him."

"Oh, I don't like him, little nymph. I'll never like any male ye fancy. Not one bit. But if he makes ye happy, I'll learn to abide by him though there'll be less room in yer heart for me with him leaning about."

Her jaw dropped. "He *does* lean, doesn't he? I noticed that."

"I'd wager he wanted ye to. And if ye were askin' for my approval to crack on, ye have it."

She'd take that. Only five more fathers to convince.

But first things first.

Waiting until Plank was completely out of sight, Ebba picked up her crimson skirt and hurried to the steep steps. Caspian and Jagger had the sword, so she wouldn't have the help of *veritas* to find the source of the shining light. But that couldn't be helped.

Ebba didn't have much time.

THIRTEEN

"Stupid dress," Ebba panted. "Stupider corset."

She'd managed to descend the steep steps without breaking her neck, but running down the path toward the stream had proved a bad idea. Her insides were squished into a tiny space and objected to the jarring movements.

Propping her palm against a boulder, Ebba held her side and sucked in large gulps of air. She strained to listen for company over her heaving pants. No one guarded their cave—there was hardly any reason to when there wasn't anywhere to go. Though she recalled Pockmark or Cannon saying the passage was guarded. Hopefully the guard's vantage point would allow her to remain unseen at the stream.

When she felt less like passing out, Ebba straightened and glanced both ways down the path. She couldn't hear anything from the direction of the ship and nothing but bubbling and popping from the stream.

No one was in sight.

She slid one booted foot in the direction of the stream. And then another before pausing to listen once more. The coast was clear. Ebba settled for a languid walk that, while it didn't decrease her slight dizziness, didn't make the feeling worse.

"Pick it up, ye blitherin' fools," came a roaring voice behind her.

Ebba stared at the damning crimson skirt and then turned in a circle, scanning the path for the biggest boulder. The largest—only the height of her shoulders—didn't inspire much confidence, but she leaped in the direction of it, skirt hoisted in both hands as she fervently hoped not to break her ankle on the uneven ground. Heavy footsteps pounded toward her. Too close. *Too many.*

Reaching the black boulder, she gathered in her skirt, tucking it as tightly to her body as possible, and crouched, hugging her knees. Peeking out to look at the troop of pirates passing by seemed like a bad idea, so Ebba squeezed her eyes shut and listened to their thumping steps, heart hammering in her rib cage.

"I said faster, ye pox'd rodents. Cannon wants us to the entrance and back in an hour."

Ebba opened her eyes. The entrance? *Again?*

Releasing a shaking breath as they passed her spot without slowing, she crept back to the path, checking both ways again.

Did they go through the passage to the entrance every day? Was it just to collect food for her crew? Ebba paused. They'd appeared awfully urgent for a food run. . . .

She waited a moment longer, listening hard for company behind her, and then set off to the stream for the second time.

Ebba paused where the larger boulders tapered to hip level. Gathering her skirt tight, she crouched and waited as the tainted pirates ran up the steps to the passage platform and disappeared through the crevice to the entrance.

They'd be back in an hour—she'd better get a move on.

She kept low—better safe than dead—and hustled to the water's edge. Tendrils of steam curled about her face. Ebba drew a hand over her forehead, wiping away the gathered perspiration. Sink her, it was hotter by the boiling water. She sucked in another breath. Blast Barrels for doing the laces so tight.

Right, the glowing damned—or thing—had been at the northern end. Without the sword, identifying the right person might not be possible. Ebba walked left along the water's edge, peering into the crowd of damned men, women, and children. Their anguished eyes bore into hers, and there was a leering edge in some of the eyes today also; whether it was because Cannon wasn't here or because of her new garb was unclear. The uncomfortable tension further emphasized that Ebba didn't want to join them, nor sentence her fathers to eternity there. Such a price was too cruel a fate for any person—though maybe not for people like Cannon and the pillars. If she saw the thunderbird again, who sorted good and bad souls in the oblivion, words would be exchanged. Or maybe she'd talk, and then he'd kill her in a monster storm.

Ebba blew out a breath, clutching her side again. Her eyes were sharp after a life spent in and out of the crow's nest. Even then, peering into the grimy black tested her limits. And she had no idea what had emitted the white glow. Well, that wasn't strictly true. The glow had moved, so that narrowed things down. Either the glow was a person or an object *on* a person.

"Ahoy," she hissed, cupping her mouth with both hands. "Is there anythin' white and glowin' in there?"

When in doubt, ask. Sometimes, it yielded surprising results.

. . . Not in this instance. Ebba glanced at the hands stretching toward her and swallowed, hoping none of them decided to take a swim today.

Sweat trickled down her neck, disappearing between the mounds of her pumped-up chest. Ebba fanned her face, pausing once more to suck in gulps of air. So hot, but she had to hurry.

Walking again, Ebba fixed her eyes on the opposite bank, systematically working front to back. Black, sooty, dirty, caked. She sighed, placing both hands on her hips.

And blinked.

There was one thing she hadn't considered. Her crew had gathered five parts of the weapon. But there was another to collect. The sixth part that they'd assumed was in Cannon's possession.

What if it wasn't?

What if she'd glimpsed it by accident from their cave?

That made things considerably harder. Not only because Ebba would need to physically go get it, but also because the part might be helping the person survive on the other side. If she was in hell with that advantage, Ebba would fight to the death to keep the part.

She continued to the northern end of the cavern, unwilling to give up just yet in case the glow had been a person. She placed both hands on her hips, panting through the muggy air.

Nope, she had to stop a minute.

Bending at the hips, Ebba rested a hand on the small boulder beneath her. Whistles crossed the waterway, and she raised her head then glanced down, realizing what the whistles were aimed at. Glaring the eight feet across the stream, Ebba bolted upright as a set of amber eyes stared back at her. Hard. *Serrated.* Before Caspian's angry gaze of late, she'd only seen such eyes once before.

She took a step closer, working her toes right to the edge of the purple stream. She couldn't step across, but she might've forgotten herself to do just that otherwise.

The person on the other side did the same, sinking to a crouch on the opposite bank. She'd never have thought such a man could crouch. The last time Ebba saw him, he'd been forcefully sat in a chair with a multitude of pistols aimed at his gut. One of which had claimed his life.

"Montcroix," she whispered.

He dipped his head.

Caspian's father was in Davy Jones' Locker. Was he the source of the glow? If not, that was a mighty big coincidence. . . .

The dead king tilted his head left and disappeared back into the midst of the damned. Ebba stared at the spot where he'd been, mouth bone-dry. Caspian's dad was here. That she'd met once. Up until the very last time he saw her, he'd thought her engaged to his son. In their last interaction, he'd seen she was a pirate, tossed her the *veritas*, and told her to look after Caspian.

"Lusty riots o' an underpaid brothel wench," she breathed.

He was Caspian's father. And he was in hell. Ebba couldn't even think of how that might mess up her friend.

Shaking herself, Ebba took the king's directive and traversed the rest of the way to the northern cliff face, glancing around the surrounding cavern and back to the passage platform to check for company. She kept a sharp eye on the shore for his reappearance. Once there, she rested a hand on the cliff face and rechecked her surroundings. The ship would be directly behind her, but boulders completely concealed it from view. But if the group of tainted pirates returned from the entrance, her skirt was a crimson flag, and she had no cover between the stream and the fifty feet to the first boulders that could conceal her.

The purple waterway at this end was narrower—only six feet—and didn't bubble and pop as much. There were far less damned here too. Ebba hadn't realized the noise they created with their moans and pleas before.

She glanced up and found the king waiting for her. He was really here. Ebba just didn't expect to see people she knew in hell. It was unsettling.

"Lady." The king dipped his head.

He didn't remember her fake name. Typical royal landlubber. "My name be Ebba. And ye're—"

"Shh," he hissed, darting a look either side. "Do not utter that name here."

The prone people surrounding him didn't seem in the listening kind of mood, but. . . . "Aye, can't say I'm blamin' ye for that. Not the place I'd want to end up in yer pos'tion."

Call her gloating, but to see the enemy of all piratekind get what he deserved was a moment for celebration. Even if he was also the enemy of her enemies. The only redeeming quality he'd displayed in her brief time cooped up in a safety room with him was his love for his children—an iceberg kind of love where only a tiny amount showed on the surface, and the rest was buried so deep and in such a cold place that she had to wonder if it was truly there. Caspian had doubted his father's love, after all. Still did.

"Why is my son here?" Montcroix whispered across the gap, crouching again. Ebba did the same, wincing as her corset dug in.

"Ye saw us come in then?" she asked.

He would've had a perfect view of the nine of them coming down the passage steps not long ago. Ebba glanced right to the southern end of the cavern and then twisted to see the west cliff faces. Cods, he could even see their cave ledge from here. King Forge Montcroix must've been driven wild by seeing Caspian up there.

Ebba chewed her lip and came to a decision. "Listen up. I'm only sayin' this once. We're on a quest to collect six parts o' a weapon that will take down the six pillars. They be an evil force with great power who have taken over the Exosian realm. Last we saw 'em, they'd stormed the castle, packed off all yer people to work in the mines. By now, mostly everyone in the realm will be tainted, from what an ex-soothsayer told us. But the pillars are after the weapon, too; it'll make them unstop'able. Mutinous Cannon—"

The king snarled, and she ignored him. He'd killed Cannon two decades ago, but it must gripe Montcroix that he had ended up in the same place and under Cannon's thumb.

"—be workin' for them. He's holdin' us prisoner here. And aside from knowin' the pillars want the parts, we can't figure out what Cannon's plan is or how we can escape with the parts."

Caspian's father didn't speak for a time, and Ebba took the chance to survey him in greater detail.

He was essentially in the same physical state as when he'd died, minus the bullet wound, unless the injury was covered by clothes. His garb, like all the others', was grimy with black dirt. The king had learned to crouch, but he'd also shirked his regal drawn-back posture. Caspian's father was a survivor, it appeared. He slumped; he crawled; he had altered to fit in. The only thing separating the royal from the other damned was that he'd taken pains to keep his face clean.

"I see," the king said quietly. "And where was my son in all this?"

Ebba narrowed her eyes. "Running for our lives like the rest o' us. And not a moment goes by when he doesn't regret it."

She couldn't glean a thing from Forge's expression. And as much as she wanted to give him news of Caspian, there were more pressing matters.

"I have questions," she said, snapping the dead king out of his funk.

He nodded. "Proceed."

Maybe he hadn't completely lost his snobbery. "How many times a day does the wind howl?"

"Four. Every six hours."

Ebba filed that away in case Barrels hadn't kept track. "When the damned die, how long does it take 'em to come back?"

A shadow of horror passed through the king's eyes. Ebba wondered if he'd jumped in.

"They'll come back with the next surge of wind. Anywhere from one minute to six hours," he answered. "And they arrive back at the start of the passage."

Ebba pressed her lips together. That wasn't ideal. If the path emerged with the howling wind, and they killed Cannon, then he'd regenerate right where they'd be escaping. "Okay."

Forge frowned. "Only the damned belong here," he called in a low voice. "Why can Caspian not leave?"

"Me, Caspian, one o' my fathers, and maybe Jagger can leave, but my other fathers have some taint in them. All o' us need to get out o' here, so we need to figure out a di'ferent way to escape." She wouldn't mention their friend on the outside. Not when any of the seemingly dead people could really be listening in.

The king's shoulders sagged. "And how is my son?"

Ebba had a list of questions the size of Montcroix's misdeeds, and all he wanted to talk about was his son, which she could kind of understand. "Caspian be stru'gling to come to terms with who he is because ye screwed him up by not showin' enough a'fection," she snapped.

Montcroix startled at her words.

"Do ye know what Cannon's plan might be?" she asked him, shoving past the small guilt she felt over her comment. He'd have eternity to dwell on that, after all.

The king shook his head. "The deal is that if we remain over here, Cannon will free us from this place. That is what he tells the damned. They believe his words."

Ebba glanced at the stream. "So ye can get over to the pirate side o' the stream?"

"We can, but then the deal is off. Everyone who isn't a pirate climbs down the cliffs from the passage platform."

"No one at all has gone over?" she said. That would be the first thing she'd do if their positions were reversed.

He tilted his head. "An eternity spent being killed by your inmates because you reneged on a deal is not desirable even though I will never believe the word of a pirate."

That made things awkward, but she felt the same way about him. "Well, don't be comin' over here. All o' the pirates on this side be tainted, and I ain't sure bein' dead will stop ye catchin' it."

She stilled. Not only was Cannon keeping her crew away from the taint, he'd kept the damned away from the taint too. That had to mean something. Why else would he take such pains?

"The black eyes and the pockmarks on their bodies. That is the taint?"

"Aye, that be the pillars' evil," she answered, casting a glance at the passage platform. How long had passed? She couldn't risk too much longer. The pirates would be back from the entrance soon.

"If the taint is infectious, how is it that you are well?" he said, peering into her eyes.

Was he checking their appearance? "Cannon put us up in that

cave ye can see. It ain't tainted. The stone this cavern be made o' ain't affected by the evil."

"A kind of talisman?"

Ebba hadn't thought of the stone like that before. "Dunno." She glanced up at the platform again.

"Does not it seem odd that you are untainted but on the tainted side?" the king murmured. "Not only does that suggest that Mutinous Cannon wants you all unharmed, but clearly he needs you untainted. Why is that?"

"Been wond'ring the same thing myself," Ebba remarked, her skin crawling. "Listen, I've got to skedaddle afore the group from the entrance comes back."

The king shifted. "They go each day at the same time."

That confirmed one thing.

"You have given me many things to think on," he continued as she started to rise. "You must come back tomorrow so we can confer again."

Ebba snorted. "There ain't no conferrin', matey. Ye're on yer own."

"Despite what I did and didn't do in my life, I still ruled a kingdom for forty years. I am versed in how the minds of the likes of Cannon work. Better still, I killed him once before."

Through sheer gunpower, no doubt. She hesitated.

"My son is over there," he pressed. "You want to get out; I want to save my son from a horrible fate. Our interests are aligned."

"Ye would've done better to save yer son when ye were alive," she told him.

The king swallowed. "No one knows that more than I."

"I'll think about it. But if I do come back, ye better make it worth my while or I won't be back a third time."

Ebba stood, her gut twisting.

Was the glowing light *veritas* showed her the king? Had the sword recognized its last owner? Because Ebba was certain Forge shouldn't be glowing with truth and goodness otherwise. Or was the sixth part with the damned, and she'd just happened upon the dead king?

. . . She'd dallied too long.

"Same spot," she told him. "It might not be tomorrow or the next day. I don't know when I'll have another chance."

The king stood and dipped his head, showing a flash of his former, regal self. "I shall be waiting. And, Mistress Pirate, please do not tell my son that I'm here."

Snorting, Ebba shook her head, not deigning to answer him. Picking up her ruffled skirt, she hurried back along the stream to the boulder path at a fast clip. A furtive glance told her the passage platform was still empty. A second glance at the perched cave told her every single one of her fathers was standing in a row watching her. Sink her, that wasn't good. But they'd understand when they heard what she'd discovered.

Her heart sank, though, recalling Montcroix's last request.

Caspian's father was in hell.

And Ebba couldn't be sure if the knowledge would hinder or help him. Certainly, hearing the news would upset him for a time. In equal measures, Caspian seemed to uphold and detest his father, craving his praise while simultaneously realizing his father's morals didn't align with his own.

Would telling Caspian help him understand his father's praise wasn't needed? Or would it push her friend to question and hate himself even further? The prince took his duty seriously. He'd been willing to die for his people. There had to be some family pride attached to that. A family pride that would be ripped away if she voiced the truth.

Jeers and laughter echoed toward her from above, and Ebba wrenched to a halt, crouching behind a rock that didn't begin to hide her as she scanned the cliffs. The voices grew louder.

Time to run!

Hands fisted in waves of material, Ebba pumped her legs as hard as she could. She wasn't far from the larger boulders that could hide her. She risked another look at the cliffs and inhaled sharply. The pirates had spilled out from the crevice onto the passage platform overlooking the cavern.

Ebba slowed to an inching pace, not wanting the rapid movement of her bright dress to attract their attention. The boulders were still on the smallish side but better than nothing. She slid between them, pausing behind each one, waiting for a handful of nail-biting seconds for shouts of discovery.

She couldn't make it all the way back to the cave like this. She was too far away.

"Where've ye been today?" someone shouted far overhead.

Ebba squeaked and plastered herself to the nearest boulder. But . . . that was Peg-leg's voice. Unlocking enough to move her head, she glanced up toward the cave perch.

Peg-leg was facing the passage platform where the tainted pirates stood. "Aye, I'm talkin' to ye, ye ugly bunch of evil buggers. Never saw a bunch 'o pirates who were harder on the eyes."

Ebba grinned as Stubby joined in, yelling across the cavern.

They were distracting the pirates.

Rising on tiptoes, she checked to confirm all of the tainted pirates were looking farther west at the cave. Ebba then ran between the rocks, hugging their shadows as much as possible.

She didn't stop until reaching the larger boulders she'd successfully hidden behind on the way to the stream. Her father's shouts cut off abruptly. She must be out of their sight.

Unfortunately, if Ebba couldn't control her breathing—which vaguely resembled that of a birthing cow—the tainted might find her anyway.

One hand to her ribs, the other one to her forehead, she stumbled down the worn path, trying to focus on not missing the smaller path to the cave. The last thing she needed was to miss it and accidentally stagger into the shipwreck clearing. The earlier dizziness was back after her sprint through the rocks. Ebba groaned, blinking furiously to bring the ground before her into focus.

Thankfully, she didn't miss the cave path.

Once around the first curve of the smaller walkway, Ebba was forced to stop and hug a boulder to remain upright. What if the tainted pirates came down here instead of returning to the ship?

She couldn't breathe.

Ebba pulled at the sides of the corset, scratching at the slippery material in an attempt to pull it away from her body. She twisted, reaching behind, but couldn't seek purchase on the tight knots and laces aligned with her spine.

Bright dots spotted her vision.

"Viva?"

Footsteps pounded toward her, but at least she recognized Jagger's voice.

She fell to her knees, forehead on the boulder.

Hands reached for her. "Viva, what's wrong?" Jagger said, spinning her around. "Tell me what's wrong!"

Her vision tunneled to his frantic expression.

"Her lips be blue," he gasped, hands searching her for injury. "Is she faintin'?"

Ebba gasped for air, only managing a weak inhale. "I ain't goin' to faint," she slurred.

"It's her corset," Caspian said urgently. "It's too tight. Rip it off."

Well, he'd probably know the most about corsets. But her skull stuck on Jagger's comment. "I ain't faintin'," she insisted. "Faintin' be stupid."

And then Ebba knew no more.

FOURTEEN

Jagger was angry; that was her first cognizant thought. Ebba brought a hand to her forehead and groaned. She had a skull full of pain.

"Ye did her corset so tight she couldn't breathe!" Jagger was yelling. "She couldn't reach the laces, ye fool. Ye nearly killed her!"

Ebba peeled back an eyelid, reasonably certain from her prone position, general nausea, and—she glanced down—where was her corset? She'd bloody fainted like a nincompoop.

She'd never live it down.

"Shh, she's waking," Caspian said, leaning over her.

Not waking. Already awake. Ebba sat, forcing Caspian back on his haunches. Jagger had Barrels pinned against a wall. Three of her fathers hovered on the point of intervening while the others were gathered around her with Caspian.

"What's this racket about then?" she croaked, wincing as the act of talking sent a spear of white-hot agony into her temple.

Jagger whirled away from Barrels, pushing between Plank and Stubby to reach her. He sank down by her side. "We found ye half-dead down the path. If we hadn't found ye, ye'd be dead already. Yer lips were blue—"

How was it that she'd nearly suffocated and Jagger was the one who needed reassurance? Ebba let herself fall against his chest. Then she frowned. His chest was bare, and hers was covered with a tunic. Her corset was gone. Those details weren't worrying, but the transition from one garment to the next certainly had her wondering what Caspian and Jagger had seen. Though she had been wearing the off-the-shoulder blouse on underneath. Was that still on?

Jagger wrapped his arms around her and sighed. "Ye nearly died, Viva."

"Aye, but it all worked out. The heat got to me, and I had to run from Cannon's crew."

His silver eyes hardened. "Don't try to make him feel better. He laced ye too tight."

Ebba pulled away. In her peripheries, she could see Barrels hovering like some kicked dog. "It was too hot. And I had to run," she ground out, setting her jaw after.

Jagger rolled his eyes, and Ebba took that as a sign he felt better.

"Mistress Pirate, are you okay? You're still very pale," Caspian said.

"I don't feel too flash, I'll grant ye."

His amber eyes were warm and showed true concern. But right now, they only served to remind her of his father.

"Why were ye down there by the stream?" Stubby asked, passing her a waterskin. "Ye bloody ran off."

Ebba ripped the cork off with her teeth and spat it away, guzzling at the contents. Never in her life had she been so thirsty. Passing the skin back, she answered, "Aye, well, I saw sumpin' with *veritas* I wanted to check out. So I went down to the stream and—"

"Ye were speakin' to someone. We could see."

She shot a look at Peg-leg. How much had they seen? A beat later, she realized they couldn't have possibly recognized Montcroix from up here. "Aye," she replied. "I did."

Jagger was watching her closely.

"Hold on, hold on," Locks said. "Ye're tellin' me ye saw sumpin' with the sword and never breathed a word o' it? That's aside from sneakin' off without tellin' us where ye'd gone. How do ye think we felt when we came out here to an empty ledge?"

Ebba's cheeks warmed. When put like that, her actions sounded a bit . . . careless. "I didn't say anythin' because I wanted to see if it was worth mentionin' first."

"What did you see?" Caspian asked.

Yer father. "A glow on the damned side o' the stream."

"Ye didn't think that was worth sharin'?" Stubby asked.

The silence on the ledge was thick. And it stuck in her gullet. "I didn't want any o' ye rushin' off to the stream."

"Ye think we want ye doin' that?" Locks shouted.

"Nay," Ebba yelled as her temper erupted. "But Mutinous threatened to chuck ye all over the other side to die and then kill yerself over and over in the boiling water, so I didn't want ye anywhere near it!"

That shut them up.

She deflated at their looks of shock. "I should've told ye where I was goin'; that was shite o' me."

Her fathers exchanged looks, and then Peg-leg nodded. "Aye, well, we supposed ye'd just run away because o' the talk about love and safe sex."

They. Didn't. Horror flooded her, and Ebba briefly contemplated pretending to faint to escape the mortifying moment. Or maybe she'd just kill them.

Six fathers grinned back at her, and Ebba received their message loud and clear: *now we be even.* Caspian's face was bright red. She refused to look at Jagger, feeling like everyone was waiting for her to do so.

Jagger was merciful. "Ye spoke to someone then?"

"Aye," Ebba said, staring in the opposite direction. "He had a few tidbits to share."

"Can't hardly trust a man in Davy Jones', though," Plank grunted, sitting down on a rock.

Barrels shuffled closer, and Ebba looked at him. "Barrels, it ain't yer fault. I didn't know either. I felt fine to start, but the stream really was warm."

Stubby waved a hand in her face. "Oi. What'd the man say?"

"Wait," she blurted. "I want to know how the meetin' with Cannon went."

Her fathers groaned.

"He took me onto the ship," Jagger said.

Ebba's eyes rounded, and she looked him over. "The ship be tainted. How do ye feel?"

He shrugged. "Aye, all right, I s'pose. He didn't take me below deck. Played me against Pockmark most o' the time. Flattered me, asked me questions about bein' immune, and then told me how we be alike."

"Ye ain't like him," she said fiercely.

His lips quirked at her reply. "Glad to hear it."

Caspian spoke. "I stayed in the clearing while Jagger went with Cannon."

"That's it?" she asked in confusion.

He shared a glance with Jagger. "Not quite. The entire tainted crew was there, surrounding me in a circle. You can imagine the rest."

"Did they shout things at ye, Caspian?" she asked him.

He straightened, the gold circlet in place on his head. "That they did. Comments about my father and my missing arm, mainly. My sisters. Then a long bout on my mother. My strength, or lack thereof. And then to top it all off, the likely fate of my people."

Ebba's hands curled into fists.

"When Pockmark and Cannon led me back, he was standin' in the same exact spot as we'd left him," Jagger said.

"Ye're okay?" she asked her friend, leaning in to squeeze his hand.

He drew back out of her reach, saying harshly, "You need not handle me so delicately, Mistress Pirate."

Pulling back, Ebba did her best to swallow her hurt. Who did he think was there worrying about him back on Zol when he'd go off by himself for the entire day, or when a string of days went by without him uttering a word? If anyone was put in the middle of a heckling crowd who jeered at their most painful memories, she'd ask if they were okay.

"She's only askin' after ye," Jagger said sharply. "There ain't no need to speak that way to her."

"Of course," Caspian replied. "Because you've never uttered a harsh word to her in your life."

"While under the taint, aye. I wager half the pirates surroundin' ye afore only said the things they did because o' the taint."

"It must be convenient to blame the taint when you're the immune. How would we even know what came from you and what didn't?"

Whoa, this was getting out of hand. Even if that same thought had long prevented her from relaxing around Jagger. "There ain't no point in gettin' angry over nothin'," Ebba said, raising both hands. "Caspian didn't mean what he said."

He stood in a burst, hands clenched into fists. "Yes, I did. Half the reason I can't get over what has happened to me—my arm and losing my father and kingdom—is because I see it in your faces each day: the pity, the worry, the memory. Would that I could start afresh with people who didn't know my past."

Ebba glanced at her fathers. They didn't seem bothered but listened intently.

Peg-leg spoke first. "I'd advise against givin' the past that much power, lad. It can't shape yer future days unless ye let it."

Caspian whirled on him, fury etched on his face. "And how do I do that? Tell me how!"

Jagger sighed and got to his feet. He leaned over and picked Ebba bodily off the ground. All she could do was stare at him, cradled in his arms, as he walked over and deposited her on the seat next to Plank.

The pirate returned to Caspian. "Ye use yer head. Sink me, ye're s'posed to rule the bloody realm, and ye can't even sort yerself out." Jagger reached out and slapped the royal upside the head.

Plank rested his hand on her knee when Ebba made to stand.

"Leave them," he breathed.

Jagger circled Caspian. "Ye stand on yer own two feet. What do ye have? What can ye use? What do ye stand to lose and gain? Ye *stop* feelin' like the damn world is against ye—because the world'll be against ye until ye die. If ye go on that way, ye'll never get anywhere." He kicked the back of Caspian's knee, shouting, "Ye're in control of yerself. Find yer bloody power and stop whining. *That's* how ye start over. These people have nothin' to do with yer weaknesses. Ye're seein' what ye want to see. *Ebba* has nothin' to do with those weaknesses either, so stop treatin' her like shite because ye're sulkin'."

Ebba groaned and lowered her face into her hands, peeking through her fingers.

With a roar, Caspian lunged for Jagger.

He tackled the pirate to the ground.

"I ain't watchin' this," Ebba muttered, standing and walking to the cave. They were acting like fools.

"You touched her with the *amare*," Caspian panted, straddling the pirate and throwing a punch with his right arm.

Jagger blocked the hit.

Stubby stepped forward. "He did what?"

This wasn't happening. Ebba veered back in a rush to smooth things over. "It was an accident. But that's how I know what I feel for Jagger. The *amare* showed me."

Caspian leaped off Jagger and faced her. "But how do you know, Ebba? How do you know?"

Because I touched the veritas and it confirmed it. The words stuck in her throat at the pain on her friend's face.

Peg-leg's mouth was ajar. "Ye already love the swine?"

Jagger had risen and wiped at his face. "Perhaps, Caspian, ye should tell Ebba about the time ye touched her with the *amare*. Ye've kept awful quiet about that."

That was ridiculous. Ebba almost laughed. Almost.

She might've if Caspian hadn't frozen at the remark.

Her eyes oscillated between the pair. "That ain't true."

Jagger stepped closer to Caspian. "At least when I did it, she knew she'd been touched."

The prince stood immediately before her and yet seemed able to look everywhere but at her face.

She gasped. "It's true? Did ye do that without my knowin'?" Ebba thought back but had absolutely no recollection of such a thing happening. "When?"

Caspian turned his face away from her. "On the rowboat," he muttered.

There was so much wrong with that; Ebba didn't know where to begin. "W-what did I do?"

He turned farther away, and she reached out and took his wrist in an iron grip.

"Ye don't get to turn away from me," she snapped. "Ye made me feel ter'ible for not feelin' deeper regard for ye only two days ago. Not only that, when I told ye what the *amare* showed me, ye told me not to trust what it had said. Ye told me to wait until I knew for sure."

"*You* doubted it too," he said, whirling back.

"And *ye* could've cleared those doubts." She withered. "Because ye already knew it worked, didn't ye? What did I do when ye touched me with the *amare*?"

She flung his arm away and waited, arms crossed.

Caspian's amber eyes were burning into her. Anger, regret, that lingering sadness, and guilt. She saw it all.

His chest rose and fell quickly as he replied, "You turned to me and gave me the hugest and happiest smile I'd ever seen. You said you would always have my back."

Aye, she probably had. *Because she loved him as a friend.* He'd interpreted that to mean something else. Or wished it. "I've never felt more than friendship for ye," she told him. "And I've been honest about that from the start."

"What about when you kissed me? That last kiss we shared, there was something there."

Locks spluttered. "She *what*?"

Cods, this wasn't happening. Ebba glanced at Jagger and saw his eyes were glittering. He'd seemed in control before.

"She and Caspian have kissed," Plank cut in, shrugging.

"Ye flamin' well knew?" Stubby yelled at him.

Her fathers erupted into a furious argument at her back.

While certain that Caspian was trying to blame her for the crappy way he currently felt, there were things she could've done better. Half she could put down to naivety, the rest to a misguided attempt to protect her friend. But on a ship, the only way everyone got along was if wrongs were righted. They'd gone through crazy things together and had come out the other side. To not give him an opportunity to make amends wouldn't be right.

As her fathers quietened, she said, "Ye've heard my opinion on how things lay between us recent-like, Caspian. And I ain't goin' to repeat what I said then. I can see ye're hurtin'; I'm sorrier than ye know to see it and to have caused it, in part. But I won't apologize for feelin' anythin' other than what I do. Ye can't hold me to the vision o' us ye've had in yer head."

Caspian opened his mouth.

"I ain't done," she interrupted with a scowl. She was livid, absolutely furious that Caspian had concealed so much from her. He'd used the *amare* to force out her true feelings about him. *Without her permission.*

"Ye've called yerself my friend for months," she said, looking up at him. "And despite what's happened o' late, I hope we can find a common ground in future days. But I'll tell ye now, Cosmo—"

He flinched at her use of the name he'd once used.

"—when ye next speak to me, ye better have a damn good apology for what ye did. Because *no* friend would do such a thing without my knowin'. When ye win, I'm happy for ye. When ye're beaten, I want to cry or rage with you. I told ye that I might be in love with someone for the very first time. I told ye I didn't know what to do, and instead o' comin' clean about usin' the *amare*, ye told me not to trust what it was tellin' me. Ye man'pulated me, hopin' that I would change my mind, Caspian, when ye could've helped. And it was all for naught. When I held *veritas* today, it confirmed everythin' I feel. I do love Jagger. In the end, I didn't need yer help, but I sure would've liked to know ye could put yer feelings aside to cel'brate mine."

Jagger approached her, but Ebba stepped back, hands raised.

"And ye can sod off, too," she told him. "If ye saw that happenin', ye should've said sumpin'. I ain't part o' a game, Jagger. Don't treat me like I am again." She took one step to the cave and paused in the shadows. "But thank ye for savin' my life."

She'd just bloody-sodding-blasted-well blurted out about loving Jagger to the whole of hell.

Ebba stormed into the cave, sick of the very sight of men—pirate, royals, and otherwise.

FIFTEEN

Ebba guzzled back some water and chewed on a dried strand of seaweed. Their food box of the day had arrived not long ago.

"How did you sleep?" Barrels asked, the first to join her out on the ledge the next morning.

"Sucky," she said. "Too much fightin' yest'rday. It don't sit well."

Barrels picked up some seaweed, nose wrinkled. "Yes, I rather agree." He slid his gaze to her. "I do apologize for nearly killing you."

Ebba snorted. "No mind. I'm right glad the others found me, though." She was still in Jagger's tunic and the crimson skirt. The combination was a lot more comfortable. Maybe even a seven out of ten.

"This is what Mutinous does best, you know," Barrels mused aloud. "Turn people on each other."

She cut a glance at him. Her fathers had turned on each other—and Jagger. Jagger and Caspian were fighting. *She* was fighting with both of them. Cannon had threatened her fathers' lives, and then she'd hidden that from her parents, which led to an argument. And Ebba assumed he'd dug at cracks in Caspian and Jagger yesterday.

"Aye, I s'pose he is at that. The pressure o' the situ'tion doesn't help any."

"No." Barrels beckoned for the waterskin. "It's different from last time, I admit. His siege is less violent."

That very thing had been bothering her. "In all o' yer stories, there was always that el'ment o' nastiness. I can see that in him now, but all yer stories had horrible gruesome acts in them. Grubby was hit, Locks dragged over the deck, Peg-leg's leg hacked off, Plank's wife was murdered. I haven't seen any o' that—aside from him killin' Pockmark, who he knew would come back anyhow. It's too di'ferent from the person ye all knew. Why is he goin' out o' his way to keep us safe?"

"You believe there's something more sinister in his lack of physicality?"

She borrowed King Montcroix's reasoning. "Why wouldn't he seek revenge by taintin' us then? Or by throwin' us to the damned side o' the river to be killed? Why isn't he hurtin' any o' ye like he did afore? He *hates* the six o' ye. He as much told me. So why is he helpin' us?"

Barrels hummed, staring at the fish in the stone box before covering his nose and mouth to lean away. "I confess I've just been so glad he hasn't hurt us yet that I haven't thought of the oddness of his behavior. But you're right, my dear."

"The man at the stream said that Cannon told damned that if they remain on that side, he'll free them all from the Locker." They knew Cannon wished to be free of Davy Jones', but she'd never actually thought he could get out. Ebba had kind of assumed the pillars would come for the root parts, and Cannon would slip the cylinders out of the barrier the same way the food came in and out.

Mutinous Cannon had some way to leave hell. And that plan had something to do with why he'd taken such pains to keep her crew—and the damned—free of taint. It had to.

She just had no idea what.

"Barrels," she said, jerking upright. "Cannon be tainted. If he can get out, so can all o' ye."

"It would appear so." Her father circled his shoulders with a moan.

Ebba got to her feet and paced. "But we're gettin' there," she said eagerly. "The man across the river said the wind howls every six hours."

"Yes, four times the last two days."

She knew Barrels would count. "And he said the damned reg'nerate with the wind."

Barrels frowned. "Is the wind magic?"

She'd seen a goat-man speak and men turn into seals. The magical status of the wind in hell was the least of her worries, especially when the queen wind sprite had been her pet. "But those who are killed reg'nerate by the entrance to the Locker, which ain't ideal."

"This man was a wealth of information, it seems."

He sounded slightly suspicious. Not of her but of the man. "Aye, we best take his words with a grain o' salt. But I said I'd head back and meet him when I'm next able."

"You think he knows more?"

Ebba shrugged a shoulder. "I said if he didn't have sumpin' good, I wouldn't be comin' back a third time."

"You do us proud when you stick up for yourself," Barrels suddenly said, patting her hand. "Despite our shock over the *amare* and whatnot, we were all behind your speech to young Caspian."

The term 'whatnot' likely encompassed all references to kissing, which Ebba was glad for. "Thank ye," she said. "I was goin' to tell ye yest'rday, but—"

Barrels smiled faintly. "We sabotaged you. Plank did warn us how it would go. So, you're in love." He frowned. "That must have been a strange transition."

Ebba blew out a breath. "It was. The a'traction part was fine. But the love part overwhelmed me. Could've done without that for a bit."

"And what does Jagger say on the matter o' love?"

Ebba scowled. "Not enough, that's what. A whole heap of pirate nothin'. I've tried to reel him in three times, and he just won't take the bait." And last night she'd gone and shouted out her love for him for all of Davy Jones' to hear.

"Perhaps he's nervous; you're quite a creature to behold. As your father, I'm biased, but you are entirely your own person, Ebba. You exude a joy that is contagious. Even with your worst face on, you manage to capture hearts. That might be intimidating to a person who has not known happiness in a long time."

"Is that why Jagger won't whatnot with me?" she wondered aloud.

Barrels winced. "As to that, I'd rather remain . . . unaware. Unless you need advice."

"Don't hurt yerself, Barrels," she said, snorting. "I'll go to whoever peeved me off most recent if I need help. That's most likely to be Stubby or Peg-leg."

She chuckled with her father.

Barrels stared past her. "Look, there they go to the entrance again. Another group of tainted."

"They go every day," Ebba said. "The man told me."

He gave her a sharp look. "Did he know why?"

She shook her head. "I'll head down to the stream once the tainted pirates get back to the ship. I don't want to risk a repeat o' yest'rday."

Caspian walked out of the cave, stumbling slightly when he saw her. Her father glanced between them and stood with a groan. "I'll give you two some privacy."

"I'm too tired to fight today," Ebba announced when Barrels disappeared into the cave.

Caspian sat in the same spot on the ledge where her father had been. "So am I. I was tossing all night, thinking on what you said."

She didn't answer. Though, in truth, she'd pondered his words too.

"I acted like a prize idiot," he said with a sigh. "Growing up, I would look at lovers consumed by jealous rage and laugh, wondering how someone could ever forget themselves enough to lose their dignity in such a way. Jealousy always seemed to stem from a person's insecurity. Whether a person was made to feel insecure by their partner or whether that person was insecure within themselves."

Caspian looked at her. "I've been acting like a jealous fool. And I acted that way and did the things I did because I am insecure."

His honesty made her want to wince. If only because he'd laid himself completely bare.

"The way I feel about myself has led me to do cruel things to someone I profess to care deeply for." He closed his eyes. "I have acted in a way I have always loathed. I've acted like my father. And that, more than anything, is a call for me to address my weaknesses, as Jagger put my situation last night."

Ebba didn't dare interrupt.

He continued after a breath. "There is one more thing I must apologize for. I'm sorry for using your kind-heartedness against you. Not only did I use the *amare* on you without your permission," he said, red creeping up his jaw, "I also used the concern you felt over my welfare to keep you close even when you told me about loving Jagger." Caspian glanced down to where he picked at a loose thread on his slops. "Maybe not in so many words, but playing to your empathy like that was pitiable. I felt, and still feel, like a coward for doing it. I want you to know that no matter what happens or doesn't happen between us, you are not responsible for my future. I want you to know that I have loved you with all my heart for months but that I hope, in time, there will be easiness between us again."

The words were hard to hear. And she'd think more on them in private. "As far as an apology goes, it's one of the better ones I've heard," she said.

Caspian smiled, eyes uncertain.

"Ye're forgiven," Ebba announced. "And I want ye to know that I heard yer words about treatin' ye with pity, like ye're dainty after losin' so much."

He ran a hand through his russet curls. “Sorry, I didn’t really mean that. Those were old wounds coming up. You’ve always treated me the same as everyone else. I was just lashing out.”

“Well, I be glad o’ that. But I want to share sumpin’ with ye. No one else knows just yet. I was goin’ to keep it to myself, but it be yer decision to make, really.”

“Should I be nervous about this?” he asked, the smile sliding off his face.

Ebba pursed her lips. “There ain’t no good way to say this, so I’ll just out with it. Yer father be in hell. Just across the stream.”

Caspian’s lips moved wordlessly.

“He’s the man I talked to yesterday. I think he was the glow I saw. Maybe the sword r’cognized him or sumpin’? The glow was either him or the next part, anyway, and I can’t see that Cannon would leave the part over with the damned if so. . . .” Ebba trailed off, realizing she was rambling.

Caspian stood, walking several steps toward the cave before turning back. “My. . . .” He blanched. “He’ll spend eternity here? He really was a bad person?”

“Few people are wholly bad, Caspian. When I looked at the damned while holdin’ the sword, most o’ the people there had some level o’ glow to them. I’d say yer father was just a little more bad than he was good.” *And he’s a bastard.*

Ebba stood. “Anyway, I’ll be goin’ to see him again. He was king for a long time and wants a part in savin’ ye.”

Caspian looked up at that. “Saving me?”

“All o’ his questions were about yer welfare,” she admitted. “He hardly wanted to speak o’ anythin’ else.”

“He was never a good parent,” Caspian said, staring at his hands. “My mother was the sole nurturing presence. In her company, my father wasn’t so cold, but when she died, it was like what little warmth he’d possessed died with her.”

“How did yer mother pass?” Ebba asked.

He glanced at her. “Childbirth. Though I was seven years old at the time, something about her death never seemed right. To my memory, she died a long time *after* Sierra arrived. Still, I was just a child then, and what do I know of such things?" Caspian tilted his head up to the cavern ceiling high overhead. "With his children, looking back, I suppose my father was as affectionate as he could be, but it never felt like love. Maybe he thought he was showing more than he actually did or that we'd understand and read between the lines. My sisters never had an issue with him. But I began to resent his cold treatment. And I began to look outward to what he was doing. I looked at the poor in the streets and at the death tolls of the mineworkers. I looked at the bursting prisons and the skeletons hanging in the cages. Each week, I walked amongst the rich of Exosia, and I did not feel one with them. Everywhere I looked, I saw lies and coldness, and I hated my father more."

"So ye ran," Ebba whispered, glancing at the cave. Barrels must've told the others to wait because otherwise, they'd have a bloody audience again.

"I ran, and you know the rest," he said. "I discovered I could not shirk my duty. I returned. And before the end I saw my father's love for me. If I had never seen it, I would not be so tortured, I think."

Ebba watched him. "Why does that torture ye?"

"Because I was content to dislike him. And then I had occasion to doubt my former opinion, yet there was not time to figure it out one way or another."

"Ye have the chance now."

Caspian answered drily, "I have the answer already. My father is in hell."

Was that answer enough? "Ye can love and dislike someone at the same time," Ebba said, thinking of the moment she found out her fathers had lied. "It's confusin', but ye can love yer father as family while dislikin' parts of him, too. The parts that don't sit right with ye. I guess ye can also even like parts o' him at the same time as well."

With a weary sigh, Caspian rubbed his temples. "I have no doubt you're right, Ebba. But I'm afraid I might need time to digest this."

Ebba nodded. "Ye don't need to come today. Ye don't need to go tomorrow even. It's up to ye."

Caspian dropped his hands, eyes dark and troubled. Her stomach twisted. No matter what he said, she would feel responsible for any of his downfalls. That was just who she was.

"Thank you, Ebba. I mean it," he said softly.

"Don't mention it," she replied, secretly hoping she'd done the right thing.

SIXTEEN

Ebba waited down at the northern end of the stream, huddled against the cliff face. "Hurry up, ye royal-lubber bastard."

She wasn't kept waiting long. True to his word, King Montcroix stepped out of the moaning masses and crouched on the opposite bank.

"You came back," he said.

"Clear-like. Any news?"

The king clenched his jaw. Whether at her tone or the situation, she couldn't tell.

"Another group returned today. I listened to them as they walked by the stream. There were multiple mentions of the number four," he told her.

Four. The first time, they'd held up two fingers. What did the numbers mean? "Any guesses?"

Montcroix shook his head. "My son. He doesn't know I'm here, correct?"

"Nay, I told him all. He be decidin' if ye're worth seein'." She regretted her words. Montcroix lowered his head, caving in on himself as though stabbed. "I just told him a couple o' hours ago, though. He's got a lot o' doubt when it comes to ye."

"I know," Montcroix whispered.

Dammit, she wasn't going to feel sorry for him. He was here for a reason. Though, if she hadn't met the thunderbird, she'd be more inclined to think the sorting process a fair one.

"What else ye got?" Ebba hissed across the bubbling water.

"Cannon needs your crew untainted to get out of here."

"Aye, we figured as much. Anythin' else? Or have I wasted my time comin' here?"

The king's eyes widened.

For a second, Ebba thought it was at her tough-but-fair attitude. Then Jagger's voice slid over her shoulders, eliciting a shiver.

"Ye can't expect too much from the likes o' him, can ye, Viva?"

Montcroix's brows slammed together. "You brought someone else?"

Shite.

Ebba turned, greeting Jagger quietly. "Ahoy."

Considering the king had killed both of Jagger's parents, she expected the anger-fueled glare. The ferocity of it still made her flinch. So busy thinking of Caspian, she hadn't stopped to consider the person she accidentally loved.

"Forge." Jagger grinned ferally at the king.

This was bad, bad, *bad.*

Ebba gripped the pirate's arm. "If ye use that name, the damned might overhear."

"Sounds like it might make his ex'stence painful," Jagger said, his smirk widening.

"Aye, and since he has news, it might make our ex'stence more painful-like. I know ye're angry, but don't lose yer head."

Jagger faced her, bringing his mouth to her ear. "Nay, Viva. I ain't angry. I'm bitter because I was cheated of knowin' my real parents. Ye have six; ye don't understand. And ye should've told me he was here."

She should have, yes. And had Jagger forgotten she was stolen from her birth parents? But there was no point reminding him of that when he was seeing red.

Ebba released him and crossed her arms, jerking her head to Montcroix. "Go on then."

"I know you," the king said, scanning Jagger's face. A crease appeared between his brows. "You were with the crew at my castle once. Flaxen hair. Silver eyes. Almost like. . . ."

"A man ye once knew?" Jagger asked. "The one ye shoved a sword through? Or do I favor his wife?"

Mouth and eyes open, the dead king stared at Jagger as though he couldn't believe the apparition before him. "Jamieson. Is that really you? I don't believe it."

"Is that my name then?" Jagger asked him. "These small details be lost when ye're raised by tribespeople."

The king blinked. "I tried to get you back after winning the battle of the seas. The tribes were too cunning. I lost too many men."

"Ye killed my parents," Jagger roared.

Ebba glanced behind her, wondering if the entire cavern had heard that.

"I did," the king said, his voice wavering. "And hell took me in return. That was the day I realized I was lost."

Jagger was shaking, but Ebba didn't remove her eyes from the path they'd used to get here. If tainted pirates at the ship had heard Jagger, they'd have to make scarce.

Somehow.

"Tell me why." Jagger's words were almost inaudible.

Montcroix held his gaze for a few seconds and then dropped his eyes to the ground. "Because I discovered my wife had an affair after the birth of my youngest daughter. She was then killed."

"Caspian thinks she died in childbirth," Ebba said, gasping. "Ye lied to him."

Montcroix's eyes glinted. "For his own good."

Her fists curled. "For *yer* own good, ye sod."

Jagger stepped closer. "Keep going."

The king tore his eyes from her. "Your father was my right-hand man. Our families had been intertwined since the beginning of the dynasty. I came to believe, most wrongly, that my queen was involved with your father and that he'd killed her to keep the secret intact. I confronted him at a time when the pirates were winning. Emotions were high. After my wife's murder, I was mourning her while feeling betrayed by her, too. It is no excuse for what I did . . . but I killed him. It was only when I held *veritas* next that I discovered how wrong I'd been. The sword confirms that which you know is true, and it did not confirm anything for me. Your father did not kill my wife, nor did he take her to bed. My wife did not have an affair. She was faithful. I never touched the sword again after that. Not until my dying day. I never found out who killed my queen. I lost my oldest and most loyal friend. That day, I lost nearly everything."

Jagger and Caspian's roles in assembling the weapon were hereditary. "Do ye know why yer families had always been together?" She butted in.

The king jerked his eyes to hers. "Because in the past, our families fought side by side against evil foes. Our histories ran parallel, until me." His eyes shifted to the perched cliff and back to Jagger. "Or perhaps they do again."

"My mother," Jagger said roughly. "Why her?"

"An accident. She attacked me after I killed Nathaniel. I pushed her, and Joan hit her head. I tried to revive her, but in minutes, she was gone, too."

Jagger was quiet for a time. No one had come running yet. His earlier shouting had gone undetected amidst the shuffling movements and murmurs of the other damned.

"Nathaniel and Joan. Those were their names?" Jagger asked.

King Montcroix closed his eyes. "Yes. I am so deeply sorry for what I did, Jamieson. It cannot undo my actions, but I am truly sorry."

"My name be Jagger. Jamieson died with his parents that day. Jagger was the child sur'ounded by people who spoke funny and ate di'ferent food and lived a life that didn't look anythin' like the life he'd known. He was forced to learn. And for that, he became much stronger."

The king surveyed the pirate. "So I see."

"I became stronger than yer son even," Jagger continued. "So here's my deal for ye, King Forge. Ye ended up in hell for killin' my parents. I can accept that. But there's still the debt against me."

Montcroix's cheeks deepened to an angry red. "You will not harm my son."

"Oh, I will. I'll be takin' pleasure in it too. He knows it's comin'; I've told him as much. Told him the debt must be paid."

Jagger was full of shite, but Ebba kept her face smooth. This was his ship to sail.

The wrinkles on the king's face deepened as his face contorted in fury. "What is it you want?"

"Ye're goin' to jump in the boiling water. Right now."

The king blanched. "That's. . . ."

"Pretty fair considerin' ye'll be alive again within six hours," Jagger said coldly. "Ye say ye're sorry. Ye act remors'ful. Prove it. Throw yerself into the water, and I won't throw yer son in instead."

Ebba gripped his sleeve. "Jagger."

"Go if ye can't stomach it, Viva. Think o' me what ye will."

She'd seen someone boil alive already; there wouldn't be a second time. As for judging him. . . . If someone killed one of her fathers, who knew what she'd be capable of.

Ebba left in a rustle of skirts, striding quickly for the boulder path. She was nearly there before Montcroix's raw screams echoed behind her. She sped up, breaking into a run, but the anguished shrieks followed her, chasing her.

She picked up her pace, sprinting down the path.

. . . Right into Pockmark.

Ebba screamed, throwing herself away from the stinking pus oozing from his face. She was on her feet in a second.

In another place, with other people, the way Pockmark scrambled away in shock—tripping over a rock and then bounding back to his feet—might've been comical.

"Ebba," Jagger called. His footsteps hammered down the path toward them.

She and Pockmark stared at each other, and she noticed the black creeping in around the corners of his eyes.

Shite. His eyes had black in them. Was Pockmark contagious? She'd just touched him!

Turning as Jagger came into view, she blurted, "Don't touch me. I just banged into Pockmark."

All blood drained from Jagger's face.

"That be right. Ye banged into *me*," Pockmark said, licking his lips. "It weren't my fault." He glanced over his shoulder and seemed to collect himself. "What are ye doin' down here?"

Jagger approached the pirate, likely seeing the black in his eyes too. "She needs the *purgium*. Now."

Pockmark edged away, glancing back again. "Nay, no need for that. It was just a little touch."

"Yer eyes have black in them. Ye're cont'gious," Jagger said, fists balling. "Ye can't tell me Cannon'll be happy if she's tainted."

"He doesn't ever have to know," Pockmark hissed, drawing his pistol out. His eyes flooded black.

Jagger might be immune, but Ebba was already tainted. She leaped for the pirate, shoving his arms over his head. The weapon fired with a crack, and Pockmark shoved her off, sending her stumbling. Ebba evaded Jagger's attempt to help her up.

What did he not understand about the taint?

The stone rattled under their feet as pirates ran toward them from the ship.

"Now ye've done it," Pockmark spat, eyes darting frantically. He dragged in uneven breaths, and some of the black receded from his eyes.

"If ye're so scared o' him, why don't ye take over his plan and do it yerself?" Ebba asked, genuinely curious.

Pockmark whirled on her. "Because I wasn't chosen by the masters." His half-black eyes fixed on Jagger. "March in front o' me. We're goin' to the ship."

They obeyed, Ebba staying well away from Jagger.

The tainted pirates sprinting their way wrenched to a halt. Those at the front threw themselves away from Ebba and Jagger.

"Get back with ye," Pockmark roared. "I've got them. Back! Ye flamin' morons."

The stampede of tainted pirates was reversed, and soon, Ebba strode into the shipwreck clearing much as she'd done on the very first day.

Except this time, Cannon was already here, his hands wrapped around Riot's throat. "Four," he seethed. "It's not enough."

"I did everythin' ye asked," Riot managed, black eyes bulging.

Cannon snarled in his face. "And yet it ain't fast enough."

Swindles approached, bowing several times. "Thirty arrived today, Captain, sir."

Cannon released Riot. "Thirty, ye say?"

"Aye, all o' them tainted. Soon our side'll be burstin'."

"*Burstin'*," he repeated with a gleaming grin. He seemed to realize Ebba and Jagger were there for the first time. Irritation flickered across his face for a second before it was gone. Ebba very much doubted he'd wanted them to hear that conversation.

"Pockmark, explain," Cannon ordered.

"I caught these two down by the stream," Pockmark stuttered, holstering his pistol.

Cannon ambled closer to him. "It was your pistol that went off?"

"A-aye. Not at them. Into the air."

Ebba snorted. Only because she'd pushed his arm up.

Cannon's eyes fixed on her. "Ebba-Viva," he purred. "We meet again. And ye're somewhat dressed as I ordered."

She remained mute.

"Pockmark, have ye negl'cted to say sumpin'?" Jagger drawled.

Cannon circled Pockmark. "It be the idiocy o' many tainted,

including the child o' my child, who think their secrets will remain so. Pos'essed by our master, nothin' will escape their notice. Nothin'. They are us. They own us."

Pockmark closed his eyes, standing ramrod straight. "I touched her."

Cannon backhanded his grandson viciously, sending him hurtling to the ground. Removing a handkerchief from his sash, Cannon wiped his hand and replaced the cloth, saying in measured tones, "Ye defied our masters' order."

The *pillars* didn't want her crew to be tainted? Not just Cannon? That was just all kinds of backward.

"Please," Pockmark begged.

Cannon looked at Riot and Swindles. "String him up." Turning to Ebba, he said, as though gracing her with a secret, "Ye would've gathered the dead can still feel pain."

"I'll be needin' the *purgium* if ye want me untainted," she stated, ignoring his comment.

Throwing his head back, Cannon laughed. "I've already given ye the *veritas,* now ye want the *purgium*. What next?"

The *scio* would be great. Ebba shrugged. "Ye'll give it to us or ye won't. Which is it?"

Was Jagger purposefully standing that close? She shifted away.

"I be thinkin' ye'd be a mite more eager to be healed than I would be to heal ye."

Ebba smiled. "I don't think so."

"And why be that?" Cannon said, face hardening.

"Because ye're surrounded by mindless cronies," she lied glibly. "Aside from those ye restrain across the stream, we be the only sane ones in here."

If she was right and the captain wanted them untainted, then all he needed was a good enough reason to agree to healing her—a reason that didn't give away what her crew had put together so far.

Cannon studied her and then Jagger. "What were ye doin' by the stream?"

Jagger answered, "Asking questions o' those across the water."

"Hmm, I don't think so," Cannon answered, nearing Jagger. He glanced at Ebba. "I don't think so. Be that the tunic ye were wearin' yest'rday, Jagger?"

She shot a look at Jagger.

"Aye," he replied tightly.

"How sad our dear King Caspian will be to learn o' this sordid affair," Cannon said, arching a brow at her. "How long have ye strung them both along?"

"Sev'ral months," she replied flatly, thanking fate that she and Caspian had already sorted through such things.

Cannon dipped his head and paced before them. What he thought of her answer, she couldn't tell.

Stopping, he spread his arms wide. "I can't deny that yer a'rival has brought more ent'rtainment than I've seen in a decade. This once, I'll grant yer boon. Once," he said, halting before Ebba and gripping her chin tight. "Ye allow it to happen a second time and there won't be any mercy shown."

Salty tears filled her eyes at his iron grip. Thank the seas she'd be touching the *purgium* soon. Ebba stumbled forward a step as he released her.

The captain clicked his fingers, and a pirate scrambled to hear his bidding.

"Get the *purgium*," he said, shaking out his ruffled tunic sleeve.

Ebba glanced at Jagger, who stared up at the ship. She followed his gaze, wincing. Pockmark had been hoisted into the air by his wrists. He yelled with every pull on the ropes, screaming as ropes trailing from both ankles were pulled tight, stretching him savagely.

"Captain, sir." The pirate slid onto his knees, black stone case extended overhead.

"Not to me, fool, to *her*." Cannon kicked the pirate, who fell back but held tight to the case.

The black stone box was presented in the same manner to her.

Ebba opened the lid and closed it, then made to grab the entire case. "Thank ye."

Cannon laughed again, sounding genuinely amused. "Good try. Do it here. I'd like to watch."

"What will it do?" Jagger whispered to her.

Who knew? It'd blackened her fingernails and leeched the color from six of her dreads. Touching the *purgium* was always a risk, but there was hardly an alternative. If she wasn't healed, she couldn't risk joining the others again, which would expose her to the risk of more taint.

Ebba opened the case and touched her finger to the *purgium.* The white-hot zap was expected. She'd felt it twice—and worse when she'd attempted to carry three parts at once.

The shivers of the intense heat dissipated, and Ebba turned to Jagger, waiting.

"Uh," he stuttered, staring at her eyes.

"Look at me," Cannon demanded.

Ebba glared at Jagger and turned as bade.

Cannon scanned her and came to focus on her eyes, too. She had a third eye, didn't she? Three was okay, but one would be an adjustment.

"The a'dition suits ye," Cannon said. He snapped the lid back on and took the case from the still-crouching pirate. "So this part can heal a person o' the taint but will kill them unless they only be havin' small amounts within them. Interestin' indeed."

Meanwhile, she still had no idea what had changed about her appearance.

"If I discover ye've been at the stream again," Cannon said to her, "for a lover's tryst, questionin' or otherwise, one o' yer fathers will join the damned. I thought ye understood me last time, but now I'm thinkin' ye haven't."

Ebba lifted her chin. "I understand ye, Cannon. I won't be goin' to the stream anymore."

Cannon grinned at Jagger, eyes remaining cold. "Congr'tulations,

Jagger. Ye've brought a wild woman to heel. I hope she serves ye well."

Heat crept up her neck, and Jagger grabbed her hand, yanking her to the path. "Aye, she will at that."

"Until next time," Cannon called cheerfully.

Neither of them spoke until they were well down the path to the cave. With a glance upward, Jagger pulled her behind a boulder. Was he concealing them from her fathers?

His hands moved frantically over her body.

"Did the *purgium* take anythin' else?" he asked in urgent tones. He palmed her sides, moving up her thighs over the skirt, squeezing her waist and moving higher still.

She slapped his hands away. "Ask afore ye touch, ye slimebag."

Jagger retracted his hands and glanced down at her. His mouth twisted. "Slimebag?"

"Ye have three seconds to tell me if I have one eye," she forced out between gritted teeth.

Jagger reached for one of her white dreads.

"One," Ebba said.

He twirled it about his finger.

"*Two*. Thr—"

"It stole a ring o' color from yer eyes. Both sides. A circle be drained to white now."

Ebba whacked him. "Ye do me head in, Jagger." She hit him again. And then a third time.

He caught her hands and held them.

"Does it look fierce?" she asked when freeing herself failed.

"Makes me never want to look away. Hypnotizin'."

And when ye maybe saw my chest, what'd ye think? Ebba sniffed. "So, how did yer revenge go?"

"It's over," Jagger said with a sigh. "Over at last. All o' my promises, gone. Debts repaid. My life be a clean slate. And I can tell ye I won't be makin' any more promises." Then he looked at her. "Or maybe just one."

The fluttering in her heart made her forget the world. Stupid Jagger tunnel. "Aye, ye silver-tongued bugger, how about ye make a promise to serve *me* and heel."

Jagger laughed, and the rich huskiness of the sound stole her breath. "Sparks flew from ye when ye said that." His laughter faded, and he added, "But do ye get what I mean?"

She patted his cheek. "Not at all."

"Not at all?" he replied, peering down her body.

Kiss me anytime, ye eejit.

Seconds went by.

Ebba sighed. "At least Mutinous conf'rmed he'll do anythin' to keep us free o' the taint."

"We can use it against him when push comes to shove. But I want to know why ye're sighin'."

Why was she sighing? Ebba scowled at him. "I told the whole o' hell that I love ye last night, and ye haven't said a soddin' word about it. Not only that, three times ye've acted like kissin' me and then pulled away. I ain't a patient woman, Jagger. I ain't meant to be with a non-kisser. And I don't understand this new feelin' any more than ye. But if ye plan on returnin' whatever this *is*—or if ye don't. . . ." Her heart sank into her boots at the thought. "Then ye best be tellin' me fast. Real fast. 'Cause there be plenty more fish in the sea."

And with that, head held high, she marched double-time for the cave.

SEVENTEEN

Ebba waved to her fathers and went straight to the cave to stew in anger. Her temper usually worked itself out pretty quickly, but while raised, the slightest provocation could have it flaring back to full fire.

She sat just inside the cave entrance, resting back in the shadows, and imagined all the ways Jagger could have said the right thing back there. Male pirates were idiots, and Ebba was glad she'd never decided to be one.

"What did ye do?" she heard Locks demand.

Jagger replied, "Nothin'."

Nothing. Exactly.

'I can work with hate.'

'Makes me never want to look away.'

I'm a pirate with muscles and big survival know-how.

Sink her, the *amare* chose her a bloody dud. Or if not a dud, then someone who was playing with her heart. Which made him an even bigger dud. There'd be no more of these boulder dalliances. She'd said her piece. The seaweed was in his net.

"But sumpin' did happen," Jagger said.

Blimey, his voice even sounded like muscles and survival know-how.

She listened as he repeated the occurrences of the day. And then after, as her fathers discussed what it all meant and ended up in the same place as she and the dud had.

"Were you speaking to my father earlier?" Caspian asked. "We watched from here."

Her fathers were silent, which meant Caspian had filled them in on Montcroix's presence.

"Aye, I met him," Jagger said after a beat.

"He jumped into the stream."

"Aye, I told him to."

Caspian didn't speak immediately. "He admitted to killing your parents."

"He did. I told him that wasn't enough. That I'd be takin' the payment from ye unless he jumped in the water."

"And he jumped?" Caspian sounded like he'd run a mile.

Jagger sounded bored. "He did."

She could imagine the bafflement on Caspian's face.

He spoke again. "Did he say why he did kill your parents?"

Ebba held her breath, waiting to see if Jagger would be cruel or kind.

"A misunderstandin'," he said shortly.

In the dark, she smiled. The *amare* had chosen her a sensitive dud.

"He deserved that," Caspian said. "For what he did to your parents and to you."

Jagger's voice wavered. "That he did."

"We've thought o' what we want ye to put on the note, Jagger," Stubby said.

Ebba exited the cave at that and sat on a rock on the ledge just outside it. "What are we tellin' Matey?"

Stubby glanced at her. "Jagger stole parchment from the ship, but it be tainted, so we're sacrificin' him to write the note because he be the immune an' all."

That was outrageous. Ebba forced her temper back.

"I volunteered," Jagger told her.

She shrugged. "Yer soul." But it wasn't just his.

Plank squinted at her. Still squinting, he walked to her. "What happened to yer eyes?" he asked.

"I had to touch the *purgium*. It took some o' my eye color." She bit her lip.

"Ye were hurt?"

"Tainted. Just a scant bit."

Her fathers fell silent.

"Does it look all right?" she asked Plank.

"Aye, I can barely look away, little nymph."

Her father had great style. With his approval, Ebba was officially okay about the new addition. The others lined up to gawk at her. Then they all gathered around Jagger, who'd poured some water onto the black stone to turn the dirt there into mud.

"What d'ye want it to say?" Jagger asked.

"We want a picture," Plank said.

Jagger cast him a flat look.

"Yeah, draw us a pretty picture, lad," Locks said.

Grubby smiled. "Ye can do it."

"We just want to let him know we're in here and alive," Barrels said. "Draw the entrance, with an arrow pointing outward, and then him waiting on the other side by the rocky path. Maybe draw a seal, too."

Jagger shook his head. "Just how well do ye think I can draw?"

"Who drew yer tattoos?" she asked, then battled the desire to groan. Sometimes she wished her temper lasted longer. She wasn't supposed to be talking to the dud.

He dug his finger into the mud and traced a curved line on the paper. "My tribe mother and my sisters."

He had sisters?

Caspian smiled. "Sisters. Good in small doses."

Jagger flashed him a grin. "Aye to that. Though they taught me to keep light on my toes for fear they'd catch me."

"Older sisters then, I take?"

The pirate nodded, digging his finger into the mud again. Ebba hated that he was touching the tainted paper. They shouldn't be taking advantage of the fact he was the immune. He could still catch the taint. They had no idea how long it had taken Jagger to beat back the evil each time and what doing so did to the pirate. "Four older sisters and five older brothers. Two younger brothers, too."

Grubby whistled. "Is yer father a selkie?"

It was a valid question. Eleven children was a . . . lot of tea.

Jagger snorted. "Nay, only four of them be children o' my parents. In a tribe, orphans are taken in by the chief and chieftess. Most are adopted, though they be treated just the same as blood kin." He sat back, holding the parchment up. "There."

Stubby peered at it. "Ye drew a sun? Nay, nay, that be the start of Davy Jones'. I see it now."

Barrels looked and cleared his throat politely.

"It can't be that bad," Ebba said with a grin. A quick glance told her otherwise. Lack of drawing skills was good, though; sometimes Jagger seemed invincible.

"But maybe the picture will make sense to Matey?" Caspian said weakly.

The crew chorused a groan. Matey wasn't exactly the sleekest ship in the seas. No way would he understand the drawing.

"Ye draw it next time," Jagger shot, rolling the parchment up.

Plank uncorked an empty waterskin and shook it upside down to dislodge the lingering droplets. "Any note will serve to tell him we're alive."

Jagger shoved the rolled parchment inside and recorked the skin, tossing it in the black case.

"Is that another group comin' back from the entrance?" Peg-leg asked, pointing.

They all turned.

"Surely not," Barrels said. "There are at least thirty there."

He was right. So many.

Jagger came to stand beside her. "I be thinkin' it be the new inmates. Cannon was happy so many were arrivin'."

"It was odd-like," Ebba added. "They all be tainted, so they'll end up on the pirate side. Yet Cannon seemed happy about that, didn't he, even though he wants everyone who isn't tainted to remain free o' it?" she asked Jagger, who dipped his head, silver eyes far away.

They watched the group trail down the passage stairs.

"Stubby, show a leg. We're headin' down to listen," Plank said, slapping her other father on the shoulder.

Stubby startled. "What? We are?"

"Aye, time for the oldies to lend a hand figurin' this all out, methinks."

Ebba smiled, not at the banter but at Plank's motivation. She'd worried after he touched the sword that it was a terrible mistake, but he'd been nothing but determined since.

Stubby didn't seem convinced.

"Listen up," Plank said, pushing his raven curls back. "This is for the old people up here."

"*Wise* people," Locks muttered.

Plank's glare shut him up. "We stood afore our worst fear not many days ago. Sumpin' none o' us ever thought to do. And since then, we've hidden up here, lettin' the younger legs do all the work. It be time to get busy, lads. We're still a crew. And we said we'd never be the kind o' parents to shirk their duty. I know that in years to come, none o' us will be dependin' on Ebba to fight our battles. We fight the battles beside her. And that be includin' now. We might've stood afore Cannon, but we've been right scared into inaction the last few days."

Ebba wasn't alone in staring at him in bewilderment. That was . . . quite the speech.

"Where did that come from, matey?" Peg-leg inquired.

Plank busied himself tucking in his tunic. "Ebba ain't goin' to say that her fathers didn't lift a finger to help. We set the ex'mple. We be the strength that she can always come back to."

Barrels was the next to venture a comment. "Did you eat seaweed this mornin', Plank?"

"Aye."

Turning to them, Barrels asked, "Did anyone else eat the seaweed?"

They all chorused 'aye.'

"That was my only theory." The eldest of her fathers shrugged.

"Are ye comin' or what?" Plank shot at Stubby. "They're nearly at the start o' the main path."

"Okay, okay," Stubby replied, getting to his feet. "I'm comin'. Not sure who died and made ye captain, though."

Plank was already at the steps. "We'll get as close as we can to the ship to see what's bein' said. We'll be back when we can."

There was a reason Ebba was happy to do the grunt work, and that was because she didn't want anyone else to do it.

"Walk on tiptoes," she called after them, following her fathers to the top of the steps. "Be careful down the stairs."

Jagger groaned. "They be grown men. Why're ye after them like that?"

"I don't know," she answered, turning back. "Always been that way."

Grubby approached and tucked her into his side. "Ye fret worse than me."

Ebba shuddered. "Aye, it ain't my favorite thing when we split up." Never had been, never would be. She stayed hugging Grubby and watched the new contingent of damned shuffle into hell.

"Something is bothering me," Caspian announced, massaging the left side of his chest.

Locks chucked the remains of his fish into the black case. "Spit it out then, man. Announcin' ye're bothered is a waste of time."

Barrels glanced around. "You have somewhere else to be?"

Locks' expression softened, and Barrels groaned. "Forget I asked."

"No, I'm really bothered by something," Caspian repeated, pacing now, still massaging his chest.

Ebba untangled herself from Grubby, alarm shooting through her. "Is yer arm painin' ye?" He couldn't be tainted, could he? He hadn't come into contact with anything, unless being in the middle of all those pirates during the meeting with Cannon was enough.

"What?" He came to a halt, blinking at her. "Oh, no. You know I always feel my arm is there. I must've slept on that side last night."

"Yer missin' arm be achin'?" Jagger asked, lips quirking.

Caspian shot him an arch look. "I know. Like it wasn't enough the *purgium* took the arm in the first place."

No bitterness stung the comment, however.

"So what be botherin' ye?" Ebba asked.

"I don't know."

Locks grumbled, "When ye do, let us know. Until then—"

Caspian resumed his pacing. "Talk again," he demanded.

"Aye, King Caspian," Jagger snorted, but he seemed intrigued by Caspian's sudden fervor. "What would ye like to hear?"

"Tell me again what Cannon said today," Caspian answered, gripping his forehead. "Replay the conversation."

Ebba and Jagger shared a glance.

Jagger took the rudder. "We walked in, and Cannon hadn't seen us. Riot was reportin' about the trip to the entrance."

"Cannon was right pissy. He was choking Riot. He said sumpin' like, 'Four. That ain't enough,'" she added.

"That ain't *fast* enough," Jagger corrected.

She nodded. "That was it. Four ain't fast enough."

Peg-leg rubbed his knee, frowning. "The only part that be makin' sense is that he was chokin' Riot. That be the Mutinous we know and hate."

"Exactly!" Caspian said. "Mutinous is violent."

"Have ye figured it out then, matey?" Locks asked.

"Keep talking," was the order.

Ebba thought back. "He seemed about ready to kill Riot when Swindles came up and said thirty had arrived. All tainted. And that their side'd be burstin'."

"Cannon repeated it and was pleased enough to let Riot scamper away," Jagger said, leaning forward on the rock he sat upon, watching the royal. "What's in yer head?"

Caspian answered, "Something big. On the tip of my tongue. Ebba, talk."

She stared at him. "What about now?"

"He healed you. That."

This was strange. But Caspian willingly read books and such, so his strangeness was no secret. "Pockmark ran into me. Well, I ran into him because I didn't want to watch yer father . . . well, die. Pockmark seemed inclined-like to hide what he'd done at first."

Jagger scowled. "He was right afraid. But he fired his pistol and brought other pirates runnin'."

"Pockmark's afraid. Mutinous wants to keep us untainted," Caspian muttered, now tugging at his russet curls.

Barrels glanced at the seaweed and then at Caspian. "Everyone else feel okay?" he ventured.

Ebba neared Caspian, hovering just out of the trajectory of his frenzied pacing. "I was talkin' to Cannon. I didn't want him to know we be aware he's keepin' us safe on purpose for his plan."

Caspian froze and turned to her. He lunged and gripped her forearm. "Safe on purpose."

"And so I pretended I thought we were just ent'ertainin'—"

"Enough," he said.

Ebba cut off. Sink her, he was a bit scary when he thought too hard. What had she once said? He'd put too many mangoes in his basket. Now they were falling out.

"Safe on purpose. Bursting with bad." Caspian tapped his forehead roughly, bending at the waist. "He wants it to burst. He's angry it's not bursting. It's not bursting fast enough."

Jagger and Barrels bolted to their feet, and Ebba shared a baffled look with the others.

Caspian straightened, grinning in a triumphant way she'd never seen before.

"The thunderbird," he declared.

Jagger whooped and Barrels was laughing.

Locks stood, his color changing from red to purple. "If ye don't tell me what's botherin' ye *right now*, I'll cut off yer other arm."

Apparently unfazed, Caspian crossed to him, clapping Locks on the shoulder. "Do you remember the thunderbird?"

Of course they all remembered. He was a power of oblivion who'd nearly killed them by creating a monster storm.

"He didn't want to let Jagger live, but when he discovered we were assembling the root that could destroy the pillars, he hesitated. He said that his job was to maintain balance in the abyss."

Jagger was grinning, too. "The abyss that was fillin' with twisted souls."

Barrels pointed at Ebba. "You were the one who asked him if there were more bad souls because of the pillars."

She couldn't recollect, but the words sounded vaguely familiar. "So the abyss he was speakin' o' is actually Davy Jones' Locker? This place?"

Caspian crossed to her. "Yes! But the rest is more important. I cannot recall his exact words, but the thunderbird said as light souls fly, the space where he contains cruelty expands. That if the light souls do not come to him, the space in the abyss would run out."

"And darkness would roam free," Jagger and Barrels chorused.

Caspian turned to all of them. "I thought the thunderbird was referring to the darkness already spreading. He wasn't. He spoke of the balance of light souls and dark souls in the afterlife dissolving. Of hell itself bursting open for the damned to be set loose on the realm."

She was following now. "Shite," she whispered.

Jagger frowned. "Cannon needs us to be untainted within the Locker, though. That must upset the balance even more, having light in a place where only darkness is meant to reside. That's why he gets so angry if the pirates come near us. That's why he's protectin' us in this cave. If we become tainted, we're o' no use to him."

Peg-leg stopped rubbing his knee. "But why keep the damned across the stream untainted?"

Ebba chipped in. "Because they ain't all bad. There be light in them too. I saw it with the sword. At least, that be my guess."

"It could be," Barrels answered, beaming.

Ebba's skull hurt. "How does knowin' this help us? If bein' light helps him, bein' dark would hinder him, aye? But I ain't gettin' tainted on purpose."

"Because we know something he doesn't," Caspian said, lifting his chin.

She looked up at him, heart hammering under her ribs.

Caspian glanced at her fathers. "Most of your fathers are still tainted. And so is Jagger. Or at least we have no idea if he's completely rid of the taint yet. If we're the centerpiece of Cannon's plan to break hell open, then he has already lost."

EIGHTEEN

Ebba dangled her legs over the ledge, the cave at her back and her eyes fixed on the path below for a sighting of Stubby and Plank. The wind had howled about half an hour ago. She'd give them another little bit and then go looking. She didn't like them being gone for so long.

"I'm goin' down to the stream," Caspian announced.

Ebba glanced over her shoulder. Was that wise? The question lingered on the tip of her tongue, but she swallowed it back. "Be careful."

"Don't get caught," Jagger added. "Cannon was clear about us not goin' down there. Even if he can't kill or taint us, I be sure there are other ways o' keepin' us in line."

"We only agreed that we wouldn't. We never mentioned the others," Ebba corrected him. "Best use that loophole if ye're caught," she said to Caspian.

Caspian hardly seemed to hear her. He'd turned, and his eyes were fixed on the passage platform. Ebba twisted to look. Montcroix stood on the platform, looking directly at their cave. He'd regenerated from boiling alive, then.

Striding to the lip of their ledge beside her, Caspian raised his hand, and then, without waiting for an answering wave, he began down the steps.

Montcroix stayed where he was for a minute longer, and Ebba tracked his movement as he climbed down the cliff from the passage platform to join the other damned. And hopefully meet with his son. Nerves twisted her gut. She hoped Caspian got whatever closure he needed from his father.

Peg-leg, Grubby, and Locks were in the cave resting. Barrels was doing the same out on the ledge, lying flat on his back and softly snoring, muttering numbers at sporadic intervals.

Ebba blew out another breath, watching as Caspian darted down to the stream and as her two fathers *still* didn't return.

"Quit worryin' yer head," Jagger said, milling over to her. "I can feel it from over there."

She eyed him. He'd found a new tunic in the clothing cases. That was a shame.

"I've tried to stop in the past, believe me," she mumbled so as not to wake Barrels. "It doesn't work. I never feel whole without them here."

Jagger sighed. "So ye'll always want yer fathers around then?"

Ebba cut him a look. "Aye, does that bother ye?" That put her in a conundrum if so.

He shook his head, saying gruffly, "Nay, I grew up in a similar situation, really, just in a forest. But I want to know if I should be makin' an effort with them or not. If ye'd just come away by yerself, I wouldn't have to."

She snorted and then choked on a laugh. "That be a very pirate thing to say."

"Aye," he said, a smile ghosting his lips. "It is at that. So, are ye game to walk down the steps a way with me? There be things we need to speak o' afore ye get violent toward me."

Ebba twisted to look up at him. Warm, teasing Jagger was back again, and she was determined not to give him any leeway. "Why?"

"Ye'll find out down there. Unless ye're scared o' movin' down the steps with me. . . ."

She scoffed. "That won't work on me."

He started to sit. "Here will do fine then. I just thought ye might wish to be away from yer fathers for it."

She cast a look at the slumbering Barrels and over her shoulder at the cave. Glaring at the pirate, she stood and strode to the steps. "Fine then. Hurry up."

He was smirking. She didn't need to turn around and check to know.

Seeing as her palms were suddenly slick with sweat and her chest was squeezing to near-panic levels, Ebba took the time down the steep stairway to collect herself. What did he plan to talk about? Was he going to break bad news to her gently? Or explain why he wouldn't kiss her?

Nausea churned in her gut. She'd never felt so nervous in her life.

She stopped a few steps from the bottom and sat, pulling her crimson skirt underneath her when it puffed out.

Jagger sat on the step above her and leaned forward, dangling his hands over his knees. "Ye never asked me why I'd be takin' pains to get to know yer fathers."

Ebba didn't answer. She couldn't trust her voice. She looked ahead at the circle of boulders around the base of their cliff perch, willing her breaths to come evenly.

He cleared his throat. "The reason I'll be takin' pains to know them is because. . . ."

She stopped breathing altogether.

". . . I'm king o' the crow's nest."

Outrage struck her in the chest. Ebba burst to her feet and whirled on the pirate, whacking him on the arm. "Ye flamin' sod."

Jagger threw back his head and laughed, leaning back on the steps. Always bloody leaning.

But a burning had begun behind her eyes. That wasn't funny. Not now. This whole *amare* thing had really put her in a spin. Why wouldn't he just tell her one way or the other and put her out of her misery?

"That wasn't very nice," she whispered, her voice wobbling.

Ebba turned on her heel and descended the last few steps, dashing for the safety of the boulders.

She only made it to the base of the steps before Jagger grabbed her around the waist.

"Wait, Viva. Don't run from me." He spun her around, and she hurried to wipe away the tears that had fallen.

His face dropped, and he reached up a shaking hand to her face. "Nay," he said hoarsely. "I didn't mean to make ye cry."

She rubbed her forehead, chest heaving as more tears burst free. "I just want it to be over, Jagger. It hurts too much."

He reeled back as though struck. "What? I'm sorry, Viva. I know I just messed things up. What do ye mean by over?"

"What do *ye* mean?" Ebba shot at him. "Why are ye stringin' me along and playin' games?"

Jagger stared at her. "I ain't."

She shook her head and made to push past him. "Ye are. And I've had enough o' it. Pirate up and tell me how ye feel. Or sod off."

Jagger hooked her around the waist again, whirling her back. "Please don't run from me, Viva. Let's talk about this."

Her chest heaved as she scowled up at the pirate. "Talk then. This be yer chance. The last one."

Watching her closely, Jagger reached up and brushed away her lingering tears with his thumb. The simple touch nearly brought her to tears again. The breath caught in her throat, and she turned her face away from him, squeezing her eyes shut.

He placed a hand beneath her chin and turned her back. "Let me see those beautiful eyes."

"Nay."

"*Aye*."

Ebba opened her eyes. Only to roll them at the pirate.

He held her chin in place, silver eyes intent on hers. "When I touched the *amare*, I felt sumpin' warm and powerful, but my immunity dampened it. That didn't matter. Because when I touched the tube, I felt nothin' more than I'd already felt for a long time."

Than he already felt? She stopped trying to pull away.

Swallowing, he rushed on, and she blinked.

He was *nervous*.

"I'd been fightin' it since seein' ye in that dress on yer birthday. And that's just when I *knew*. A part o' me must've realized afore then. Sumpin' drove me to collect yer beads. Even when I couldn't see anythin' else, I could see yer face. Yer eyes. I knew I should protect ye with my own life. That ye were precious beyond anythin' else. Ye assumed that I continued this quest for my tribe. But that ain't true. I continued it for ye."

Ebba sucked in a ragged breath. She had no idea what to say. His words bounced around her skull, replaying over and over, making her feel as light as a feather. How had he felt so much for so long?

He mimicked what she'd done a minute before, turning his face away.

She dragged his face back to hers. Now they both had a grip on the other's chin.

"Why did ye fight it?" Ebba demanded. She didn't like that. Which might have been classed as hypocritical.

He licked his lips. "For the same reason I won't kiss ye or touch ye overmuch. I was tainted. I didn't know I was the immune for a time. I didn't know if I'd ever be rid o' it, and I couldn't risk spreadin' it to ye. Then I wasn't sure if the taint had gone. Ye're meant to be joyful, Viva. And when ye ain't, it crushes my very soul. I'd break open Davy Jones' myself if it meant preventin' that. I'm furious at myself for makin' ye cry just now as it is."

He breathed as hard as her.

The pirate released her chin. He still clamped her against him with one arm about her waist, but he brought the other hand to rest against her cheek. In a daydream, she released his chin, gripping the front of his tunic in both hands. He licked his lips, and she traced over his high-boned cheeks, his liquid silver eyes, and the tangled strands of his flaxen hair.

"Viva, I love ye with everythin' I have," he told her, voice guttural. "I love ye with everythin' I thought I didn't have left."

A lump rose up her throat, but she'd had enough crying for one day. Ebba forced the lump down.

Jagger hadn't kissed her in order to protect her. She hadn't thought there was any valid reason he could give for avoiding that, but he did. Jagger had an answer that Ebba couldn't even find a depth to. His words, his very tone, stole the ground from under her. They frightened her; astonished her. She wanted to seize that emotion with both hands yet handle it with exquisite care, lest too rough a touch should break the fierce feeling running rampant in her chest.

A smile curved her lips. A smile she couldn't have stopped if she'd used both hands and thought of dying birds. She made a sound that was half laugh and half sob, releasing a hand from his tunic to cover her mouth.

She sucked in a shaking breath and this time fully laughed. With joy.

"Viva," Jagger said mildly. "Could ye say sumpin' soon? Ye're killin' me."

That smile crossed her face again, but this time she didn't hide it. Dropping her hand, Ebba let Jagger see it. She laughed again as he all but sagged with relief.

How did he think she'd felt after shouting her love for everyone to hear?

"Jagger," she said, aware and uncaring of the breathy quality to her voice.

She felt like she'd run for a lifetime and was just slowing down.

"It's all very sudden for me," she told him. "And I can't say that if I hadn't touched the *amare* and then the *veritas* that we'd even be havin' this conv'rsation for another ten years, but though it be ac'idental, I can feel the right o' it."

Reaching out, Ebba rested a hand against the pulse in his neck.

"Ye feel right. And I feel strong when I'm about ye." She frowned, thinking of the crow's nest. "Except when—"

He flipped her hand and yanked her into his arms. "Let's stop there, aye?"

Ebba shut her gob and buried her face against his chest, overpoweringly aware that the tattoos she'd always found fascinating were just on the other side of his tunic. Sometime soon, when all of this was done, she was going to stare at them for a good long time.

He stroked her dreadlocks, lingering on each of her beads. "Do ye love me then, Viva?"

"Pretty sure I shouted it out the other day," she grumbled.

Jagger chuckled, the deep sound sending a bolt of longing through her. "Aye, ye did at that. Don't think I've ever felt so relieved in my life. And even then, I had to work up the courage to tell ye the same. Somehow I convinced myself ye hadn't meant it."

"I love ye, Jagger," she told him, pulling back.

He smiled at her. "Thank ye."

"So we've professed our love for each other. Do we go back and fill in everythin' else or what?" she asked, closing her eyes and breathing in the salt-and-rope scent of him.

He snorted, resting his cheek atop her head. "I can't say I've thought much past kissin' ye."

"Why did ye write the note then?" She pulled back, glaring at him. "If ye weren't tainted afore, ye'll be tainted again. Yer eyes ain't black. I say we risk it."

"I won't be kissin' ye until I know for sure. Cannon tainted his crew through addin' a drop o' blood to the grog barrels. When the tainted pirates' eyes be black, ye can catch it from their skin, but blood and spit work di'ferent. I won't risk it, Viva."

"What if I be willin' to risk it?" she countered, nuzzling into his chest.

"Then I still won't kiss ye," he said flatly. "Though it ain't pleasant to say no when ye look at me all 'Jagger, kiss me.'"

Her jaw dropped and she pulled back. "I don't speak that high."

"Ye get all breathless. And yer mouth makes that 'o.'"

Her cheeks burned. "I don't."

He quirked a brow and bent his head, resting his cheek against hers. "Ye make me burn."

"With want? Or at the stake?"

She linked her hands behind his neck, savoring the intimacy of his face against hers. It was all the action she'd get until they busted this joint. Just one more reason to escape hell.

His chest rumbled. "Both, I guess. Ye make me feel desperate love."

Desperate love. That was a good description for what she felt. "I second that, m'hearty."

"So I think I'll start takin' pains with Barrels first. That one really dislikes me."

"*Barrels?*" she scoffed. "He's a big sweetheart."

"Nay, he be a sweetheart to ye. To everyone else, he looks like a savage pirate in fancy dress."

Ebba laughed at the image, then glimpsed Jagger's serious expression. "Ye're kiddin' me. Barrels?" she pressed, jerking her thumb overhead to where her father had slumbered out of view. "That Barrels?" She paused and then laughed again. "Ye ain't afraid o' my fathers, are ye?"

"I defeated Ladon single-handedly. What do ye think?"

"I be thinkin' that Sal was there to help ye."

"Aye," Jagger's silver eyes gleamed. "But she used her magic, not her bare hands."

Stubby's voice floated through the boulders toward them. "This uneven ground be hell for my hips. I didn't even know I *had* hips until hell."

Ebba leaped away from Jagger as though branded, bolting for the steps. "Make smart!"

"Ye're not afraid o' them, are ye?" Jagger mocked her, ambling after her up the steps.

She caught her giggle at the last second and morphed it into a snort. "If ye ain't afraid for yer future health, I best be afraid on yer behalf."

Reaching the top, she settled next to Barrels, grinning at Jagger when he appeared and leaned against the cliff face next to the cave.

Stubby and Plank reached the top of the stairs a minute later, and Ebba's chest loosened. Both looked weary but unharmed.

"What took ye so long?" she demanded, crossing the space to hug them both.

"Learn anythin'?" Jagger said. He shot a smile at her.

What was that for? She smiled back, unable to help it.

Barrels started, cutting off mid-snore. He rolled over and looked at them all. "Whaz going on?"

Stubby hobbled around the ledge. "Bloody sat in one place overlong."

"We watched the group come in to make sure they didn't spot Caspian down at the stream," Plank said, appearing as limber as when he'd left.

Ebba tensed. "They didn't, did they?"

Plank shook his head. "Nay. Anyway, Riot came on ahead o' the others. Turns out the pirates escortin' the new inmates had a di'ferent number to report. Cannon was shoutin' the number three. He wasn't happy. Shot five pirates after."

"There ain't enough space on the shipwreck for the new ones to caulk, so they've set up in the clearin' and boulders around the ship. We had to wait until they were sleepin' to get away."

That would make sneaking around harder, especially if more of the tainted arrived each day. And if the pirate side of the stream got as crowded as the damned side, remaining untainted would be a true feat.

"The number's gone down from yesterday. Four to three," Jagger said. "What does that mean?"

Plank scooped up a waterskin. "Nay idea. There be far too many myst'ries for my likin'."

"Oh," Ebba said, straightening. "But Caspian figured sumpin' big out."

She brought the others up to speed, leaving Jagger and Barrels to answer their questions. To simplify things, Ebba was just going to think of what was happening as a scale. On one end was evil, and the other side was light, and when evil grew heavier, hell would burst open.

"None o' it changes the fact we don't have the root parts," she said, interrupting Barrels. "We know Cannon be bustin' out to take the pillars the parts, but we don't know how to stop it. How do we prevent bad people gettin' in? We can't fight against so many in here. There have to be upward o' three hundred pirates on just this side."

"More than that, methinks," Stubby said. "With more and more arrivin' each day, there could be a thousand o' them in no time. Enough to match the number of damned across the stream."

Ebba shook her head. What could they do against such numbers?

Plank smiled at her. "Don't worry yer head, little nymph. Today, we know a lot more than we knew yesterday. And if our luck be holdin' true, we'll know even more tomorrow."

She forced her lips into an answering smile.

But what if time ran out?

. . . What would happen then?

NINETEEN

After collecting the black case of food from the bottom of the steps, the crew crowded around as Peg-leg sifted through the seaweed.

"Any note?" Locks whispered.

"Give me a scant second, ye impatient bugger." Peg-leg rifled a moment longer and then shook his head. "Naught that I can see."

Barrels frowned at the case. "There are any number of reasons why Matey mightn't have gotten a note to us."

"But if he doesn't get a note to us again, we can't assume he'll be there to aid our escape," Jagger said.

Caspian rasped from the cave, "I figured something else out. Or I *think* it's something."

Large shadows bruised the area under his amber eyes. Ebba hadn't heard him return last night. She desperately wanted to ask how things with Montcroix went. One week ago, Ebba wouldn't have stopped to think otherwise. But despite the truce they'd arrived at, she felt their friendship was out of reach—like there was a boundary between them that wasn't there before.

"The numbers," Caspian said.

Plank cut in. "Went down to three, Cannon was sayin'."

Caspian nodded. "That is what my father heard, too."

"See," Stubby blustered. "What was the point of us sittin' behind a rock for hours when he found out the exact same thing? Waste o' bloody time."

Plank rolled his eyes. "Please go on, Caspian."

"First the number was two. Then the number was four. And then three."

Locks sighed with gusto.

"I shared some of our theories with my father. And it was he who made the connection. If Cannon wants to break the abyss open in order to release the damned on the realm, what is the one thing he'd test?"

"How many be gettin' out," Ebba answered.

The others stared at her.

"I don't know why ye're so supr'sed," she said, folding her arms. "Who do ye think has collected most o' the information so far?"

Barrels hummed. "That's true, my dear. We don't give you enough credit."

No. They didn't. She was much smarter these days.

Jagger squatted beside her, and for an intense stuttering heartbeat, all she could think of was their recent conversation. She slid a glance his way.

He winked at her.

"One problem with that, matey," he said to Caspian after. "Thirty tainted people arrived yesterday. One hundred the day afore that. The number that can get out should've gone up if yer theory be correct, not down."

"*Unless*." Caspian held his finger aloft. "Something occurred to affect the balance between tests."

Barrels' eyes flew to Caspian. "Jagger wrote the note. Jagger was tainted again."

"I believe so," Caspian replied excitedly. "Before he penned the note, he wasn't tainted. Afterward, he was."

At least someone was excited about that news. Ebba let her eyes rest on Jagger with the weight of a thousand accusations. He slid a look sideways and cast her a drawling smile.

Soon, she would take kissing matters into her own hands.

"So we can keep taintin' Jagger over and over again to screw with Cannon," Peg-leg said, grinning.

"No," Ebba said, leaping to her feet.

Everyone stared at her, Jagger with a wide grin.

She slowly sat. "I mean, nay. That be mean. We can't be abusin' his immune power. We don't know enough about how long it takes him to battle the dark back. It ain't right-like."

"Are ye sure that be what ye're really worried about, Viva?" Jagger murmured.

Six pairs of eyes snapped to him. If Jagger was hoping to win her fathers over, he wasn't going about it the healthy way.

"I ain't sure it'll come to that," the pirate added, seemingly unbothered by the blistering tension. "If a little taint in me could lessen the number able to get out, even with thirty bad comin' in, the fact that five o' us are tainted should be enough to control the sit'ation until we figure out how to get the parts and escape. If it ain't, I can taint myself here and there."

Taint himself here and there?

Did he even hear himself? He might be the immune, but the taint wasn't something to toy with. Each time he caught it, he carried the scars from battling it back. Jagger would always recall the horrors of what he said and did during those times.

"If I was those three or four pirates testin' the entrance, I'd bolt away from Davy's and never come back," Stubby said.

Peg-leg pursed his lips. "Aye, but ye ain't controlled by the pillars. All o' them, barrin' Pockmark and Cannon, are gone to the taint."

Caspian shook his head. "Yes to all of that, but you're not seeing my point. When we arrived, no one could get out. With more arrivals, two could. Then four. And now three, but tomorrow, maybe five will be able to get out."

"If we keep comin' back to those same numbers, I'm leavin," Locks said.

"There are *five* of us who are tainted," Caspian said. "If Jagger is rid of the taint soon, we won't even need all five spots. We could escape the Locker. We could take those spots."

That shut everyone up well and good.

Stubby scratched at his stubble. "Barrels, Caspian be much smarter than ye."

"I don't see how that's relevant," Barrels spluttered.

The prince's cheeks reddened.

"Just pointin' it out," Stubby replied. "If all this supposin' be right —and I'm guessin' that be a big *if*—then we've got the makin's o' a good plan. All that be left is to get the parts back."

Right.

Ebba deflated. The parts. Her mind had already leaped to running through the entrance, sprinting down the rocky path, killing the Satyr, saving the female Capricorn, and freeing the realm.

"If we leave and Davy Jones' doesn't burst open," Plank said, arms folded, "then the parts would be trapped in here."

Peg-leg tutted. "We still need 'em to be rid o' the pillars out in the realm."

"True. And I guess this place will burst in time anyway."

Jagger shifted. "I'm thinkin' Cannon holds the weapon parts below deck. It'd make sense. It ain't a place we can easily venture. And close to him."

If he was about to say what she thought, he could go to Davy Jones'. Or stay here. Whatever.

"Nay," she said again.

"It ain't abusin' my immunity if it be the only way," he countered.

He would go into Cannon's hell ship over her dead body.

Stubby said, "But what are ye talkin o'?"

Ebba flung an arm wide, gesturing to Jagger. "He wants to go and get the root parts himself."

Stubby appeared to mull this over. "I'm okay with that."

Everyone but Plank and Caspian added their hearty agreement.

"Uh." Caspian drew out. "Only Ebba can pick up multiple parts. Well, if I've assumed correctly from what happened to Grubby. Regardless, we haven't tested that theory, and this isn't the time. Jagger would have to make six trips."

Jagger stood. "Then I best get started. Especially if we can be leavin' in the next couple o' days."

She blocked his way. "Nay, ye ain't doin' that. We need to think on it more."

He twirled one of her white dreads around his fingers, and she slapped his hand away.

"Watch me, Viva. We're gettin' out of here."

As she bent her knees to leap at Jagger and physically stop him, someone began to clap—a slow, steady sound that stole all other noise from the ledge. A sarcastic applause that seized the very breath in her throat.

Ebba whirled, one of Jagger's arms drawing her back against him.

Mutinous Cannon walked up the steps, joining them on their cave ledge. He didn't stop his clapping until he was immediately before her.

"My, my," he said, smiling down at her. "What a lucky day for me." Reaching into his sash, he drew out a piece of pale, folded seaweed.

Ebba's heart hammered as she took in the ink stains covering it. Matey *had* sent another note; the message just never reached them.

"Ye've been keepin' a fair share o' secrets, it seems," Cannon said, his tone gleeful. "Ye should know the pillars always find out. Esp'cially ye, Jagger."

Jagger's grip tightened around her waist.

How much had he heard? She didn't dare utter a single word until he'd shown more of his hand.

"Five o' ye are tainted, did ye say?" he said, dispelling her small hope that he'd only heard the part about Jagger sneaking onto the ship.

"Ye've put everythin' together by yerself. Color me surprised," he continued, head tipping to the stream in the distance. "Though ye had some inside help. Did I hear that Forge was over there? What an *honor*. I'll be sure to visit him. Well, now the fish is out o' the net, I'll be tellin' ye a few things more. I can't deny I've waited a good long time to do so."

Gone was Cannon's restraint. He'd made a decision, and by the dread filling her boots, she knew the decision didn't bode well for her crew.

Fear now froze her to the spot.

"More'n forty years ago," he said, stalking through their midst, "I lay half-dead at the bottom o' a cliff, an attempt to steal plunder gone awry. It was there that the pillars came to me after ten years o' searchin' the realm for a body. They said that if I accepted their help and lent my help in return, not only would they save me, but I would have unparalleled riches and power."

He was telling them how it all began? Ebba couldn't deny her curiosity. She'd wondered too often about how the pillars managed to secure a foothold after being defeated once.

"I accepted them into my body, and they saved me as promised. With their power and guidance, I rose through the pirate ranks and soon ruled the seas. I thought I'd reached the top after killin' the king at the time, but his son declared war against all piratekind in revenge. And over the years, my power swelled until I was the last pirate left standin' against that son, King Forge, in the Battle for the Seas. The pillars had offered me ultimate power, but danger was closin' in on all sides. They needed time for their power to grow. To kill Montcroix for good, to kill the entire royal line, they needed an object. My masters showed this object to me at every wakin' moment. A silver tube with a pearly sheen o' the like I'd never seen."

Cannon placed his hands behind his back, eyes trailing over her fathers. "It took two years to track down where the tube was while battlin' off and evadin' the navy. And when I did find it, unable to risk leavin' the ship in the midst of war, I sent six o' my crew to collect it."

Ebba stilled. Six of his crew? He was talking about her fathers.

"The six pirates betrayed me, taking the op'ortunity to flee with the treasure—as my masters then thought. Only in later years did they discover that wasn't so. Instead o' takin' the *purgium*, the traitors took the child I'd ordered them to kidnap for bargainin' power."

That was her. Ebba glanced at Stubby, and he answered with a grim look.

Everything could've been so different if her fathers hadn't run with her.

"My masters were d'spleased with me," Cannon said, face contorting. "I'd failed them. But they were willin' to show mercy. One more chance. There was another object. One I succeeded in attainin', though I lost half my remainin' crew in the battle for it. But now I'd earned the pillars' trust, and they told me more."

Sounded more like the pillars had strung him along from the start.

"Regainin' their power would take far longer than the battle would wage. And if they died within me, our efforts would be lost. The object I'd found would help them destroy all o' my foes, but objects of immense power could be tracked by those of similar power. And those powers wanted the pillars destroyed. The power o' the tube would give away their location and make them vulnerable, *us* vulnerable."

Ebba had always believed the pillars could drain the weapon parts, like how they drained Locks' girlfriend, Verity, of her power; like they had to drain *all* immortals and mortal-immortal mixes. But now that she thought of it, that was an assumption. It sounded like the pillars could only collect the root parts when they became strong enough to defend themselves against the powers of oblivion. Giving up their location prior had posed too much risk.

"There were six such parts, my masters told me. Six parts that formed a weapon o' vast power. A weapon only one o' immortal flesh could yield. The weapon belonged to them, stolen away long ago by three thieves." Cannon's eyes trailed over her, then to Jagger. Ebba followed his bloodshot gaze to Caspian.

He knew who they were, not just Jagger. Fear trickled down her spine.

"They'd already located other parts. One o' the objects was with their ally, Medusa, in her lair. Another resided with Forge, a sword ripe for the takin' whenever they gained enough power to take his throne. I had one part. The six o' my trait'rous crew were thought to have another. And the other two objects were lost as o' yet. Findin' them was imperative, but the three watchers who defeated the pillars hundreds o' years ago had taught my masters caution. They were not content to rely on just one plan. They knew if their enemies were to find three parts, they'd be led to the remainin' parts already hidden by my masters.

"I was given the honor of ensurin' they could never be destroyed. I was to take the object in my pos'ession to a place where none o' black heart could leave, and none o' power and goodness would dare enter for fear of unleashin' the damned on the realm. But I needed to die to enter such an abyss."

He'd definitely been swindled.

Cannon's mouth twisted as he spoke faster. "The pillars emptied the wisps o' their beings from me to my son, leavin' me only with the taint and not the insight o' their minds. My son and his crew hid away on the pillars' orders to wait out the wrath o' King Forge against our kind. Playin' my part, I lost the Battle for the Seas and ended up here, in the Locker with one o' the six parts under my guard."

He had the sixth part. Ebba's eyes widened.

So thick was the tension that Jagger's voice from behind nearly made her scream.

"How do ye know what came to pass between then and now?" he asked. "How did ye know o' our presence in the Dynami Sea? Some o' what ye say could be from Pockmark, but not all."

Cannon studied him, and his eyes glinted. Ebba got the feeling that he really had waited decades to gloat. Or even just to say he'd lost the final battle on purpose. For a man who'd never lost, purposeful failure must've stung.

Cannon answered, "Ye're right. The pillars sent messages with the tainted who ended up here over the decades. The tainted arrivin' spoke of Medusa bein' thwarted; they spoke o' a crew I was familiar with who'd collected most of the pieces." He smiled. "Pockmark arrived and divulged their names, and I grew eager enough to meet ye that I made my own plans, usin' the Satyr that had long been my servants on Medusa's orders for a new purpose—to bring me the crew o' *Felicity*. I would have my revenge on the pirates whose mutiny put me in here. I'd take the ultimate prize to my masters and receive all that I desired at long last."

"What do ye desire?" Jagger asked, voice low.

"Have ye learned then, too, Jagger? That the key to controllin' a man be through knowin' his wants?" Cannon asked. "Ye seek to bring me down as I would ye if our sit'ations were reversed. Yet I own less of my will each day and so care less about petty 'desires.' Soon I'll only know my masters' wants. Either way, my desire is realized. I will finally be free o' the Locker. There is no way I can lose."

"Ye and Pockmark be di'ferent from the others," Plank said from her right.

Cannon sneered. "Ye've paid att'ntion, Plank." He didn't offer any further answer.

To her, Cannon and Pockmark both seemed more resistant to the taint. Where the other crewmates' eyes were black, their eyes were yellowed and bloodshot. And yet Cannon had been in hell amongst tainted pirates for nearly twenty years.

Did Cannon and his grandson have a natural resistance?

Jagger was the only immune, but Ebba knew from her time on *Malice* that everyone succumbed to the taint in varying time. Some two days, some a week, some a month—like Verity.

"What happened to yer son?" she asked, swallowing.

Cannon fixed his attention on her, and she immediately regretted making a sound.

"The pillars were weaker when with me, and I withstood them better. My son was theirs when my masters were still growin' strong enough to leave a human body. He was lost to the taint and became useless within a matter o' years. My masters ordered Pockmark to be rid o' him and he ended up here with me," he said.

Was that part of why Cannon seemed to detest Pockmark more than any of the others? Because Pockmark killed his son?

"Pockmark had the fortune o' bein' the pillars' body when they were able to flood the ship as well as him. There wasn't so much to take. My son be restrained below deck on the shipwreck. He often dissolves into the berserk rage o' the taint—as ye saw Pockmark sink into not long ago. I can't have the pirates here goin' berserk, and I grew rather tired of wastin' bullets on my son."

If it were anyone else, Ebba might feel sorry for Cannon. Preyed upon while dying and offered his life back. Swindled by a cohort of greater minds and powers. Fed upon and convinced to give up his life and reside in hell indefinitely, sacrificing his son's soul in the doing. Made to believe he was in control at every turn.

Ebba shoved away the pity. The state of the realm was past the point of pity. Cannon wouldn't hesitate to end her life once her use ran dry. She couldn't relax her hatred of him. A victim he might have been, but there was no going back to that day, over forty years ago, when he'd lain half-dead and made the wrong choice.

Cannon's yellowed eyes trailed over each of them in turn. "And now ye know all. Ye know yer lives have always been part o' my masters' plans, o' *my* plans."

Is that how he saw it? What about her fathers' choice to snatch her and run?

"Pockmark," Cannon bellowed, making her jerk.

"Aye," came the faint call from below.

Cannon drew his pistol, and Ebba stopped breathing as he pointed the weapon directly between her eyes. "Fetch the *purgium*. I *will* get out o' this hole. And we be havin' some tainted guests I didn't know about afore. I think a trip to the entrance will do them nicely."

TWENTY

If Ebba was honest, she'd hoped to walk back through the narrow crevice to the entrance under different circumstances. Not shuffling in a line led by Pockmark, Swindles, and Riot and backed by Mutinous Cannon. And with much more of an escape feel to the return journey rather than the creeping sensation she and her crew were squeezing between two cliff faces to their doom.

Since her time on *Malice*—maybe even since her conversation with the Earth Mother—Ebba had wondered how the pillars were allowed to get a foothold in the realm again. Verity had told her some of how their power had grown since the wall crumbled, but now she knew the entire story. If the pillars had caused so much anarchy before magic was locked away, how was it possible the evil force wasn't watched and followed and checked by the powers of oblivion after? The pillars, being the weakest of magic at the time, had returned first to the realm when the wall holding the creatures back crumbled, but what about the years after that?

She'd looked at the six pillars as a passive evil, not one with their own agenda. After Cannon's recount of how they'd taken root in him and his line, one thing was obvious.

The pillars didn't mean to repeat their mistake, and if they seized possession of the weapon parts, that was it. For good. The realm would forevermore be governed by evil. They sent Cannon to Davy Jones' Locker two *decades* ago to ensure just that. And if the pillars did that twenty years ago, who knew what other plots were circulating around the realm that she was ignorant of.

"I must thank ye all for solvin' one problem," Cannon said, resting a hand on one of the cliff faces. "I couldn't understand why only a handful o' my crew were able to set foot outside. Hell should've burst open a day or two after ye first arrived."

Ebba peered back through the dim light at Caspian, who walked immediately in front of Mutinous Cannon. He'd been right about the numbers. The tainted pirates were going to the exit each day to see how many of them could get through.

Cannon's eyes cut to her, and she quickly whirled to look at Peg-leg's back again, stumbling slightly on the sandy floor of the crevice.

"All that's left," Cannon continued, "is to decide which o' ye betrayed me most when ye mutinied. Was it Barrels, my timid quartermaster? Ye must've figured out the log'stics o' the escape. Or was it the sobbin' Peg-leg or the weak-stomached Locks? Was it Plank? But that's o' no matter, I s'pose. I've already taken my revenge on him. Several times, if memory serves right. Ye named yer next ship after her, nay? *Felicity*."

At the front, Plank whirled around, shouting wordless fury. He shoved past Locks, lunging in Cannon's direction. Ebba yelled with the others, jumping back into Barrels as Stubby shoved Peg-leg, who stumbled back.

Righting herself, she scooped both arms under Peg-leg's windmilling arms to steady him.

Jagger had taken Plank to the ground, and Locks and Stubby were scrambling to help keep him there.

"Aye, I've taken my revenge there well and truly," Cannon crowed from the back.

Ebba released her father, turning to the pirate. Heat flooded her cheeks, and her hands shook with repressed rage.

His eyes passed over a stern Caspian, a shivering Grubby, and a quiet Barrels. Then scanned Peg-leg and Locks, Jagger and Plank, and finally, his bloodshot orbs came to rest on Stubby. "My former first mate," Cannon said with a smirk. "I entrusted ye to keep the others in line when I sent ye to Pleo. Aye, that seems about the right size to me. Stubby, the biggest mutiny belonged to ye."

Cold dread filled her stomach. What would he do to her father?

She turned back to the front, the coldness like a dagger between her shoulder blades. Jagger righted Plank. She watched as the younger pirate pushed her father in front of him.

"Just around this bend, Captain," Pockmark called back, undisguised glee in his voice.

Ebba's heart hammered.

"Good," Cannon purred. "Very good."

Something terrible was about to happen; she was sure of it. Her breath came fast, her chest rising and falling in a way that should have her breathers filled with air, except nothing seemed to be happening.

Barrels whispered in her ear, "Are you all right?"

Nay. She managed a nod, blinking through the dizziness assaulting her senses, the visible signs of the absolute terror she felt for Stubby.

Ebba stumbled around the bend, resting a hand on the cliff faces either side of her in the narrow passage. Her heartbeat filled her head, obscuring the sound of her crew's footsteps and their quiet murmuring.

"Stop there, ye miserly sea pigs," Pockmark snarled.

She inhaled sharply, pulling up short behind Peg-leg.

"Manners, Pockmark," Cannon said mildly. "Or did my son raise ye to be a savage?"

Who was he calling a savage? To her, it seemed like Cannon had no feeling except for his own ambition to get out of hell. What was more, his ambition wasn't blinding. Cannon knew everything he was. That was true savagery.

Pockmark's face reddened, but he appeared to recover, ordering them out of the tight confines of the crevice and into the larger area immediately before the entrance to hell.

The space was just as she recalled. Only enough room to fit a rowboat, with no wind, smell, or sound to hint at the realm on the other side of the sheer black-and-crimson stone wall.

So close.

She could get out. Caspian and Grubby could get out. Maybe even Jagger.

But that wasn't enough. Still wasn't enough.

"Jagger," Cannon said, rounding the back of their row to stand before them. "If our positions were reversed, what would ye do?"

"Lay over and die, I s'pose," Jagger replied with a shrug. "I would've already given my body to the pillars, so it wouldn't make sense to pretend I had a spine at this point."

Ebba's eyes rounded. She gasped, her shock over Jagger's reply momentarily cutting through her terror.

Grubby snorted once. Twice. A high-pitched wheezing emanated from his lips before loud, uproarious laughter spilled out. Dread filling her boots, she turned to her doubled-over father, who was slapping his hand on his thigh.

"That's a right good one, Jagger," Grubby choked. "No spine."

Barrels turned away from her, gripping Grubby's forearm and whispering urgently in his ear.

Ebba's chest tightened as she glanced back at Cannon for his reaction.

His eyes weren't fixed on Grubby though her father's ill-timed hilarity bounced and doubled through the passage, back the way they'd come. His eyes were on Jagger.

Cannon ambled closer to the pirate, a curious smile quirking one side of his mouth. Reaching out, he stopped just shy of touching Jagger's chin. "How I would've loved to meet ye outside o' this place.

Then the dec'sion would've been a fair one." He leaned in, his face level with Jagger's.

"What dec'sion?" Jagger asked in a steady voice. Ebba didn't know how he remained so outwardly calm. *She* wanted to go over there and drag him farther away.

Cannon smiled and stepped back. "Pockmark. The *purgium.*"

Pockmark did as bade, snatching the black stone case from Swindles. He swaggered up to Cannon, opening the lid.

Cannon peered into the box and then turned to stare at the entrance.

Back rigid, he extended an arm as he walked toward the solid rock. When he reached the sheer wall, his limb slid through like a hot knife through butter. Though she'd known some of the tainted pirates could now get out, the reality of it still unsettled her. As subjective as the thunderbird was with sorting people into the Locker, she was under no illusion that the majority of the inmates hadn't done something horrible in their time to warrant being here.

A sigh escaped Cannon's lips.

"I used to come here each day in the start," he murmured, shoulders sagging. "Once I claimed my territory, I would test the passage. Doing so nearly drove me mad, and the temptation became . . . a weakness I couldn't afford others to see. They couldn't know how much I wanted the entrance to open. They could not guess my plan. I have done this for my masters, *I* alone. They will reward me. Exalt me as they promised over forty years ago." The muscles around his shoulders leaped as he moved the hand no longer visible on their side of the wall. "I feel the wind on my skin. I feel the sting o' cold. Rubbin' my fingers t'gether, I feel the grittiness o' salt. No pirate should be chained. We ain't meant for cages."

No, they weren't.

Cannon inhaled and drew his hand back in, bringing it to his mouth. "I *taste* the salt from outside. Freedom be within my grasp at last. At long last." He curled his fingers into a fist and lifted his head to look at Stubby. "And I will have it. Stubby, my disloyal first mate.

Step up." Cannon gestured to the black stone case. "It be yer lucky day. Ye're about to be freed o' the taint."

Ebba stared at Cannon, buzzing filling her ears as she shifted to look at the box holding the *purgium* and then her father. "Nay," she said.

Cannon slid his yellowed eyes to look at her. "Aye. My orders were not to harm any o' ye because to harm ye would just bring more evil to the Locker. My masters were needin' ye free o 'taint for hell to burst open." He looked over the line, lingering on Jagger's end. "But five o' ye be tainted. And to my way 'o thinkin', that means the rules be changed."

Ebba swallowed, unable to glance away. Unable to say a word through the vise of fear around her throat.

"Yet killing him won't achieve your purpose either," Caspian said, stepping forward, determination etched in his face.

"King Caspian," Cannon said in greeting.

Caspian didn't show any reaction to the remark. "We were warned by a great power that healing any of Ebba's fathers would kill them."

Cannon tilted his head as though contemplating the words. Ebba inhaled as quietly as possible, as though that could upset the balance of what happened next against her crew.

Cannon's mouth twisted, and he barked in laughter.

"He be o' equal use to me tainted as if he were dead. I need him pure. So tell me, great king, what have I to be losin' by havin' someone place the *purgium* on his skin?"

The hope in her chest withered and died. He'd already made up his mind.

But that wasn't happening. It couldn't. She wouldn't let it.

She slid a look at Peg-leg and Locks, who gave shallow nods.

"Now, now," Pockmark said. "None o' that." Drawing out his pistol, he released the hammer, aiming the weapon at Ebba's head.

She clenched her teeth. Did he really think that would stop her? It might stop her fathers, but nothing would prevent her from attacking whoever tried to harm one of her crew. Rage unfurled in her gut as she crossed up to Pockmark.

The words out of her mouth were so filled with anger, she barely recognized her voice. "Ye better go on and pull that trigger then, Mercer, because I'll hap'ily kill ye four times a day for the rest o' yer damned life rather than see my father hurt."

Doubt flickered through Pockmark's face.

"Do it," she shouted at him, stepping so the muzzle was a mere breath from touching her forehead.

Cannon called lazily, "Unless ye wish to lose a daughter and one o' yer crew, I'd suggest ye control her."

Ebba managed to evade Barrels' swinging arms. In a swish of skirts, she dodged around Pockmark, ducking Peg-leg's attempt and skirted around Locks' stocky frame.

Stubby stood by the box, looking inside.

Then Jagger blocked her view. "Nay, Viva."

Ebba stared up into his silver eyes. "Ye best be gettin' out o' my way, Jagger. Nothin' comes between me and my fathers."

They both ignored Cannon's laughter at her comment.

"That's where ye're wrong," Jagger said, low and fast. "I'll always come between ye and danger. Even against yerself."

Ebba transferred her weight back to dart around him but trod on the back of her skirt. The hem tore, and as quickly as she managed to regain her feet, it wasn't quick enough. Arms clamped around her from behind.

She glared up at Plank. "Let go o' me!"

"Be smart, little nymph," he whispered.

One of her fathers was about to die. Ebba thrashed in his grip, relishing the yells of surprise for an instant before Peg-leg had a hold of one arm and Locks the other.

"Ye touch him and I'll rip yer soddin' head off," she screamed at Cannon. "I'll hunt ye to the end o' yer damned days. When I'm done with ye, even the Locker will spit ye out!"

Cannon's laughter swelled, and true amusement glistened in his eyes as he surveyed her. "Now there's a pirate I could have used. Think o' what ye could've been." He circled behind their ground, but she paid him no mind.

"Ebba," Stubby said, glancing over to where she struggled.

She paused, her aching heart reaching for him.

"Ye can't reason with madness, lass," Stubby said, a wry smile on his face.

Panic obliterated everything. Her reason, her love for the others around her, her very life. "Nay," she shrieked, ripping her arms from her fathers with a strength she hadn't known she possessed. "Nay!"

"I love ye, lass. Never forget it."

Ebba lunged for her father as he touched the *purgium*.

White light exploded in a roaring wall of heat.

Swindles was flung past her by the force of the eruption. She heard her fathers' faint yells over the roar as they, too, were shoved away by the invisible power of the *purgium*. But Ebba wasn't flung back. No. She was jerked *forward*.

Against her control, as though a hand reached under her ribs, Ebba was yanked toward Stubby so hard she bodily left the ground, hurtling toward her father.

High above her crumpling father. . . .

. . . Where she was flung, *thrown* down onto the ground, against the black stone.

TWENTY-ONE

"Who let Grubby make the grog?" Ebba whispered, trying to move her mouth as little as possible as she formed the words. Any jolting of her body was bound to hurt her skull.

"She's awake," someone called.

"Flamin' hell, shut yer gob." Ebba groaned, clutching her face.

She pressed on her forehead and yelped, her eyes flying open from the pain.

Bad idea, bad idea. Ebba closed her eyes again, rolling onto her side.

"Little nymph, how are ye farin'?"

Plank.

"What happened to my face?" she rasped. If her fingertips were correct, she had a bruise the size of Locks' hidden birthmark on her face.

"Ah, well. . . . Ye were thrown into the ground."

What? Ebba lifted a hand and pried open one eye to look at him. "Ye're kiddin'?" She trailed off, looking past her father at fiery stone.

Her heart began to thunder as the last moments of her flight flooded back to her. Ebba bolted upright, sore head forgotten. Black blanketed her very soul before she frowned, feeling her torso.

She glanced up and jerked to see six faces staring back at her, not including Plank. Six was too few. And yet. . . .

"Stubby be all right," she said, sighing in relief.

Peg-leg and Locks exchanged a look.

Then Barrels cleared his throat. "Yes, my dear. But, if I might ask, how do you know?"

"Where is he?" she asked.

"Inside," Grubby said. "He's been sleepin' three days, like ye."

Three days? "He's okay, though? What did the *purgium* take from him?"

Silence reigned.

"He's unconscious, lass," Peg-leg said before the quiet became too awkward. "But from what we can tell, he hasn't lost a thing. From his body, anyhow."

Ebba held a hand to her head again and looked over everyone. Caspian and Jagger were accounted for, too, though Jagger stood half in shadow. She couldn't see his face. Was he hiding something?

"So what happened then?" she asked. "The *purgium* healed Stubby. There was the explosion, and Mutinous just decided that was enough for the day?"

Caspian approached and crouched by her side.

She looked into his amber gaze.

"Sorry, Ebba. You can consider us a little confused by your calm. And I'm with Barrels . . . how did you know Stubby was okay?"

I felt it. "I'd know if he were gone," she answered, unsure how to describe the happy stability in her heart. Actually, all things considered, aside from her head, she felt great—lighter than ever, though she wouldn't have said she felt bogged-down beforehand.

Silence reigned again.

Caspian's eyes were slightly too wide. "When you . . . flew into the stone, you weren't in great shape. We managed to convince

Cannon that it was in his interest to let us tend to you. I guess that, considering Stubby was alive and now 'pure,' he relented."

Cannon hadn't healed any more of her fathers. Ebba sagged in relief, then stilled. "Stubby was healed o' the taint," she said excitedly.

Grubby passed her a waterskin, and she threw him a grateful look, uncorking it and taking a small sip.

The others weren't as excited as her.

"We don't know how he is," Barrels gently reminded her.

She frowned at him. "He's fine."

"Who let Grubby make the grog?" came a pained groan from inside the cave.

Ebba folded her arms, raising her brows at the others.

Stubby stumbled out of the cave and staggered toward her. She handed him the waterskin without a word.

He took a sip, blanched, and spat the water out, spraying liquid over Barrels and Locks. "I'm alive." His gray-blue eyes were wide as he patted himself down and held out both arms. "I'm alive."

Stubby glanced up. "How am I alive?"

"*And well*," Barrels muttered.

"What do ye mean 'and well'?" her father asked.

Peg-leg stood. "Ye were healed by the *purgium*, ye dolt. It should've taken sumpin' from ye in return. Sumpin' big-like."

Stubby paled and resumed his body search. Once he'd looked down his slops, he sat down heavily. "I don't understand."

"We don't either," Caspian assured him. "We've only been able to come up with one theory in three days."

"Three days, ye say?" Stubby arched, moaning. "That explains a fair lot about the state o' my back. Go on then, what be yer theory?"

Locks muttered, "Wait until ye hear it."

Ebba glanced around the crew. "Spit it out then." Her eyes roamed of their own free will to where Jagger stood in the shadows of the cave. What was the matter with him? Why wasn't he coming out to see her?

"They be thinkin' that ye took the rap for Stubby," Jagger answered from the darkness.

She took the rap? Screwing up her face, Ebba turned to Caspian.

"You didn't see it," he told her. "All of us were thrown back, but it's like you were lifted and flung. Stubby just crumpled in a heap, as though he slept. *You* were unresponsive for three days. And," he said with a pointed look to the others, "is it mere coincidence that you woke minutes before Stubby also regained consciousness?"

Ebba stared at him. If truth be told, she'd known for a long time that the connection between her and her fathers went a step beyond the norm. When the crew was apart, she didn't just feel sadness but borderline panic. When one of them was hurt, she could barely think straight. "What does it mean?"

He blew out a breath. "I'm not sure. It's like the two of you are connected somehow. Linked. But that makes no sense."

Stubby was shaking his head. "Are ye sayin' the tube took sumpin' from Ebba instead? She wasn't the closest to me. And the *purgium* ain't never done that afore."

"But is that true?" Barrels interjected. "When Grubby touched the *purgium*, Ebba was out for several days also. He just slept, like Stubby."

Her brows rose. That was true. But. . . . "I hit my head then too." Ebba paused. "Though that injury wasn't really bad enough to be out three days."

She turned to Barrels. "Do ye think there be sumpin' in that? Like I'm truly linked to the six o' ye somehow?"

Jagger stepped out onto the ledge. She took one look at his white-lipped expression, and her heart sank. If Ebba had to guess, she'd say the pirate was mightily peeved over recent events. And she had an inkling all that anger was directed her way.

All Ebba wanted was for him to close the gap and wrap her in his strong arms, but as the seconds went by, it became clear she wouldn't receive a single look.

"Ye forget," Jagger said, "that she ain't just mortal. She's one o' the three watchers. We don't know what she's capable o'. Or what her role entails."

There were too many unanswered questions in that for Ebba's liking. "Does it really matter? Stubby's alive *and* healed—"

"O' course it matters," Jagger snapped at her. "What if Mutinous heals the rest o' yer fathers and the same thing happens four times over?"

Ebba blinked. "Why are ye in a shite?"

She hadn't done anything wrong, had she? Hard to with being unconscious and all, but Ebba was mostly sure she was in the clear.

Barrels leaned forward and took her hand, drawing her attention. "We've been worried about you. We didn't know if you'd wake up."

Understanding dawned. "Ah, I see." Ebba knelt and hugged her eldest father. "I'm okay."

She went around to each of her fathers in turn and stopped before Caspian, eyes asking him a silent question.

He opened his arm and she leaned in, hugging him with her right arm as per their usual custom. The hug was slightly awkward, but the physical touch felt good. As though they'd navigated another swell in regaining their friendship.

Then Ebba turned to Jagger, who'd returned to his shadows. "Stop sulkin'," she called ahead.

That drew him out quicker than salt on a leech.

"I ain't sulkin'," he said, glaring.

Ebba pushed his arms open and fell against his chest, pressing her cheek to the area over his heart. "I'm okay, Jagger, ye nincompoop. Why're ye puffin' up for?"

He stiffened. "I ain't puffin' up."

"What do ye call this then?"

His arms encircled her tightly. "I call it ye never listen to me."

Her eyes narrowed and she pulled back. "Ye tried to stop me gettin' to Stubby."

"Ye wouldn't've stopped me?" he asked.

She huffed and resumed her position on his chest. "Don't turn the tables. This is about ye."

Jagger stroked a hand over her beads, resting his head atop hers. "Aye, Viva. It's all about me." He brought his lips to her ear. "I thought ye'd died."

A shiver assaulted her. Now that he'd put the notion in her head, it wasn't hard to imagine *that* situation reversed. Ebba breathed through the horror induced by the mere thought of Jagger being asleep for three days after something like that.

"Well," she said softly, "I be right sorry ye were worried."

"Okay, enough o' that," Stubby said. "My head be too sore for that sight."

Ebba rolled her eyes and untangled herself from Jagger. Her fathers should be glad she hadn't given in to her feelings completely and kissed him for all she was worth.

Stubby glared at them. "What else have I missed then?"

"The tainted pirates have been searching for my father," Caspian said, turning to look out over the Locker. "They haven't found him, but none of us have left this ledge since Stubby was healed."

Peg-leg clapped him around the shoulders, nearly sending Caspian over the edge. "Don't worry, lad. If the tainted pirates didn't have orders to the otherwise, they'd already have crossed the stream to collect yer father. If he be smart, he'll stay in the thick o' the damned there. Whatever else yer father was, no one disputed his cunnin'."

"Sometimes I wonder if it was his only redeemable quality," Caspian said, face falling.

Ebba interjected. "That and lovin' his children. But that aside, I think ye're ten times the man he is, as ye well know."

Jagger stirred at her side and she glanced across at him. Blank face. Her favorite expression on him.

She sighed, and his lips twitched.

"Am I a lot to handle, Viva?" he whispered, running his hands over the beads in one of her dreads.

A lot to handle? A scalding pot full of boiling water was a lot to handle. He was like one of the thunderbird's storms. Ebba sniffed and focused on ignoring the handsome pirate who had now picked up one of her hands and was stroking each of her black nails in turn.

That felt . . . incredible. Relaxing.

Grubby raised his hand. "A crack appeared in the black rock when Stubby was healed. Right through the middle."

Shite. That wasn't good. "It doesn't open all the way to the Dynami Sea?"

Peg-leg answered, "Nay, just a rivulet from top to bottom. For now."

"Riot be dead-dead," Locks piped up.

"Wait, what?" Ebba blurted, leaving Jagger to go to her father.

"He was the one holdin' the box with the *purgium* in it. When Stubby touched the tube, white light exploded, and the rest o' us were thrown back. But after all the chaos, we looked back and only a pile of ash remained where Riot had been." Locks shrugged.

"He hasn't come back?" Stubby asked.

"Not that we've seen," Plank said. "But Cannon hasn't made contact with us since. Just been sendin' Pockmark with food and to ask about Ebba."

Ebba whistled low. "So the taint doesn't go well around the white light?" If so, that was good to know. She had a promise to keep to Cannon, if her fathers didn't make her get in line behind them.

"Hold on a minute," she exclaimed, an idea coming to her. "Don't ye think that Riot could've been the one to pay the sacrifice?"

"We did contemplate that," Caspian said, righting his crown. "But how do you explain what happened to you?"

She lifted a shoulder. "Magic weirdness?"

Caspian hummed in reply.

Even she knew that fobbing off recent events as magic weirdness was no longer an option. They had to figure this out before more tainted pirates got out of here. "It's been three days since Stubby was healed," she said suddenly.

Plank grimaced. "Aye, little nymph. It has."

"Well," Ebba pressed, "how many are gettin' out?" If Stubby was free of taint now, that meant the scales had slid in Cannon's favor—even with the possible 'real' death of Riot lessening the tally of evil within the Locker.

"They haven't been fillin' us in," Plank said then hesitated. "But this mornin' we counted one hundred goin' to the entrance. And only seventy yesterday. Plus, each day, more and more tainted have been arrivin' in the Locker." He tilted his head over the ledge.

Still reeling that the number of tainted able to leave the Locker had leaped up so quickly, Ebba neared the edge of their perch. She gaped at the sight below. When they'd first arrived in the Locker, the far side of the stream was covered with damned while the tainted pirates on this side remained mostly confined to the ship. No longer. Now, tainted pirates spread out through the boulders nearly all the way to the stream, partway where their cave path branched off from the main walkway.

Both sides were as packed as each other. There had to be nearly one thousand tainted pirates below.

"So many more," she said, her voice a hollow echo. How could they ever beat or escape that many?

"We be thinkin' the pillars are killin' the tainted on purpose unless there be some type of battle afoot," Peg-leg said.

"If one hundred pirates can get out, then so can we." She bit her lip. But how was that possible when Cannon had the root parts? And with the tainted pirates sprawling through the boulders, her crew's jaunts down to the water had just become significantly harder.

The situation felt out of control. Utterly. And the urge to open the vote to abort their quest hovered on the tip of her tongue. Yet Ebba swallowed it back. A pirate might take a while to dedicate themselves to a venture of this like, but once a pirate gave her word, a pirate saw the job through. She'd known when they decided to pursue all this that they were likely signing over their lives. Ebba was okay with giving her life to save her loved ones.

She just wasn't okay with her loved ones giving their lives to save hers.

Crossing to the top of the stairs, Jagger jogged down, disappearing from sight. He reappeared soon after and then crouched by Plank. "No one be listenin' on the steps. I'm goin' in tonight," he said in undertones. "I'll try to find the parts and get as many out as I can without detection."

"Nay," Ebba said immediately.

"What? Ye're allowed to risk yer life, but not me?" he answered her, eyes calm.

She stared at him. Had he just read her mind? "Ye've risked yer life plenty-like, haven't ye?"

"Aye, we're in agreement there. And if someone else was immune to magic, I'd be for sendin' them in instead, never doubt that."

She didn't. He was a pirate, not an idiot. "But what if ye're tainted badly? Like ye were at the start." That Jagger had been out for himself and, on occasion, had done mean things for the apparent fun of it. Letting her beads roll out of the scupper being one of them.

"I won't lose control," he said, pressing his lips together.

"That be well and good, unless ye can't," Locks replied.

Jagger fixed him with a look. "Do ye have a better idea, matey?"

"No man that hugs my daughter, who ain't one of my co-parents, is a matey of mine," her father scoffed. "But nay, I reckon that be our best shot. Though I be concerned it won't be enough."

Ebba paced in the only clear section of the ledge. "O' course it be a terrible idea! Ye expect him to sneak in and out six times? Are ye all mad? Cannon overheard our plan three days ago. Ye think he'll have forgotten that?"

"Shh," Caspian said, glancing over the side. "Lower yer voice."

"Don't tell me to lower my voice when the plan be stupid."

Caspian's jaw clenched. "There won't be any plan unless you keep your temper."

Since when did Caspian speak to her like that? Ebba scratched her chin, scrutinizing him, and then blew out a breath. "I vote nay. We'll find another way."

"One more load o' tainted come in, and Davy Jones' could burst open," Stubby said with a look her way. "And if that don't work, considerin' the crack in the wall, Cannon'll be back here to heal more o' us. I don't know if Ebba just took the hit for me or if that ain't the case or what. But if she did take injury so I could heal, I be worried she'll take it for the rest o' ye, too."

"Aye," chorused her other fathers.

Ebba stood, her fists furled. "So ye'll sacrifice Jagger just to save me."

"Do ye need us to answer that one, lass?" Peg-leg asked.

Barrels stood, looking at her. "We've got to put our personal feelings aside. This is bigger than us."

And the fact Barrels disliked Jagger had nothing to do with his opinion whatsoever.

Ebba snorted derisively, placing her hands on her hips. It wasn't that she didn't agree. Saving the realm *was* bigger than them, and they'd all signed up for it. But there were some people, namely everyone on this ledge, who she couldn't bear to lose. Three days ago, she nearly did, and the incident had brought an icy realization to what they were doing. At many points, her crew's lives had been placed in harm's way. But never, *never* had she experienced the blinding, furious panic of three days ago. Where that came from, Ebba didn't know. Her instinct told her that her crew dying was a bad, bad idea, and not just for the normal sadness. Ebba had come so far. Not all of that way with her fathers' help. Or the help of Caspian or Jagger. Should she ignore her instincts now just because this was 'the only plan'?

No.

"I vote nay," she repeated.

One by one, the others mumbled their votes.

Turned out hers was the only no.

"It be settled," Jagger said.

She ignored his attempts to catch her eye. If he wanted to go and kill himself, he could do it knowing she was raving mad at him. And then when he died and ended up here, she'd let him know all about it for eternity.

Caspian nodded, leaving the edge. "You'll go in tonight." He glanced around the rest of them, his eyes flickering as they met hers. "But you won't be the only person doing something. If this is going to work, we'll all need to help."

TWENTY-TWO

"Are ye still angry at me?" Jagger whispered as they crept down the path to the crossroad.

Ebba pressed her lips together. "Are ye still goin' to creep onto the ship?"

"Aye."

"Then *aye*," she mocked. Her eyes narrowed at the rumbling sound in his chest. He'd better not be laughing.

Amusement laced his deep voice. "I'll have to come back and make it up to ye, will I?"

Ebba glanced back at Grubby, Plank, Caspian, and Stubby to make sure they weren't in earshot. Like she and Jagger, they were quietly creeping from boulder to boulder down the cave path. Well, mostly quiet.

"Ye can try," she answered him. "If ye're in luck, I mightn't have moved on to the next lad afore ye return."

This time he chuckled low. "I'll have to come back with riches."

Ebba doubted there was any gold or priceless gems in hell. But his comment reminded her of Plank and his wife and how her father must have once joked about the same thing. "Nay, Jagger. Just come back to me. Come back to me as ye are, and I'll forgive ye on the spot."

She didn't much feel like joking any longer.

"And what if I be changed, Viva? What then?"

A tightness saturated his words as though he was slightly nervous. So Ebba thought some about her reply. "I'll chain ye down until ye're normal again. Then I'll kiss ye. After I punch ye in the gut."

A moment of quiet passed. "Sounds reas'nable."

It was. Ebba wasn't happy about the plan whatsoever. *Happier* because the rest of them were helping, but still angry that Jagger would be right in the belly of the tainted ship, surrounded by the evil damned. Still, a vote was a vote, and she was willing to admit to herself that her feelings were clouding her judgment. In her defense, she'd be exactly the same if one of her fathers or Caspian were going inside.

There hadn't been enough discussion of the consequences for her liking. Odds were, unless they got extremely lucky, that Jagger would be discovered before extracting all of the parts. What then? Things wouldn't just go back to normal. Cannon and even Pockmark had minds of their own. They wouldn't let this go without repercussions.

Ebba slowed as they reached the crossroads.

There would be tainted close by, so none of them spoke. The rest of her crew sidled up beside them, and they all watched as Jagger leaned down and patted the ground. Straightening, Ebba's brows shot up as he rubbed his hands over his eyes.

What was he doing?

She leaned in and saw his eyes were watering furiously. Had he just rubbed dirt in his eyes? They were kind of bloodshot now. Not yellow, like Cannon's, but somewhere in between. Ebba shook her head.

He removed his tunic and gave the garment the same treatment, rubbing it over the black stone and encrusted dirt before shrugging the garment back on.

Did he honestly believe a bit of dirt would save his gullet? Or was she not giving him enough credit, considering he'd survived two years serving under Pockmark?

He tucked in one side of his tunic, and then rubbed his dirty hands down his already stained slops. Then Jagger straightened and looked straight at her.

Be careful, she mouthed, her chest tightening.

Jagger winked and then, with a nod at the others, hunched over and shuffled left down the path. She watched him go, frowning. How had he done that? From the back, *Ebba* would have a hard time distinguishing him from the other tainted pirates.

Too soon, he disappeared from view.

Plank beckoned them back the way they'd come, and once far enough away from the main path, he crouched down. Ebba joined him between Caspian and Grubby.

"All right, lads," Plank whispered. "Ye know the plan—"

It was a stupid plan, in her pirate opinion.

"If we make a ruckus, Cannon'll know it was us. Even if Jagger gets the parts out one by one, we'll still draw the wrong kind of attention," she said.

"We're all ears if ye have sumpin' better to offer, lass," Stubby said.

Ebba desperately wanted a better plan. Just the thought of Jagger shuffling his way through a crowd of slumbering tainted pirates was enough to make bile rise through her throat. She'd seen the way Pockmark went berserk when she'd needled him. And the other pirates, Cannon aside, were completely gone to the pillars and lost control much easier.

She shuddered, imagining the entire Locker chaotic with berserk tainted. "We don't want Cannon to know it were us that started a ruckus. If he comes out and hears us makin' a ruckus, if he thinks it just be the tainted fightin', he may not think anythin' o' it, and won't go searchin' for Jagger. Or us."

Grubby nodded beside her. "I like it."

Plank and Caspian shared a look.

"That be solid pirate logic there," Stubby said, smiling at her.

Well, she wasn't stupid, just a genius who worked within pirate parameters. When given a strong enough incentive.

"We start a fight with them," Plank ventured, tapping his mouth.

Caspian cut in. "We start a fight between them."

Ebba grinned and saw the same expression echoed on the faces around her. "It's a plan."

Stubby cocked his head. "I dunno about ye, but I haven't heard a peep from the d'rection o' the ship. Where do ye think Jagger is?"

"He should be on the ship by now," Caspian said. "How long should we wait?"

"We don't want to move too soon. He needs to be below deck before we draw everyone out," she said quickly.

"We'll wait another ten minutes or so." Plank straightened, rubbing his knees.

Her other fathers did the same, but Ebba remained crouched by Caspian.

He nudged her with his stump. "You really love him. I've only seen you fret this much when your fathers are in danger."

Or when Caspian had been infected by the taint. But perhaps saying such a thing wasn't wise. Ebba didn't want to confuse their new territory. And, in some ways, it was different with Jagger. With her fathers, the thought of them dying made her feel like she would cease to be. With Caspian, it would be like losing a limb, one of the greatest friends she'd ever had. Barring an alcoholic wind sprite, the *only* friend she'd ever had. With Jagger. . . . With Jagger, the thought of never having the opportunity to feel the love she'd witnessed upon touching the *amare* was the source of her terror. To have that ripped away; that hope, that discovery, and the unknown. That was what caused her anger and terror now.

The possibility of regret and a life without him. Emptiness.

"Aye," she said. "It's a funny thing. I have all the feelings for him but so few experiences for feelin' that way just yet. It's as though I've skipped to the end."

Caspian swallowed, but nodded. "I can imagine it's like reading the last chapter of a book."

"Can't say I've done that, yet, but I'm guessin' so." Ebba smiled at him. He'd changed. Since his shouting fest on the ledge, and since visiting with his father, Caspian was altered. Not that he'd ever been a rollover, but in the last week, he'd seemed . . . more in charge. Almost assertive. She liked the change. Surely this new confidence was a good beginning.

Caspian searched her face and glanced away.

Just as she was about to stand, he said softly, "I wouldn't worry about skipping ahead to the end, Ebba. Once this is all over, you'll have your entire lives to fill in the gaps. To know that you have found your match is a great gift."

A gift.

A wrinkle appeared between her brows. To this point, she'd thought of touching the *amare* as more of an accident than a gift. "Aye, I'm s'posin' so," she mused, then glanced at Plank. "But knowin' I only have one perfect match, if Jagger were harmed, I'd just live my life wantin' to be with him. That doesn't seem like a gift. It seems cruel."

A ghost of a smile graced his lips. "I've thought much on the subject of late. The beauty and savagery of such things lies in their mortality."

"Ye're goin' to have to pirate that down," she grunted.

"If love was safe, whether for a family member, siblings, or a partner, it would not be half so treasured. The uncertainty of love, the risk of allowing ourselves to feel, is what propels our emotion to such beautiful heights; for tomorrow, all might be gone. We must be grateful each day that we can love someone and be loved in return."

A lump rose in her throat as she stared at Caspian's shadowed profile. His high forehead was creased, and the too long russet hair curled around his face. The amber eyes that first gave her pause were distant, the mind of their possessor turned inward.

Ebba nudged his stump with her shoulder. "That was like a poem. Pretty. And I can see what ye're sayin'. Except I find it hard to be grateful for the gift when I'm so afraid." Not just for Jagger, for everyone.

"I think we get better at not being afraid," he answered, blinking and turning to look at her once more. "When we've known loss, maybe we learn not to be afraid of it. Pain of loss reminds us we loved. And in our case, there is no fear of the unknown. We know that there are birds—the thunderbird's vessels—and the Locker. We know the souls of our loved ones end up in the sky as birds." His eyes drifted in the direction of the stream.

Ebba shook her head. "That makes it worse for me. I've a feelin' everyone I know but ye would end up here. Well, not Stubby and Grubby, mayhaps, now they be free o' taint. Still, ye never know, the thunderbird may wake up on the wrong side of his nest and decide to send everyone to hell for it."

Caspian's face darkened. "That bothers me a lot. You have to wonder how many of these people actually deserve to be here. What does anyone do to deserve imprisonment in hell? There's no way to atone. Endless penance is cruel. Why would anyone repent without an end in sight?"

She'd had similar thoughts herself. But the darkness on Caspian's face bothered her more. Bookish people thought far too much. She'd seen it with Barrels. They were so good at thinking that they didn't just think *their* thoughts; they thought of everyone else's thoughts too. Too smart for their own good.

"Ye know what I'm wonderin'?" she said to him.

"What's that?"

"How big the thunderbird's nest be and if he has to constantly remake the thing after beating his wings to create a gust."

Caspian grinned, displaying a flash of white teeth. "Maybe that's why he sends everyone to the Locker."

Ebba grinned with him.

Plank bent down. "Show a leg. Time to weigh anchor. Gather some small stones. We're goin' to spread out and toss a few pebbles at the tainted and see if we can't start sumpin'."

She leaned down, scooping up a few stones. And a couple of larger rocks in case one of the tainted went for her.

"Ebba and I will head through the boulders on the other side of the path," Caspian said.

"Aye, we'll branch out through this side. Be careful, mind," Stubby replied, his hands filled with pebbles. "And once the fight starts, meet back up at the cave in case Cannon comes lookin'."

They crept back up the cave path toward the main walkway and split up. Crossing into the boulders on the opposite side of the worn route, Ebba slowed to a shuffle, creeping forward foot by foot.

The tainted could be anywhere around here.

Caspian gripped her arm and jerked his head to the boulder in front. The arm of a tainted pirate was visible from where they stood. Ebba's heart pounded at the sight. She crouched, scanning the area before them. They had to start the fight farther in. They wanted as many tainted involved as possible.

Tapping her shoulder, Caspian tilted his head to the left, mouthing, *I'll go this way.*

She nodded and remained crouched, squinting into the boulders. There were another couple of tainted two boulders up. She'd head to the right and circle around them.

On silent feet, Ebba circled to the right, nearly gasping when she caught sight of a pirate's bare foot. But, she surveyed the area, there were at least six tainted here.

It would have to do.

Ebba glanced back to check what cover she'd have. She had to be located between the shipwreck and the stream, though the broken vessel was hidden away in the towering boulders from her view. To her left was the main path to the stream. Then to her back was the stream itself. She had enough exits.

A yell went up from where her fathers were positioned.

Shite. Ebba selected a small pebble and, taking aim, threw it at one of the middle pirates.

Another yell went up from across the way.

She selected a larger pebble and tossed it at the same tainted pirate. He didn't budge.

Sink her, how deeply did the pillars' minions sleep?

There was definitely movement up ahead now. Ebba had no idea where the others were, but if this was to turn into a crazed brawl, she had to play her part. Taking one of the larger stones, around the size of her fist, Ebba cocked her arm back and let the rock fly.

She winced as the rock crunched against the tainted man's head.

Ebba ducked.

His eyes flew open, and he roared, glancing around and searching the ground. When his back was turned, she let fly with her other smaller stones, pelting at least two of the others. One woke and leaped to her feet. Her eyes landed on the already standing man with the large stone in his hand.

She held her breath as the tainted woman launched herself at the man with a furious screech. Backing into the shadows, Ebba didn't stick around to see if the rest would join in. The others were waking; she had to get out of there.

She spun around a boulder and pressed herself against it, taking a deep breath.

Ebba raised a foot, ready to sneak back to their cave, but a flash of white caught her eye. Her jaw dropped as Caspian sprinted down the path, just a flash between boulders to her eyes. Why was he running? The tainted would hear him.

She didn't have long to wonder.

Feet stampeded in a growing tumult down the path. Ebba peeked out from the boulder and glanced back to see that the tainted she'd woken had abandoned their fight and were running to the path after

Caspian. Pirates hurtling after her friend were the source of the pounding footsteps.

"Nay," Ebba whispered, her face falling. There were so many of them.

Abandoning her boulder, she began running, too, weaving between boulders and jumping over smaller loose stones. She weaved between the boulders parallel to the tainted on the path, legs pumping as fast as was possible without breaking her neck.

Caspian would be trapped against the boiling stream. He could perhaps make it back to the cave by dodging through the boulders on the opposite side of the path and doubling back. But if he did, he'd lead berserk tainted to their only safe point.

"Shite, shite, shite," she panted.

The boulders tapered in size as the stream loomed ahead, and she scanned the area for Caspian, spotting him running down her way. Why was he running away from the passage platform? He should be running for the entrance!

Shrieks jerked her back to the present. Risking a glance through the boulders behind her, Ebba jolted. Some of the tainted had changed direction and now pursued *her*. Their eyes were flooded black. Berserk, they shoved at each other, pausing to fight amongst themselves, but clearly, Caspian and Ebba were the ultimate prizes. She renewed her pace, bursting out through the last of the boulders.

"Caspian," she called between puffs.

He caught sight of her, and his eyes widened as she skidded alongside him.

"What are you doing here?" he gasped, holding his side.

The mort pertinent question as they sprinted toward the sheer cliff face of the northern end of the cavern was. . . , "What happens at the dead-end?"

"I was going to jump the stream down there," he answered.

Jump the— "Ye be aware it's boilin'?"

"Yes. But narrower down this way. Only six feet instead of eight," he said.

Ebba glanced over her shoulder and blanched. "Uh, better pick up the pace."

He cast a look at her and then did the same, peering back. She gripped his belt as his feet faltered.

"Right, so it's six feet," she said, eyeing the gap that suddenly looked more like seven feet. While talking to King Montcroix, the space hadn't seemed all that large. Now. . . .

"How good are ye at jumpin'?" she asked.

"You go first," Caspian ordered. "We don't want to bump into each other on the way over. The tainted might follow us over. We'll have to disappear through the crowd of damned once we get across."

"Ye'll be jumpin, though, aye?" she said, eyes narrowing as she hurdled a knee-high rock.

He nodded.

The space before them dwindled, and the footsteps behind were far too close to risk a glance back. The pirates' shrieks and roars echoed through the cavern, and Ebba imagined hot breath on her neck. She imagined what would happen if the tainted got hold of her.

"Jump as hard as ye can," Ebba ordered him.

She picked up the pace, and when in front of Caspian, she angled inward to the very end of the purple, boiling stream, lining up with the narrowest part of the water. Arms pumping, feet digging in and pushing off the fiery stone as fast as she'd ever run, Ebba brought both feet together and shoved down, flying through the thick air.

The ground disappeared from under her. For a moment, steam curled about her, obscuring her vision. And then the steam was gone.

Over the water, Ebba landed. Bending her knees, she rolled once and sprang to her feet, searching for Caspian. She saw the moment he jumped as she just had, sailing through the air. His gold circlet flew high, disappearing from sight. But Caspian was twisting in the air, eyes rounding in panic.

He wasn't going to make it!

Mouth dry, she surged forward, screaming as he landed right on the water's edge. He windmilled his arm, and Ebba lunged for his belt, planting her feet and throwing herself backward.

Caspian landed on top of her.

Except Ebba wasn't looking at him. She peered over his shoulder at the berserk, black-eyed tainted jumping across the stream after them.

TWENTY-THREE

"Get off, get off, get off!" Ebba yelled at Caspian, shoving at him though she knew it was too late. The tainted were nearly on them, eyes flooded black, teeth yellowed, and clothes frayed and slick with grime.

There was a roar from behind. And then Ebba was staring at the underside of someone's boots as they leaped overhead. Other damned followed the first, thundering past where she and Caspian lay.

What was happening?

"That was all of them," Caspian said, head raised, looking behind her.

He rolled off, and Ebba knelt, eyes wide as she looked to the stream. The damned were helping them, standing in a line and shoving the tainted back into the water. And at their center was King Montcroix.

She glanced down the length of the stream and saw the tainted were trying to leap the boiling water south of their spot too. Some managed to cling to the damned, pulling them into the scalding water with them.

"Son," Montcroix shouted. "Get back. Climb the cliffs to the passage. Get to the entrance."

They couldn't leave her crew.

"Get help. Come back!" Montcroix yelled. "Fight another day."

The tainted were relentless, but they—and the damned—could still feel pain. Their screams and shrieks filled the air. Though their brethren melted before their very eyes, the pirates didn't stop attempting to reach the other side.

"What have we done?" Caspian said in horror.

The wrong thing. But there wasn't any point lingering on that now. "Come on, matey. To the cliffs, like yer father said."

"But my father?" Caspian said, aghast.

"Yer father already be dead. Don't be a fool. He'll come back; you won't." Ebba grabbed his arm. "I will drag ye to the cliffs if ye make me."

Caspian looked at his father and then her. The desperation faded from his eyes, and he nodded curtly, lips pressed together. "Let's go."

Ebba turned, still holding the prince's arm, and wrenched to a halt.

Damned, too many to count, stared at them. And she stared back. By the looks, they'd been drawn to the fighting.

"What do we do?" she hissed from the corner of her mouth.

Caspian stood beside her. "I guess we just walk through. They aren't attacking. Just standing there."

Mutinous Cannon's words from what must be nearly two weeks ago replayed in her mind. Namely the part about the damned tearing people apart. Swallowing the lump in her throat, she started forward. When she reached the line of damned, they stood aside to let her pass. Ebba ignored a few leering looks, squeezing between males, females, and children from all walks of life.

"Ahoy," she greeted them quietly.

She squeezed Caspian's arm, and he shifted so that they held hands.

Sucking in, Ebba stepped over a slumbering damned. A hand snaked out, gripping her upper arm.

"Tell me, wench," an orange-bearded man snarled in her face. "Is the entrance open yet?"

Ebba jerked free. "Who're ye callin' wench, ye fire-jawed bastard?" She wasn't telling him anything. Or anyone here. She had no wish to die as they stampeded out.

Caspian slid between them. "What she means to say is yes."

She inhaled sharply. "Nay, I didn't."

"Outside the entrance, the path to safety only appears once a day. There is only just enough time to cross to the next island," Caspian blurted to the stranger. "The entrance will only let out so many. Cannon plans to leave the damned here and free the pirates."

The bearded man froze. So did she.

"Are you sure of that?" the man demanded, ignoring her completely to address Caspian.

"We figured it out. Why do you think the tainted were chasing us?"

. . . Not strictly true. Ebba was proud of him.

The man studied her friend intently. "I knew Cannon was up to no good."

She winced as a series of ripe expletives left his lips.

Caspian said, "You just need to make sure the tainted pirates don't get out before you. Or all will be lost."

Ebba remained mute, letting the prince run the show. He was playing with more fire than they'd already played with—and that hadn't turned out too well. If he wasn't careful, he'd start a riot.

"I thank you for the information." The bearded man bowed to Caspian. "Where are you going now?"

"To the passage platform," Caspian answered. "Our friends are back across the stream, and we must reunite with them."

The man nodded. "I will take you there."

Ebba waited until he'd turned to lead the way before whispering, "What are ye doin'?"

Caspian hushed in her ear. "We can't stop the tainted marching out of this passage. But the damned can. They equal the number of pirates."

"But they'll *become* tainted."

"The taint is already here," he said, looking back the way they'd come. "And that's my fault. It's only a matter of time until everyone on this side catches it."

Ebba stared at him, realizing what he'd already put together. King Montcroix was now tainted. But Caspian was right—on both counts.

Ebba exhaled. "All right. Let's get back to the others and see if Jagger had any luck."

They trailed after the huge bearded man, easing between the curious and filthy occupants of hell. The cloying crowd of damned obscured the distance. Orienting herself was impossible. On the pirate side, she could have run along the stream from north to south in just a few minutes. On the damned side, with the sheer masses in a smaller space, the journey to the cliffs felt four times that.

A high-pitched whistle cracked the air, and Ebba halted.

"Pistol fire," she said, glancing around.

There was a second high-pitched *crack*, and the damned around them huddled to the ground. Ebba jerked Caspian down. She tucked in her crimson skirt as tightly as possible.

"Where'd the pistol fire from?" she asked.

"The passage platform," Caspian replied flatly.

Shifting, Ebba lifted her head.

A buzzing filled her ears.

At the top of the cliffs where they were headed stood Mutinous Cannon. At his side was Pockmark, who held Jagger at pistol point. Her fathers stood in a row along the platform, blocked from escape by hordes of tainted who milled on the steps down to the other side of the stream.

"I be lookin' for two people," Cannon called lazily over the pregnant silence. "One o' them, a man, has naught but one arm. The other, a small woman with black dreadlocks and green eyes."

The orange-bearded man, crouching ahead, turned back to look at them.

"If they are harmed and if they are not returned to me, none o' us will leave this place," Cannon continued.

Ebba couldn't glean anything from his tone, but with a sizeable number of his tainted victims in the boiling stream and the simple fact he'd had to physically address the damned, she guessed Cannon was furious.

She swallowed as the surrounding damned set their eyes upon her and Caspian.

"No one says a word," the bearded man ordered. "Cannon doesn't mean to let us out of here. He's lying."

The damned around her seemed torn. She didn't blame them; *she* was torn—just not over the same thing. Up there was nearly everyone she cared about in the whole world. But what would Cannon do if they joined her fathers and Jagger?

Caspian whispered, "Jagger's bleeding."

Ebba squinted at the pirate and gasped. Bleeding was an understatement. His entire face was covered with blood, the red staining his flaxen hair. "What if his wounds get inf'cted with taint?" He was immune, but tainted wounds acted much faster than just absorbing the taint. His recovery could take much longer if his injuries were infected.

Ebba checked the row of her fathers. None of them appeared worse for the wear. Yet. Continuing down the line, she focused on the string of tainted pirates on the cliff steps. They covered the fifty-foot steep stairway entirely, spreading across the base of the cavern on the other side of the water. Clearly, only a small fraction of Cannon's force had been swept up in the earlier stampede.

She focused on the tainted closest to her father, stilling.

"Look," she breathed. "The ones at the top o' the steps have the cases."

Jagger had gone in for the six parts, but now it appeared as though they'd been brought out. "Why would he bring them out into the open?"

Caspian answered immediately. "He means to leave. Or he didn't have enough tainted left to guard them while he came here."

Cannon spoke again, and Ebba listened, rubbing her temples.

"No?" he called out. "Ye have nothin' for me? Perhaps ye wish to break our accord? Perhaps ye mean to stay here for etern'ty."

A shudder of dissent rippled through the damned.

"They're here!"

Ebba whirled, scowling at the child behind her. "Ye soddin' brat."

The child bared her teeth.

"There they are." Cannon snapped from above. "Get them."

Ebba turned to Caspian. Their trip here hadn't been a waste. Perhaps the man with the orange beard would spread the news. That might buy Ebba and the others some time to get out of this mess.

"Wait," Caspian said, eyes focused on something past the bearded man. She followed his gaze to the passage cliffs.

"Sink me, it's Forge," she gasped.

Caspian's father scaled the cliff face of the semi-circle platform. He climbed up the very eastern part of the jutting cliff, so the curve of the platform concealed him from the pirate side of the stream.

The crowd of damned could surely see him as clearly as she and Caspian, but they didn't utter a single word. They were hedging their bets. For now.

"Come on, we'll distract Cannon," she said. There was nothing for it. They wanted to be up there, and Cannon wouldn't rest until they were up there. Their interests were briefly aligned. Though Ebba could guess that today's events wouldn't go unpunished.

The cowering damned parted for her and Caspian as they strode to the base of the cliff. Ebba glanced at the prince's stump. "Ye go up ahead of me. I'll give ye a boost when needed."

"No, that won't be enough," he said. "Cannon!"

Pockmark appeared over the edge.

"Unless your grandfather means for me to fall and die, he can toss the *dynami* down here. I can't climb with one arm," Caspian shouted.

"Ye think he's goin' to chuck a part down?" Ebba said.

He shrugged his shoulder. "Depends how much he wants us alive. The taint is on this side. If Cannon has kept the damned safe from taint because they have good in them, he's going to lose their light in short duration. If we're down here, too, we'll also be tainted. The scales will tip against Cannon. The entrance could close."

Ebba exhaled shakily. "He has to be goin' for the entrance now."

Pockmark reappeared with a black case. He tipped the open case forward, and a tarnished silver tube she hadn't seen in weeks tumbled out, spinning end-over-end toward them. Caspian took two steps to the right and caught the part in his outstretched hand.

"No funny bus'ness," Pockmark yelled down.

Caspian tucked the part in his belt and turned to her. "I don't know what my father is planning, but he's going to help."

Ebba nodded. "We have the *dynami*, and only so many tainted pirates can fit up on the passage platform. Most o' Cannon's crew be confined to the cliff steps or the other side o' the stream. The higher ground will be easier to defend, and the crevice to the entrance, easier still. If we can get the upper hand on the platform, we could get to the entrance with the parts."

"You're right," Caspian said, voice tight. "This isn't the plan we'd hoped for, but we'd be foolish not to take advantage of it." Determination settled heavy on his face. "Yes, we've got to take the opportunity. But . . . he'll expect it."

Assuredly. Ebba placed both hands on the cliff. "He will. Let's go."

Regardless of the *dynami* in Caspian's belt, she remained slightly below him on the way up, ready to grab for him if he should fall. But no strain was detectable in his arm or legs during the fifty-foot climb. He shoved his hand into the black-and-crimson stone as if it were flour, punching his feet into the cliff face as he worked his way upward. Sweat beaded on her brow before long as she heaved herself up the stone cliff, focusing on the deep crimson hue as she reached for each jagged hold.

Ebba peered up at the lip of the platform, her chest tightening as the distance between her and her crew shrank. Nearly there.

Seeing her friend struggle to heave himself over the top lip, Ebba scrambled past him up the cliff and swung her body onto the ledge. Ignoring everyone, she hastened to help Caspian, gripping his belt and pulling him onto the shelf, too.

She rolled to her feet and looked over her fathers.

They were okay. She sagged in relief. Pale-faced, but her initial scan from below had proved right. None appeared harmed. She nodded at them, letting her eyes linger on Stubby for several seconds. His gaze sharpened, and he turned to murmur to Barrels.

They'd be ready.

Ebba looked at Jagger next, and the stone all but disappeared from under her. What had they done to him? Whether forced to his knees or there because he couldn't stand, she didn't know. Jagger had been cut. His face, at least four times, but also on his arms and legs and across his torso. Her heart sank.

He lifted his head and stared at her, black shadows beneath his eyes. Was he tainted? She couldn't tell from where she stood. He looked out of it. Judging by the red staining his tunic and slops, he'd lost a lot of blood.

"Ye've made quite the mess of things," Cannon said, lips curling though his eyes glittered dangerously. Was it just her, or was he looking a smidge more tainted tonight?

Caspian crowded her to the left, and Ebba took the hint, stepping farther around so Mutinous Cannon would turn away from where she assumed Montcroix waited to attack. She'd lost sight of the king on the way up.

"Your tainted nearly killed us," Caspian said.

"Don't test my patience!" Cannon boomed, black creeping into his eyes. "Do ye take me for a fool?"

Ebba's throat tightened.

"Do you?" he shouted at Caspian.

"No," the prince answered. "Many things, but not a fool. Or perhaps you are a fool, but your masters are not. Any victory you have will never be yours, after all."

Ebba winced, itching to warn her friend.

But then she saw a twitching of the shadows behind the seething captain. That had to be Montcroix.

"*This* victory shall be mine, boy," Cannon spat. "When I am free at last, all will know it. All will know I never lost a battle."

He was really hung up on fake-losing that fight. "But no one will," she found herself saying. "Everyone be tainted. Ye feel it, and ye see it in yer pirates. They ain't there. They don't know the di'ference between losin' and winnin'. They only know darkness."

"Silence," Cannon said, teeth clenching as he stepped in her direction.

The shadows behind him twitched again, a little closer.

Cannon lowered his head until he was level with hers. Ebba struggled not to fidget, keeping her breaths steady.

He smirked. "This is how things are goin' to be happenin' from now on."

TWENTY-FOUR

Mutinous Cannon straightened and sauntered down the row of her fathers strung out along the open edge of the passage platform. Ebba's small sigh of relief to no longer be the focus of his attention took on a wheezing quality as she contemplated how easily the evil captain could push her parents to their deaths. She cast another look to the shadows where King Montcroix lurked. Cannon had moved away from the king's hiding place. Montcroix wouldn't attack just yet.

"I'll be leavin' this place tonight," Cannon announced. "The pillars won't let me out without their army at my back and the root o' magic in my grasp. If I wait for more tainted to enter the locker, I could be in here for months to come. But I've figured it out at long last."

Caspian threw a veiled look at her.

He'd been right.

Continuing, Cannon said to her fathers, "I'm about to heal every one o' ye."

So far, Jagger hadn't uttered a word. He did now. "Ye can't," he slurred. "It'll kill her."

"Nay, just . . . hurt her a bit." Cannon smirked.

"She was unconscious for three days from ye just healin' Stubby," Jagger said through clenched teeth, wavering on the spot.

Ebba crossed to him and reached out.

"Nay, Viva," he said softly. "Don't be touchin' me now."

His eyes weren't black. He wasn't contagious. But he'd been worried about transferring taint through blood and spit before. Touching him would worry Jagger even more. But that was all she wanted to do. All she'd wanted to do for weeks. "Are ye sure ye won't fall on yer face, matey?" she said tremulously.

Weak amusement curved his lips, and fresh blood oozed from a vicious cut on his cheekbone.

"Ah, Jagger," Cannon said, circling behind him. "Yer future doesn't lie with Ebba-Viva. Haven't ye gleaned that much?"

Black edged the captain's eyes, and before she could shout out, Cannon rested both hands on Jagger's shoulders. One of his tainted hands directly over a bleeding wound.

Foggy horror gripped her, and her eyes lifted of their own accord to Jagger's.

There was no way the taint wouldn't enter that wound. Like a snapping mast, Ebba unfroze and shot to her feet. "Get yer hand off him!" Fists balled, she leaped at Cannon, but the air whooshed from her breathers as an arm clamped around her waist.

"Let me go, Caspian," she said in a warning tone. "I'll hurt ye."

"No, you won't," he said matter-of-factly. And then in her ear, "He knew the risk. You know he can beat the taint back."

Was that meant to make her feel better? Each time Jagger came back from the taint, he was a little less. Jagger still had to live with himself after. And he could only beat it back when removed from the source.

Caspian let her shake off his grip.

Ebba glared at Cannon, shaking from head to toe. She was going to kill him. Actually, at this point anyone could kill him and she'd be happy.

Cannon didn't shift his hands as he spoke. "Ye'll have seen how difficult tainted are to control. Prone to violence. A single comment can make them go berserk and forget their orders. It be the caveat to my masters' control. Even they can't control the spread o' their taint." He peered down at Jagger. "That be why they collect people like me and like Jagger here."

A high ringing took up residence in Ebba's ears. Why was he looking at Jagger in that way? Like he knew something none of them did.

"The pillars have plans for ye," Cannon sang in Jagger's ear. He released the pirate, shoving him to the ground.

Ebba dropped by Jagger's side again as Cannon's booming laughter echoed through the Locker.

Jagger groaned and rolled onto his back, locking gazes with her. She stretched out a hand, but he didn't return the gesture. He wouldn't risk it.

"What do ye mean?" Stubby demanded.

Cannon was still smiling. "To the pillars, Jagger is a prize only second to the weapon. With his resistance to magic, he alone will have the power to retain some o' his reason over the years. And then his child after that, and the child o' his child. Only his bloodline can resist the taint. So they will always be alone, the sole partly aware human in a realm o' tainted souls."

The heavy horror of the picture he painted robbed Ebba of speech. She didn't move her eyes from Jagger's. An ache filled her chest at the dullness of his gaze. He'd already been alone for years. Jagger had given enough to keep the realm safe by now. This time, someone else had to pay the price. She needed time with him; she needed *him*. Her breath came fast. Mind seizing, all Ebba could do was look to her fathers for answers.

They appeared as lost as she was. But Barrels stepped forward. "You said that Jagger is a prize only second to the root of magic. You know that Jagger is the immune. So you must know that he is only one of the three watchers needed to assemble the root. I'm assuming that your masters don't want all six individual parts but the weapon itself. Only the three watchers combined can put the parts together."

That stopped Cannon in his tracks.

He turned to look at her and lifted his gaze over her shoulder to where Caspian stood. From the corner of her eye, she saw Peg-leg slap Barrels upside the head.

"True enough, my old quartermaster. True enough," Cannon said quietly. "To taint them might make them useless. Yet healin' the rest o' ye might risk her life."

"Yes," Caspian blurted. "So you need to heal them individually and wait for her to heal."

"Nay," the captain replied, tilting his head. "I just need the three watchers to assemble the weapon afore I heal them. Then it don't matter if the wench be dead."

Sink her.

Locks slapped Barrels upside the head.

With a pained groan, Jagger rolled onto his stomach and got onto all fours. "Nay, I'll come with ye," he said. "Ye know where Viva and Caspian be if ye need them. Easy enough to sail back later."

"Pockmark," Cannon snapped, ignoring Jagger. "Bring the cases forward." He looked at Ebba. "Get up. Ye're the assembler."

"I am?" she asked in a daze. They'd taken a stab in the dark after overhearing the Satyr talking about them, but Cannon sounded confident that was indeed her role.

"O' course ye are," he snapped. "Ye have six fathers."

What did that have to do with anything?

Caspian helped her up. Ebba felt weak, drained, as though Jagger's wounds were her own and the blood spilling onto the black stone belonged to her also.

"We don't know how to do it," Caspian said. "We know nothing about putting the weapon together."

"Ye don't know anythin'?" Cannon asked, searching their faces.

He tipped back his head and laughed. "Ye're tellin' me that ye be sailin' the realm, collectin' the parts, but have no idea what to do after?"

Heat crept up her neck as his laughter continued. It wasn't like they'd had any help. They'd been only days from discovering answers before the Satyr caught them. Matey had said his grandfather had records, and Sally had promised to scour wind sprite archives for anything about the three watchers. Worrying about how to put the weapon together was pointless when they didn't even have the parts —though knowing *something* of what came after would have been a great reassurance.

And a great help right now.

Six black cases were laid out before them.

Just like that, the parts they'd spent months in pursuit of were there. At her very feet.

Ebba lifted her chin to look at Jagger and then Caspian. The same awe was in his amber eyes. How many times had they nearly died to attain these? They'd been tainted, beaten, and kidnapped; ridiculed, imprisoned, and threatened on too many occasions to count.

Now, right here, were all six parts of the root.

She crouched down and opened the first lid, staring at a part she'd never seen. "*Fortudo*," she sounded out.

"Bravery," Caspian told her. "Amongst other meanings."

That was straightforward. She could do with some of that.

Furtively, Ebba reached out and gripped the tarnished silver cylinder. She waited, expecting a rush of courage, but nothing happened—that she could detect.

"Hurry, girl. The next one," Cannon snarled, stepping forward to peer over the lip of the platform. "Swindles, give the order. If any of the damned start climbin' the cliffs, they're to be shot."

Ebba glanced back, noticing the loud murmur in the Locker for the first time. The damned were talking, and their hum of dissent was growing steadily louder. Was the orange-bearded man spreading the truth of Cannon's plan?

She opened the next case and immediately recognized the *purgium*. Reaching out, she ran a finger down the curving name etched on the side. How long ago it felt since they'd entered a different cavern in search of this to heal Caspian.

She held up the *purgium* and *fortudo*. One had two flat ends, the other one flat and one pointed. Ebba brought them together with an experimental *tap*.

Tap. Tap.

Nothing.

Clearing her throat, she tried again. *Tap, tap, tap.*

Nope, not a thing.

There were other parts with a flat end, however. Maybe these two parts weren't meant to fit together. Already, Ebba was envisioning how *veritas* would fit with the other pieces. How would that work? What did the weapon look like? Some kind of sword with a really long handle?

Ebba opened the third box and recalled something else.

Caspian beat her to it, speaking low. "You can't touch more than two, remember?"

Remember? Hard to forget the worst pain she'd ever experienced. The resulting explosion had blinded her for nearly an hour. Yet, she frowned, hovering her fingertips over the *scio*, last time she'd felt . . . uneasy just before touching the third part. That same uneasiness wasn't there now. Though she held the *fortudo,* which might be making her falsely brave.

"Don't do it, Viva," Jagger rasped, still on all fours.

She'd trusted her instincts before Jagger, and she trusted them still.

"No," Cannon said. "King Caspian. It's time you passed over the *dynami*, don't you think?"

Caspian's face smoothed, but he slid the *dynami* he'd used to get up the cliff from his belt, setting it on the ground.

Ebba touched the third part.

Her fathers surged forward, yelling. Caspian reached for her. Even Jagger lifted his head. But Ebba smiled, holding up the *dynami*.

She could hold three of the cylinders.

. . . What had changed?

"Why did ye all yell?" Pockmark demanded, speaking for the first time. He and Cannon had stepped back against the passage.

Caspian opened the fourth case, and the warning twinge in Ebba's gut was immediate. Apparently, the *fortudo* hadn't been at work before.

"I can't touch that," she announced.

Judging by the crease between Caspian's brows, he was about as confused by the development as she was. Her only guess was that she had to touch the extra part once, be blown up with each one, and then the next time she'd be able to touch another part without issue. That didn't bode well for her lifespan.

"What are ye waitin' for?" Cannon asked.

She sat back and looked up at him, jerking at the sight of black further encroaching his eyes. The dark nearly touched the outer ring of his irises. If Cannon went berserk, this situation would go from bad to worse.

"I'm the bearer," Caspian said slowly. "Maybe I have to help?"

Ebba shrugged. "Worth a shot." The flipping of her stomach said otherwise.

"If she touches another part, ye'll all be incin'rated by the white light like Riot was a few days back," Jagger gasped, clutching his side.

One of the three parts she held was the *purgium*. True, the white light that occurred when she touched too many parts was just like the one that came when Stubby was healed. And the same as the light when she, Caspian, and Jagger touched. Or so Ebba assumed. They hardly knew anything about the white light, but hopefully Cannon didn't either. And if Cannon got close enough, she could heal him. He'd come back when the wind next howled, as Pockmark had, but that would be ample time to win or lose the battle to escape.

The prince wasn't slow to follow up on Jagger's words.

Caspian gripped the *amare* and immediately held the cylinder out to her.

A pistol cocked. "No closer, King Caspian," Cannon said dangerously.

It wasn't needed; the warning in Ebba's gut was working overtime. She couldn't touch that without being severely injured. Maybe even killed.

Maybe they could try touching Jagger? Or would that just result in all three watchers being tainted?

Caspian lowered his arm. "Then we are at an impasse. Ebba cannot assemble the weapon alone. If there is a way, we don't know it. And if she continues, you risk her life and whatever is left of yours."

Peeking up at Cannon, she watched as the captain stared at Caspian, gripping his pistol several times. The black was now *touching* his irises.

"Back to the or'ginal plan then," Cannon said, jaw clenched. "Takin' the pillars the weapon would've been ideal-like, but I'll take the next best option. There be other a'semblers. She's replaceable."

Whoa, Ebba had a little something to say about that—except she really had no idea if he was right or wrong, so she stilled her tongue.

He swung the weapon on Barrels. "Touch the *purgium*."

"I will not," sputtered Barrels. "I will not knowingly hurt my daughter."

Ebba got to her feet, sliding the *dynami* and *fortudo* into the waist of her skirt. Caspian did the same with the *amare*.

Pockmark scowled at them. "Put them back in the cases. All but the *purgium*."

She eyed his hand that rested on his pistol and sighed. Keeping them was worth a shot. She bent down and replaced the *dynami* and *fortudo* in their separate cases.

Cannon swung his pistol back to point at her. "Ye'll touch the *purgium* one way or another. In one version, yer daughter be alive. At least for now. In the other, she be dead and ye still touch the *purgium*. Which would ye prefer? If she dies, I'll still have more good souls than I was havin' afore."

Maybe this could work in their favor. If her fathers were healed in the vicinity of tainted pirates, they'd be rendered to ash. Hopefully.

She caught Locks' eye, widening hers slightly.

Barrels glanced behind him, and in turn, Locks, Grubby, Plank, Stubby, and Peg-leg exchanged long looks and nodded.

"I shall touch the *purgium*," Barrels said, clearing his throat. "Only me."

Cannon shouted, "Ye ain't givin' orders here. Touch it or she gains a bullet in the skull. Ye can watch her rum spill over these rocks right now." He stepped back to the far end of the platform, as far as was possible from Barrels. Bugger, he was ready for the white light. But now Cannon stood close to the shadows where King Montcroix lurked.

If Montcroix was waiting for a good time to attack Cannon, then this was about as good as it would get. What was he stalling for?

Barrels hastened to stand before her. "Away from the cliff edge," he murmured to her. Last time she'd been dashed into the ground. A steep fall wasn't the ideal place for what might happen next.

Barrels led her to the start of the passage and sighed. "I'm so very sorry, my dear."

Stubby had touched the healing part. And Grubby. But there was no surety, other than the feeling in her gut that Barrels would live to tell the tale.

"I love ye," she said, swallowing hard.

He reached a hand to her cheek. "And I you."

Barrels reached a hand out toward the *purgium*.

And all hell broke loose.

TWENTY-FIVE

Ebba whirled at a roar from the far side of the ledge. Despite knowing he'd hidden there in waiting, a gasp left her lips as King Montcroix threw himself from the shadows, lunging for Cannon.

"They mean to leave us here!" the king boomed to the damned. "Attack the tainted or be left behind for eternity."

He seized hold of Cannon's doublet and attempted to drag the pirate with him over the cliff edge.

Cannon wrestled for the upper hand.

With the growing murmur of dissent from below, it appeared the damned didn't need any further encouragement. Ebba turned toward the anarchy, heart hammering as she watched the damned jump the stream where she and Caspian had escaped earlier. She stood, chest rising as they flooded the pirate side of the cavern, the tainted meeting their attack.

The rest of her fathers turned to the steps, picking up stones to brand them at the closest pirates.

"Touch it," Pockmark yelled at Barrels from close to Cannon. His weapon was trained on her. Ebba gasped at his eyes. The tiniest ring of yellow remained; the rest was solid black.

She leaned forward and scooped up the *purgium* to placate the pirate, tucking the tube in the waistband of her skirt.

Caspian took a step in his father's direction.

"Stay back, son. He's tainted," panted Montcroix, breaking away to stand between Cannon and Caspian. "I bested him once; I'll do it again."

Cannon laughed, drawing his cutlass. "Ye didn't best me, foolish king. I went wi'lingly to the grave. But here be sumpin' I've been wantin' to do for some time."

The cocking of the hammer and the pulling of the trigger blurred into one sound. In a flash and a flurry of smoke, a pistol was fired.

Caspian cried out, running forward as his father staggered back.

Pockmark pivoted, training his pistol on the prince, eyes flooded black. *Berserk.*

"Caspian!" Ebba screamed and reached out for Barrels' hand, bringing his fingers to the *purgium* tucked in the waistband of her skirt.

Ebba's breath was dragged from her mouth as a searing pain squeezed her heart, like metal pouring over her chest.

White light exploded.

Barrels held fast to her at first. But the tightness of his grip lessened until his arms fell away. This time, as Ebba flew forward, the force only knocked them to the ground.

Barrels was immobile beneath her. But that hardly registered. She screamed, clutching uselessly at her chest as the molten-metal feeling coated her insides, cooling and leaving only raw, blistering agony in its wake. Ebba ignored the hands touching her, curled in a ball, her mind shocked to numbness.

Rolling onto her back, Ebba blinked through the double vision that was edged with black. She was still conscious, but she wished she wasn't.

Her head lolled to the side.

On his knees, Caspian stared at the body of his father.

Jagger was on his feet, hands around Cannon's throat. Ebba

twitched her fingers, straining in his direction as Cannon brought the butt of his pistol down on Jagger's head.

Her pirate crumpled to the ground.

"Where be Pockmark?" Cannon shouted, firing at the hands of the damned reaching over the ledge.

Swindles was firing, too. His pistol clicked onto an empty chamber, and he drew his second pistol. "Over the edge, Captain. Dove out o' the way when the white light exploded. He be climbin' up now."

Damn. She'd intended to kill Pockmark. But at least Caspian was alive.

Pulling her eyes from Jagger's unconscious form, Ebba looked up at her fathers, who'd abandoned the fight at the top of the steps to run to her.

"Grab the cases and Jagger," Cannon ordered the tainted pirates, picking up a case himself. "Into the passage. Now!" he roared.

Swindles yanked several of the tainted surging at the top of the stairs forward. "Ye heard him. Grab the cases and the pirate."

Cannon kicked Caspian, who skidded face-first along the ground by his father's body. "Up, ye snivelin' landlubber. Into the passage. All o' ye into the passage."

Stubby lifted Ebba into his arms, and her head lolled back. Close by, Barrels was in a similar state, conscious and supported between Locks and Plank.

The prince was right. Each time the *purgium* healed one of her fathers, Ebba was affected. They were definitely linked somehow. She just didn't know how. Or if that was part of being the assembler.

Then the cliffs of the narrow passage closed around her. The light dimmed. Fiery stone either side extended for as far as she could see. Footsteps thudded. The ragged breath of many filled her ears, but just who was in the passage, she couldn't be sure.

With colossal effort, she shifted her eyes to look behind Stubby at a pale-faced Caspian.

Hold on, he mouthed to her.

Ebba planned to, but she must've lost consciousness because when she awoke, they were much farther down the passage than could have been possible. Ebba peered up at the rocky entrance, her vision clearer than before.

She stared in mute horror at the huge crack running vertically through the middle of the entrance to hell.

"The crack be bigger," Stubby said hoarsely.

He passed her to Peg-leg, shaking out his arms.

"Stand me up," she whispered. She had to see what was happening.

A misty-eyed Peg-leg obeyed, setting her upright and looping an arm around her waist. Ebba peered ahead.

Everyone was here, Mutinous Cannon and Swindles included. Pockmark staggered behind them, looking worse for wear. Tainted filled the passage crevice back as far as she could see, and the sounds of fighting echoed toward them. The damned were still battling their way to the front.

Cannon turned in the slightly larger space before the wall. He scanned over her head. His eyes fell on Peg-leg.

"More," he whispered.

Cannon trained his pistol on her father. "More! Touch the *purgium*."

Peg-leg stiffened, and Ebba took matters into her own hands, seeing the scant sliver of yellow remaining in Cannon's eyes. Those behind him would be on a rampage, and her crew was trapped at the mercy of the captain's pistol.

She let out a shaky exhale, bracing for pain.

Under the guise of squeezing Peg-leg's hand, she yanked his hand to the *purgium* tucked in the waistband of her ruffled skirt.

White light erupted once more, and her head snapped back.

The black stone underfoot vibrated with the force of a quake, and Ebba fell forward, white spots filling her vision. The molten metal swept through her, and she screamed anew, throat ripping at the sensation of her already raw and blistered insides burning a second time. The echoing shouts and screams mixed with pistol fire and the ring of cutlass against stone was a blur.

Even then, a tiny part of her mind could acknowledge that this time wasn't as bad as the last.

A frantic Stubby rolled her onto her back. Her limbs had been drained of strength. Peg-leg lay slumped against the gateway.

The crack in the entrance was larger. Light streamed through a tiny hole, impossible to miss in the otherwise dim space. Cannon stood before the crack, laughing. Pockmark limped up to join him.

Her head fell to the left, looking back through the narrow confines of the two sheer cliff faces. Two tainted pirates had Jagger strung between them, dragging him along the ground toward the entrance. Plank and Locks had planted themselves in the bottleneck of the passage farther up, swinging tainted cutlasses at the tainted cloying to get out.

"Again," Cannon bellowed at them, shooting the ground at Stubby's feet. Black filled his eyes.

He was one misplaced word away from going berserk.

"Easier each time," she mumbled up to Stubby. A pirate truth, to be sure. The pain was less each time. But experienced one after the other as it was, Ebba could feel herself sliding into something murky within herself, something dark and empty.

Stubby seemed to understand what she was saying. He glanced at Peg-leg, who had already struggled to his feet.

"Locks!" Stubby shouted back through the passage. "Get back here. She needs to heal all o' us."

Ebba watched listlessly as Plank grabbed Locks by the collar and threw him in her direction.

Stubby spoke over her head, his urgent tone reflected in Locks' answer.

Then Locks was where the cook had been, eyes wide and fixed fearfully on her as he touched the *purgium*.

Numb.

Dark.

Cold heaviness filled her. The white explosion lifted her body toward Locks, but like a sack of potatoes, Ebba was heaved up and dropped.

Her eyelids were heavy, her vision blurring—the only sense remaining to her. It was as though the sound in the space before the entrance had been switched off.

Her head lolled to the left again. To the tight, dark passage.

Plank.

Plank still fought against the tainted pirates there.

One more father and she was done.

Plank had to heal.

Then they were free.

The muteness as chaos reigned was peaceful, coupled with the bright light pouring into the space. There was light in hell, actual light—not the fiery replica illusion created by the red tinge to the black stone.

Something about that should be important.

But it wasn't. It only confused her. Because Ebba watched her father as he swung the cutlass back and forward through the filtered mass of crazed tainted and the desperate damned. She watched as he fully turned to glance back to where she lay.

As the tainted sprinted for her, his mouth formed five words.

I love ye, little nymph.

And even when she didn't want to see, horror forced her to.

Unable to scream, unable to move, she watched as the tainted surged forward, enveloping Plank; *trampling* her father as they stampeded for freedom.

ACKNOWLEDGEMENTS

Pirates of Felicity is my longest series yet. While I knew a bigger word count would allow me to delve deeper into my characters and plot than a trilogy, even I was taken aback by how deep. Drawing in the various threads from the last five books in the series for Eternal Gambit made for one explosive writing experience. If you finished and feel like your head is spinning and your heart is pound-ing, be assured that is exactly how I felt too.

I'd like to thank my husband, family, and friends for their understanding, support, and love.

An extra big hug and thank you to my beta team and advanced readers who are SO much fun.

Thank you to my author friends for supporting me in this industry with their banter, time, love, and knowledge. A special shout out to Raye Wagner, Leia Stone, and Kim Loth for being inspiring humans and authors.

My swashbuckling manuscript team:

Editor One

Melissa Scott

Editor Two
Robin Schroffel

Proofreaders
Patti Geesey and Dawn Yacovetta

Map Illustrator
Laura Diehl

Cover Designer & Illustrator
Amalia Chitulescu

To my readers … please don't throw things at me for the ending.

Happy Reading!

Kelly

ABOUT KELLY ST. CLARE

When Kelly is not reading or writing, she is lost in her latest reverie. Books have always been magical and mysterious to her. One day she decided to unravel this mystery and began writing.

The Tainted Accords was her debut series. Her other works include *The After Trilogy*, *The Darkest Drae*, and *Pirates of Felicity*.

A New Zealander in origin and in heart, Kelly currently resides in Australia with her ginger-haired husband, a great group of friends, and some huntsman spiders who love to come inside when it rains. Their love is not returned.

ALSO BY KELLY ST. CLARE

The Tainted Accords:

Fantasy of Frost
Fantasy of Flight
Fantasy of Fire
Fantasy of Freedom

The Tainted Accords Novellas:

Sin
Olandon
Rhone
Shard

The After Trilogy:

The Retreat
The Return
The Reprisal

The Darkest Drae (Trilogy) Co-written with Raye Wagner

Blood Oath
Shadow Wings
Black Crown

Pirates of Felicity:
Immortal Plunder
Stolen Princess
Pillars of Six
Dynami's Wrath
Veritas
Eternal Gambit
Mortal Trinity

www.ingramcontent.com/pod-product-compliance
Lightning Source LLC
Chambersburg PA
CBHW020933310726
48980CB00007B/760/J

* 9 7 8 0 6 4 8 3 3 4 4 4 6 *